One year ago, Vince Knight walked away from his role as crime lord of Port Knot. In his absence, the gangs he founded went to war, and frightening new factions have risen from the ashes to tear at the town's throat like hungry wolves.

Now Vince is back and has taken command of the Watch—working side-by-side with the very people who spent years trying to put him behind bars. Unbeknownst to him, Captain James Godgrave has been given his own team to deal with crime in the town, but while he and Vince share a common goal, they are not allies.

The murder of one of James's crew puts Vince in a delicate position. Facing pressure from the council, the townsfolk, and the Watch itself, Vince must find the killer because if he doesn't, James will, and Vince's tenure as Watch Commander will be the shortest in history.

As Vince and James clash in their public and private lives, Vince starts to understand the damage caused by his abdication as crime lord, James sets about putting down the gangs once and for all, and the mysterious power behind the new factions exacts a terrifying plan that will change Port Knot forever.

Note: This is a spinoff of *The Moth and Moon* series. It is not necessary to have read that series before this book, however those who have read it will recognize former villain Vince Knight, who is now trying to make up for past mistakes.

THESE YOUNG WOLVES

The Knights of Blackrabbit, Book One

Glenn Quigley

A NineStar Press Publication

www.ninestarpress.com

These Young Wolves

© 2022 Glenn Quigley
Cover Art © 2022 Jaycee DeLorenzo

First Edition, December 2022
ISBN:

Also available in eBook, ISBN:

CONTENT WARNING:
This book contains sexual content, which may only be suitable for mature readers. Depictions of guns/gun violence, murder, and death of a secondary character. Mention of past trauma.

This book is dedicated to the memory of Damian Whyte. I will be forever grateful for his help, his support, and most of all for his friendship.

Author's Note

From the moment Vince Knight first walked onto the page in *The Lion Lies Waiting*, I knew there was something special about him. Some characters require a degree of finessing and moulding to reveal their true selves. Not so, Vince. He appeared fully formed and ready for action. It is a genuine thrill to be able to bring you this, the first in his adventures as head of the Port Knot Watch.

The Knights of Blackrabbit series is set in the Pell Isles—a group of islands situated off the coast of Cornwall. The isles and their inhabitants have been heavily influenced by the Cornish language and culture. As such, you will see words such as *backalong* and *bleddy* crop up in the dialogue. These are Cornish words which have been adopted by everyday Pellans.

Backalong means *in former times* and *bleddy* is simply the word *bloody* in the local vernacular. Other words and phrases have been rewritten to make their meaning clearer, but I felt it important to leave some elements of the local dialect intact.

It is important to note that in this world, an event named "The Illumination" coincided with the fall of the Roman Empire and ultimately led to the abandonment of religious practices across the world. In England, in the year 1141, Queen Matilda passed a law declaring women equal to men with no restrictions placed on their education or the roles they could hold within society. The dearth of religious doctrine led to those who experienced life outside of the traditional to blossom and become accepted as simply another part of life. Prejudice based on gender, race, or sexuality became almost unheard of.

This story begins on 23rd October 1781, the day after the events of *We Cry the Sea*. It is not essential to have read that book, nor the rest of the Moth and Moon trilogy, though doing so will provide a more detailed insight into how Vince Knight came to arrive at his current position in life.

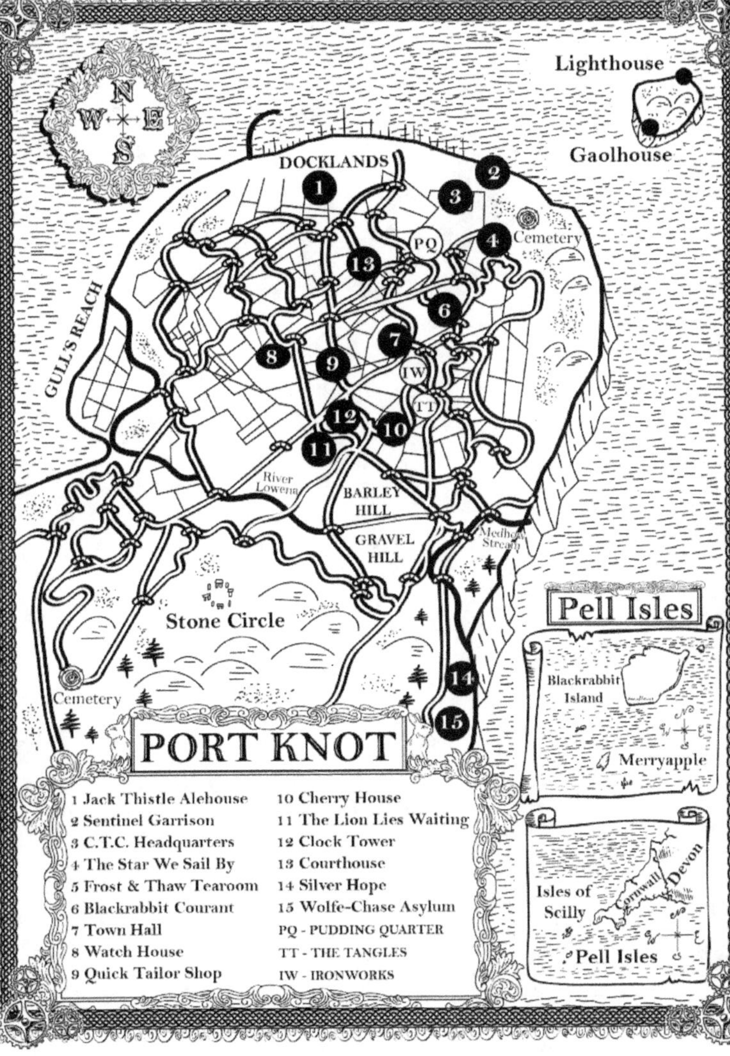

Lighthouse
Gaolhouse
DOCKLANDS
PQ
Cemetery
GULL'S REACH
IW
TT
River Lowena
BARLEY HILL
GRAVEL HILL
Medhow Stream
Stone Circle
Cemetery
Pell Isles
Blackrabbit Island
Merryapple
Isles of Scilly
Cornwall
Devon
Pell Isles
PORT KNOT
1 Jack Thistle Alehouse
2 Sentinel Garrison
3 C.T.C. Headquarters
4 The Star We Sail By
5 Frost & Thaw Tearoom
6 Blackrabbit Courant
7 Town Hall
8 Watch House
9 Quick Tailor Shop
10 Cherry House
11 The Lion Lies Waiting
12 Clock Tower
13 Courthouse
14 Silver Hope
15 Wolfe-Chase Asylum
PQ - PUDDING QUARTER
TT - THE TANGLES
IW - IRONWORKS

CHAPTER ONE

HE CLICKED HIS pale, meaty fingers twice, sending Crabmeat running along the narrow Entry while he hurried up the dry, cobbled road. He readied himself at a corner and stuck out the tip of his octopus-handled cane. A young man with a thatch of blond hair slammed into the cane at full speed, turning head-over-tit onto the cobbled road. A necklace and a handful of coins spilled out of his pockets, splashing into a horse-made puddle. Crabmeat—a tubby, short-nosed little bulldog—darted after him, barking furiously.

The young thief rolled onto his back, holding his shin and crying out, before being lifted wholly off the ground and slammed against the nearest wall. Vince Knight spoke with a voice like rolling thunder, "Assume you know the way to the Watch House?"

No one in the town of Port Knot could remember a warmer October than that of 1781. As the hazy sun rose in a saffron sky, the harbour stretched its cranes like waking arms and prepared for another day. Already several tall ships had docked and become targets for hungry gulls searching for scraps.

The briny air, awash with the stench of yesterday's catch, stung Vince's nose in a familiar and welcoming way. With his bag over his shoulder, he took the thief by the scruff of his neck, and marched deeper into town.

The crowds of traders, dockworkers, and sailors sundered themselves before him and fell quiet when he drew near. He kept his head down and carried on walking. He no longer needed the aid of his cane but thought it added some sophistication to his appearance, especially given his newest acquisition of a patch over his left eye.

Had he not already towered over the townsfolk, his clothing would still have set him apart. Sartorially speaking, he never truly overcame his brawler beginnings. His cream-coloured top shirt had seen better days and his black trousers had long ago begun to fray their edges. Yesterday, he'd attended his brother's handfasting on the nearby island of Merryapple, and he'd accidentally left his favourite claret overcoat behind. Not that he needed it that morning. His tricorne cap, cracked and scaly in places, covered his snowy white hair and kept the morning sun from his lone icy blue eye.

Port Knot's sole Watch House sat at a crossroads on the west side of town. Three storeys tall, it had a low front door painted in cornflower blue and a single window set with rusted iron bars. Above these, the sand-coloured bricks rose to an arch and then to a gable, in a wholly unnecessary architectural flourish. Like most buildings in town, thin copper pipes ran across the surface like veins under sallow skin.

The bridges of Port Knot infested the town like rats. Long, short, arched, flat, and each one different from the last. Lickbeer Bridge connected the road above Vince's head to the first floor of the Watch House and protruded from the side of it like a hernia. The arch had been carved to resemble the open mouth of a bearded man, swallowing all who travelled through.

As with the rest of the town, the Watch House had been built too close to the surrounding premises, and indeed the entire street had the appearance of an overstuffed bookshelf.

Within, Vince found a grimy pit of browns and mustards. The Watch House saw hardly any sun, so a plethora of lanterns fought bravely against the gloom.

Vince all but threw the thief onto a chair. "Stay," he said, pointing. "Or else."

Crabmeat sat in front of the thief and growled.

Vince let his bag of clothes slump to the dusty floor. He tapped his octopus-handled cane on the knotted wooden floorboards. "Anybody in?"

A voice from a backroom called out to him and presently a slim, dark-haired woman in her early twenties greeted him. She wore oversized tan trousers held up by braces, a striped shirt splattered with oil, and a pair of goggles perched on top of her head. She gripped a hammer in one hand and scowled.

"Got you a present," Vince said, nodding to the thief.

"Ah, sure that's very kind of you, altogether." She raised the hammer a little and steadied herself. "And who might you be, now?"

"Vince Knight. Watch Commander."

She recoiled but caught herself and recovered. "Oh. Oh!" She set the hammer on a table and cleaned her hand on an oily rag. She shook his hand, hers so tiny in his. "I didn't know you were coming today. I'm Sorcha Fontaine, Watchwoman. There's no one else here; the others don't start until nightfall. I came in early to fix the plumbing. It's not very reliable."

The thief rose from his chair. "I can see you have your hands full; there's really no point in me hanging around."

Crabmeat barked at him and he sat back down immediately.

"I must admit, it was a surprise to hear you were taking over," Sorcha said. "It wasn't so long ago we were trying to arrest you." She tried to laugh but it didn't come out right. Too dry.

"Things change." Vince strode around the Watch House, taking it all in. It held a few tables, a few chairs, and not much else.

"Well, I suppose it takes a criminal to catch a criminal," the thief said.

"What did he do this time?" Sorcha asked.

"Helped relieve a woman of her purse and necklace," Vince said.

"It wasn't me, I swear! I didn't do anything!"

Vince rushed over and grabbed the thief's arm, pulling up his sleeve to reveal a vambrace. "Explain this."

"I'm looking after it for a friend..."

"Frogblade," Sorcha said. "Nasty little things, they are. Tool of choice of the Clockbreakers. A twist of the wrist is all it takes for a little arm tipped with a razorblade to flash in and out, quick as a frog snatching a fly. The blade slices the pocket of the unsuspecting victim, their wallet slips out into a hand or an open bag, and the victim is none the wiser. How long did it take you to learn not to cut your own hands open with it?"

"Longer than you'd think..." the thief said. Faded white lines crossed his palms.

"Clockbreakers?" Vince asked.

"It's what they call themselves now," Sorcha said. "I thought you'd have known all about them?"

"Been away from town for a while." Vince had spent most of his fifty-three years living in the town but recent events had taken him to the countryside for a spell.

"All the pickpockets, housebreakers, and shoplifters banded together last year, after you and Councillor Mudge... well...left. They started using all this fancy horological technology, thanks to Flowers and his contacts in the industry. And they've been a right pain the arse ever since, haven't yis?"

Vince wrenched the frogblade off the thief's bony arm.

Sorcha rooted in a deep drawer and withdrew a set of rusty shackles. "Now, we'll just trade your bracelet for these and drag him to the magistrates for sentencing. Then it's off to the gaolhouse with him."

"Him has a name," the thief said. "It's Walter. Not that anybody cares."

"I already know your name," Sorcha said. "And if I thought it mattered, I'd have used it." She clamped the manacles onto his bony wrists. "Who do you report to? Merlin or Flowers?"

"Flowers," Walter said.

"Know him," Vince said. "One of my boys, once."

"He's moved up in the world since then," Sorcha said. "He's one of the higher-ranking Clockbreakers now."

"Knew he had potential."

"You taught him well," Sorcha said.

Vince wasn't sure if he was supposed to hear that. She was right though. Vince had taught Flowers everything he knew. Taught him how to be a thief, yes, but Vince had taught him how to live in the corners of society. How to make a life for himself in a world that insisted it had no place for people like him. Vince had done the same for so many people, taken so many lost souls off the streets and given their lives purpose and meaning. And now he was going to betray them. Every single one.

CHAPTER TWO

"YES, ALL OF them! Why would I want only some of the ratlines inspected? See to it this deck is spotless by the time I return. I want a full inventory of ammunition and rations, and I expect to see those spars repaired." Captain James Godgrave descended the gangplank of his ship, the *Lancelot Striking*, and wrinkled his nose at the odour of the bustling docklands. Overhead, cranes turned, lifting goods from ships and depositing them on carts. Dockhands scurried past, ferrying ropes and other odds and ends. Ahead, market stalls plied their wares to feverish shoppers. A skinny greyhound tied to a butt by a frayed piece of rope whimpered at anyone who caught its gaze.

James's lieutenant approached, turned out to the nines. "The carriage is just up ahead, sir. As they said it would be."

Shiny black and with the seal of the Chase Trading Company emblazoned on the door, the carriage stood out from its grotty surroundings like a marble headstone on a muddy grave. James climbed into the plush plum interior and thumped the ceiling with the underside of his fist.

The coachman took them along Quarrier's Run, the twisting main road leading from the long, curving swathe of docklands to the centre of town. James had been there only twice before and found it busier each time. The roadsides swarmed with people going about their day. A trading town with a busy harbour, Port Knot also had numerous quarries and mines farther inland. The town found itself caught between the land and the sea in more ways than one.

The copper pipes around every building clattered with the water they carried. To his left, workers laboured to tear down a house. To his right, construction continued on a new one. His lieutenant, Pertinacity Hancock, ignored most of the activity.

"Has it changed much since the last time you were home?" James asked.

"Not in any way that matters," she said.

A man cried out from a side street, evidently the victim of a robbery, and he dashed after two young girls who bundled a coin purse and expensive cane in their arms, giggling all the while.

James leaned his head out of the carriage window. "I say, Perty, shouldn't we stop and help?"

"No point," Perty said. "They'll be in the Entries by now."

On the balcony of a theatre, a set of horological automata played instruments. Tin mice and copperplate cats blew into horns and plucked strings, seemingly producing the sounds of one of Handel's operas, albeit greatly reduced.

The carriage took them through the centre and to the south side of town, where the architecture underwent a marked change. The businesses became fewer, the noises quieter, and the houses bigger. Many sat in their own grounds, surrounded by high iron fences. They came to a stop outside one such mansion.

A footwoman with the most remarkable hazel eyes James had ever seen welcomed them. She escorted them through the gates, up the winding flagstone pathway, and through the arched front doors of the buff-coloured mansion. The hallway, a pleasing sea green, held oil paintings of stern-faced aristocrats and oddly thin dogs.

In a cheery drawing room, James discovered a decanter with brandy and poured some into a tumbler. He caught himself in a gilt looking glass and checked the ends of his moustache and the point of his short ducktail beard. Always broad in the beam, he'd put on a little more weight at sea, not an easy thing to do. His uniform bulged slightly at the buttons.

"Captain Godgrave, such a delight."

He turned to find the nude form of Mrs Dorothea Chase walking towards him, hand outstretched. He grinned widely. "A pleasure to see you again, Councillor Chase."

"I must insist you address me as Swan, Captain. Standards must be maintained."

"Of course, I wouldn't have it any other way. This is my lieutenant, Pertinacity Hancock."

"Oh, now, you must be a local with a name like that."

"I am, ma'am." Perty hovered awkwardly by the window until beckoned to sit. "Port Knot, born and bred."

A woman in her late forties with a round face and a fuller figure, Dorothea Chase's inclination towards nakedness was well known but James had never witnessed it before today. Unburdened by prudishness or an overdeveloped sense of shame himself, he found it rather delightful. Perty appeared less than impressed, which came as no surprise. James had always found her a touch stuffy.

"How are you finding your new position on the council?" James asked.

"Chaffing," she said. "But not without its uses. I hope you both won't object to my attire or lack thereof? I dislike clothes at the best of times, and I find this heat to be simply unbearable."

"I believe we should all be as comfortable as possible in our own homes," James said. "Shall I pour you a drink?"

"It's a little early... Oh, why not? This is a special occasion."

Every member of the ruling council of Blackrabbit took on an animal name. As Swan, her responsibilities lay in managing the waters around the island. A very useful position for the owner of a shipping company to be in. James handed her a drink, and they sat facing one another on matching pink satin settees.

"Captain, you probably won't have seen much of the town yet, but let me assure you it is in turmoil," Swan said. "For the past few months, we have been held to ransom by the whims of warring criminal cabals. For a time, we didn't dare to leave our homes after sunset for fear of being caught in their crossfire. Every morning brought with it a fresh body on our streets. Now, rumour has it they've settled their differences and have re-organised themselves. No home is safe from thieves. Every road out of town is fraught with highwaymen, and who knows what manner of illicit goods pass through our harbour every day.

"The local Watch is woefully incapable of dealing with this problem and now Rabbit has appointed a criminal to command them. I find this to be a disgrace I cannot long tolerate. A fish rots from the head down. Where Port Knot goes, so follows the rest of Blackrabbit. In short, I believe we deserve a better town protector. I wish it to be you."

"I'm flattered, of course," James said, taking a sip of brandy, "but why me? Surely there must be plenty of Blackrabbiters who could fill the post?"

"We have met several times before and I find you to be an upstanding person with a firm moral backbone. And a company man, through and through. I believe the Chase Trading Company is best equipped to protect the town and the island. After all, we practically built it. Without us, this would be a scrub of shale and grass like Merryapple. My family put too much into this town for me to stand by and watch it crumble. Do you accept my offer?"

"I do."

"Excellent. I will garner support from the rest of the council, and when the time is right I will see to it that you are appointed. Until then, I should like to keep this discussion between us. I suggest you think about who among your crew would be best suited to aid you in this endeavour. Once you're appointed, the *Lancelot Striking* will be assigned a new captain."

"I'll be sorry to say farewell to the old girl." James raised his glass and smiled. "Still, onwards and upwards."

They sat and talked for another hour or so before returning to the waiting carriage. James rifled in his pocket, lifted some snuff from a silver box, set it on the back of his hand, and sniffed. He offered some to Perty, who declined, as she always did. "I should very much like you by my side, of course."

"Oh," Perty said, shifting about in her seat. "I see."

"Is something the matter?"

"No, it's just... I joined the C.T.C. to get away from this place."

"I can always ask someone else."

"No, no," Perty said. "It's just a surprise. It would be an

honour."

"Splendid," James said. "Keep it to yourself for now. I have some idea of who I'd like to take with me but I'd be interested in hearing your thoughts. Draw up a list of who you think might be best suited. About a dozen or so should do it. I want Spradbery. He's overdue for promotion."

Perty picked her fingernails. "Sir, what about the town Watch?"

James shrugged. "We'll get rid of them, first thing. I assume it's the usual collection of useless reprobates and old codgers. Hardly a great loss."

CHAPTER THREE

VINCE HAD LOST his connection to the town. Since last Midwinter, he had been living and working at the newly founded Wolfe-Chase Asylum in the countryside. His mother had been put in charge of running the place, and she'd hired him as a porter, security guard, and general workhorse. He'd kept himself away from society as much as possible. An easier task than he'd expected as his mother had always found plenty of work to keep him busy.

Just before sunset, he leaned against a wall, arms folded, with his one good eye to the door. Sorcha sat at a desk with her head resting in her hands and a massive grin on her face.

Within minutes, the Port Knot Night Watch arrived. The group waved to Sorcha who smiled and pointed behind them. They jumped when they found Vince staring back at them, stony-faced and silent. One of them, a stout, tattooed woman in her forties, immediately raised her fists.

"Now, Ruth, there's no need for that," Sorcha said. "This is our new Commander. Vince Knight, this is Mrs Ruth Whimple. She's been here longer than I have."

Sorcha gestured to a pair of men around Vince's own age. "Messrs Frank Rundle and Clive Hext are our newest recruits, fresh in from the war with the Dutch. Or against the Dutch. I'm not sure which. Both wounded in the same battle by the same shot, if you can believe it."

"It went through my hip and into his leg." Frank Rundle dropped the top of his breeches to show Vince the wound, a round white lump amidst a field of curly black hair.

"Put it away, Frank; we've all seen it," Sorcha said.

"Took my leg clean off below the knee," Clive Hext said. "Frank kept me sane until help arrived. I lost my leg and my heart on the same day." He leaned over, took Frank by the hand, kissing it.

"Sappy eejits, the pair of yis," Sorcha said. "And this here is our stalwart beadle, Mr Jack Norton."

They all shook Vince's hand except for Mr Norton, a portly middle-aged man with little hair on the top of his head and none whatsoever on his face. He turned the key on a striker-lantern at his desk, flaring the candle within to life. "So, you're the one Rabbit brought in to keep an eye on us. The great Mr Invincible Knight."

Vince straightened up, growing even taller. Already bigger than anyone else on the island, he did it to intimidate people, and it always worked. Well, nearly always.

Mr Norton eyed him up and down, from the tip of his boots to the snowy hair on his head. "We never needed any help before."

"Never had gangs running wild in the streets before," Vince said.

"Because you were always around to keep them in line. Shouldn't you be out there with them?"

Vince lifted his chin, addressing the whole room. "Get something straight from the off. Rabbit put me in charge because you lot failed. Walking around busting up tavern brawls isn't enough anymore. Gangs ran rampant for weeks. People were scared. Couldn't rely on you to protect them. Watch is going to have to toughen up or this town is going down in flames. Don't like it, door's behind me."

"I'm not going anywhere, big man," Mr Norton said. "I've been a Watchman for fifteen years, and I'm not about to let a jumped-up lout like you run me off."

Vince leaned over him, fists clenched. Mr Norton, short and round, barely came up to his chest, but still, he stood his ground.

"Oi, oi, late again," Ruth said.

"This is the last part of our little team," Sorcha said. "Vince Knight, meet Mr Alfie Exeter."

"It's the third time this month," Mr Norton said, pointing and ignoring Vince. "I'm docking your pay."

Alfie Exeter nodded to Vince and scowled at Mr Norton. A young man around Sorcha's age, with masses of dark hair swept back from his handsome face and away from his piercing green eyes. He winked at Sorcha as he passed by and took his seat. "Mr Norton," he said, "Port Knot is a pit of iniquity, a cauldron of the criminal class. Whether I arrive ten minutes early or ten minutes late makes no appreciable difference whatsoever in stemming the tide of malefaction breaking over all of us."

"You can explain it all to the people of the Tangles tonight," Mr Norton said. "Ruth, you too."

"What did I do?" Ruth asked, throwing her hands in the

air.

"Nothing," Mr Norton said, "but someone has to keep an eye on him."

Vince's brow furrowed as he scanned the room. "The rest?"

Sorcha pursed her lips. "The rest? Oh! No, this is it. We, ah, we had three people resign when they heard you were taking over. All of them had been with the Watch for years. They objected to serving under you."

"Perfectly understandable, if you ask me," Mr Norton said.

"Some of us are thankful to have some proper leadership." Alfie Exeter shot daggers at Norton. "Finally, we'll get something done around here."

"It's not like you to want to do something." Clive's accent singled him out squarely as a local. From the south of the island, Vince guessed.

"Not all of us are content to hobble our way round, putting in the time before we fill our grave," Exeter said.

"Watch your tongue, boy," Clive said. "We fought wars for you, you know."

"You fought in one war, and you got sent home after a week," Exeter said, holding up a single finger for emphasis.

Clive put his foot on a chair and rolled up his trouser leg, revealing a brass pegleg, close to the natural colour of his skin. He clanged it with his fist. "I got this for you!"

"Oh, you really shouldn't have." Exeter held his hands open. "I didn't get you anything."

"I told you not to bang on it so hard!" Sorcha knelt by Clive and examined the leg. She unlocked a hatch in the calf and checked the pistons inside. "If you want it to keep working, you have to treat it gently. Otherwise, it's back to the wooden one for you."

"Any relation to Nurse Hext?" Vince asked.

Clive frowned at him. "My nephew," he said. "He works at the asylum. He told me about you. How you'd lurk around the gardens and corridors, scaring the patients."

The patients at the asylum were mostly prisoners transferred from Blackrabbit Gaol who required specialised help. Some of them had a tendency to kick up from time to time. It had been part of Vince's role to keep them in line.

"Local boy?" Vince asked.

Alfie Exeter stood and straightened his waistcoat. "Born and bred."

"Barley or Gravel?"

Exeter grinned and licked his teeth. "Gravel. How did

you know?"

The wealthiest areas of the town were Barley Hill and Gravel Hill. In Vince's experience, they bred a singularly cocky type of young man. "Experience," he said. "Hadn't you better get going?"

Exeter took Ruth by the arm and marched her to the door where she pulled free of him. "I told you before not to do that," she said.

"Dammit, Ruth, I love you, and I don't care who knows it." He laughed and smiled at Sorcha, who brushed some stray hairs behind her ear.

"You're a bottle-headed rake," Ruth said. "And if my husband catches you talking like that, he'll knock out what little brains you have." She shoved him in the back, and they were on their way.

"Don't mind him," Sorcha said. "He's only here because his da insisted on it. He wanted him to have some sort of *real life experience.*"

"Rich people talk for actual work," Clive said. "He's slumming it down here with the rest of us before he takes over his family mining business."

"Thought the name sounded familiar," Vince said. "Small mine on the west coast?"

"The very same." Frank lifted a staff and together with Clive, they walked slowly out of the Watch House.

Vince frowned as they left. "Not much use in a fight, those two."

Sorcha rocked her head from side to side. "Their heart's in the right place though."

Vince lifted his hands. "Rather have heavy fists than a good heart in this battle."

JAMES TOOK THE list from Perty and quickly scanned through the names. "Yes, these are all who I was thinking of. The perfect roster for this fight. Except for Tresome. Do you believe she'll be capable?"

"She's a fine officer," Perty said. "She hasn't been given much of a chance to shine on board the *Lancelot*. I think with the right encouragement she could prosper."

"I'm sure she'll flourish under your tutelage."

A knock at the cabin door stirred them.

"Ah, Spradbery, come in, come in," James said.

A bony chap, Carter Spradbery had shoulder-length flaxen hair and a sort of wet look about him but had proven himself a thoroughly capable sergeant nonetheless.

James rested his ample backside on the edge of his desk. He took a pinch of seeds from his palm and fed them to his peregrine falcon, Maclaren.

"She's a beautiful bird, sir," Spradbery said.

"Isn't she just? When I last visited my family home in Scotland, I took quite a shine to her. It took me no time at all to train her. I've been training birds since I was a lad, you know."

"I don't think I've ever known a peregrine to be taken to sea, sir."

"My father assured me the bird would not survive on a ship for months. I must confess how delighted I am in proving him wrong."

"I saw the drawing Tresome made for you of Maclaren in flight, swooping around the rigging. Truly brilliant work, I'm sure your father agreed."

James stood and brushed the bird seed from his hands. "You would have thought so, wouldn't you?" James still took great delight in the bird, but now when she soared around the deck and out over the sea, he found his pleasure tainted by his father's indifference to the artwork James had sent to him. "Sit, please."

Spradbery pulled his chair from the desk and slightly away from Perty.

"I believe Perty has brought you up to speed?" James asked.

Spradbery avoided looking at her. "She has, sir. If I might say, I'm surprised at you accepting this role."

"How so?"

"You always struck me as having saltwater in your veins."

James smiled and sat behind his desk. "When the order arrived some weeks ago to come to Blackrabbit, it contained no information pertaining to the reason. Now that I know, I find myself relishing the opportunity it presents. I love the sea as much as the next sailor, but there's no feeling quite like watching the sun set on your own land. Feeling the soil between your fingers when you plant a tree. The stewardship of animals that would otherwise starve without you.

"I can easily picture myself taking a house in the Blackrabbit countryside. Some grand place with acres of rolling grassland and a staff of dozens. I am perfectly at home at sea but the truth is I can make my home anywhere."

James's father, an admiral in the royal navy, had instilled

in him a drive to succeed, raised him to believe the world was his for the taking. James saw no reason to dispute it. At forty-five, he was a captain. By fifty, he would be an admiral. Sooner, if he impressed in his role as town protector. No matter what it took, he would look his father in the eye as an equal—at last. "It's an exciting opportunity for a young officer like yourself. I know a hungry heart when I see one. So, do you have an answer for me?"

Spradbery took a deep breath. "I have some reservations, sir."

James sat back in his seat and rested a hand on the arm-rest. "Oh?"

Spradbery looked at the desk, the floor, the wall—anywhere but at Perty. "I don't know if I'm the best person to have on your team, sir. I think... I think I might prefer to remain at sea."

James furrowed his brow and nodded to Perty. "You mean you don't relish the idea of working with Lieutenant Hancock?"

Spradbery's face turned red. "I never said as much, sir, I..."

"You didn't need to say it," James said. "Unspoken words can be clearer than any statesman's speech. I don't know what's transpired between you two, but it's hung over the ship like a cloud for months now."

Perty cleared her throat. "A simple clash of personalities, sir."

James's voice grew sharper. "There's nothing simple about it. Now look here, the pair of you. You're two of my best officers. I need you by my side. I want you to take yourselves off to somewhere private and hash out whatever this is between you. Scream at one another, shout, hurl abuse, throw fists, sleep together, whatever it takes to clear the air. Do you hear me? I won't have my officers behaving like children."

Perty lifted her chin while Spradbery bit his lip—both of them trying to compose themselves.

"There's an alehouse I know of," Perty said.

Spradbery finally looked at her and nodded.

"Splendid." James shook Spradbery's hand. "Mum's the word for now but I hope we won't be kept waiting for too long. Just between us three, this should grease the palm of the admiralty for us. Port Knot is the home of the C.T.C. This is where we'll make our names; mark my words. If we do good work here, we'll be off to bigger and better things in no time."

CHAPTER FOUR

VINCE SAT IN the sickly yellow gloom of the Watch House while his dog slept on the feet of a thief. Not exactly how'd he pictured his first night in his new role. Walter squirmed in his chair, trying to get comfortable without waking Crabmeat. The ticking of the clock on the wall grew louder every hour, Vince would swear it.

"I really do think I should go," Walter said. "I'm sure you have bigger things to worry about than me."

"He can't stay here forever, you know," Mr Norton said. "He'd be better off in the gaolhouse. At least he'll be fed and watered regularly. Which is probably more than can be said for his home life."

Walter rolled his eyes. "That's the best I can hope for, is it? Just to be fed and watered? Like an animal? That's all I am to you?"

"Oh, no," Mr Norton said. "Animals are useful."

"Gaolhouse," Vince said. "Learn to be a better thief in the gaolhouse."

"People like him have to learn it somewhere," Mr Norton said, "since you will no longer be teaching them."

"Not as if I trained each and every gang member," Vince said. "Only the special ones."

"There goes what's left of my self-esteem," Walter said, rolling his eyes.

Mr Norton's quill scratched across the pages of the book in front of him. The shelves behind him held stacks of similar books, all bound in indigo covers.

"Didn't know you kept records," Vince said.

Mr Norton held up his quill. "Everyone who comes through our door goes in here. I expected you to be in here, sooner or later. Though not on the roster, I must admit. Why are you sitting here, by the way? Shouldn't you be out on patrol?"

"Waiting for the right time," Vince said. "No sense

blundering around, picking off strays. Need to strike at the heart of the gangs.”

Mr Norton rolled his eyes and returned to his writing.

“You lot waste your time on people like me—victims of circumstance—when the real criminals run riot,” Walter said.

“You are a real criminal, Walter,” Mr Norton said. “You’ve picked every pocket in the Entries.”

“But it’s not as if I’ve killed anyone,” Walter said.

The door to the Watch House suddenly slammed open, thumping against the wall. Ruth held one hand on the frame, panting for breath. “The docks,” she said. “We’ve found a body at the docks.”

Vince and Mr Norton glared at Walter.

He held up his manacled hands. “It wasn’t me, I swear!”

Vince leaned in and snarled at him. “Better not have been. Else you’ll be a victim of more than just circumstance. Crabmeat, stay. Keep an eye on him.”

Vince followed Ruth out of the Watch House and down Rope Burn Road, his boots scraping on the cobblestones. It would still be a few hours before the sun rose but every taverner, barber, apothecary, and chandler in town hung candle lanterns outside their doors until daybreak. They provided much-needed light, for even at such a late hour, the town had plenty of life about it.

Bakers struggled with their ovens, bedworkers plied their trade, and drunken people staggered home, had arguments, and relieved themselves in doorways.

"I suppose this is a new experience for you," Ruth said.

Vince frowned at her. "Don't understand you?"

"Hurrying towards a dead body, instead of away from one?"

A deep growl rumbled in Vince's chest. She wasn't frightened of him in the slightest. "Seen you before," he said. "From the other side of the law."

"Oh yes? I can't say I've ever set eyes on you before."

"By design," Vince said. "Some of my best people have run afoul of your mace. Always thought one day I'd have to buy you off or put you down."

Ruth smirked at him. "Pity you never got the chance to try. Down there, between those old barrels."

Under the pier, Alfie Exeter stood guard. Vince shooed some gulls away from the corpse. A man in his late twenties or early thirties, Vince guessed.

"Poor bugger got drunk and drowned when the tide came in," Ruth said.

"Not likely," Vince said, leaning the body forward.

"Unless he could sleep with a knife in his back."

"Looks recent," Exeter said. "Plenty of blood around. No sign of the knife, though. What about his purse?"

"Gone," Vince said, checking the victim's pockets. "No jewellery, either."

"A robbery, then," Ruth said. "They can turn nasty, sometimes."

The dead man wore the black boots, cream breeches, and emerald-green overcoat of the Chase Trading Company.

"Didn't mention he was a greencoat," Vince said. "Complicates things. Just stumbled across him?"

Ruth shook her head. "We overheard some men talking in the Tangles. A sailor named Winkleigh said he'd seen a body down here but didn't want any fuss so he didn't report it to anyone."

The sea sloshed towards them, kissing the corpse's feet.

"Need to speak to the harbourmaster," Vince said, looking out to sea. "Don't move the body soon, it'll be washed away."

"The harbourmaster won't be on this late," Ruth said. "There's an undertaker on Crowstone Row. I'll go fetch them."

"Won't still be open, surely?" Vince asked

"They're used to working late these days."

THE HALF-TIMBERED town hall, like most places in Port Knot, sat askew, as though it were a cake threatening to topple over. Unlike most places, it had a ring of iron railings and a smattering of marble columns. Not long after dawn, Vince adjusted his eyepatch as he climbed the half-dozen stone steps and passed through its front doors.

Portraits of past council members, each wearing their mask of office and long since dead, hung on the walls with an air of historic significance laced with displeasure. Vince felt they were all disgusted by his presence in their expensive mosaicked hallway.

Mrs Agatha Samble, chairwoman of the island council, had been talking with two dreary men when she spotted him. A sombre woman with grey hair worn in a simple style and with deep wrinkles about her eyes, he addressed her by her official title of Rabbit.

"Mr Knight, this is a surprise."

"Need to talk," he said. "Privately."

She beckoned him to follow her to her office on the next floor. They passed by more than a few council workers who gave them a wide berth. Vince ducked under the beams of the bright hallways.

"Wasn't expecting a personal welcome." Vince sat in a leather chair that likely cost more than he could expect to earn in a year.

"And I wasn't expecting to provide one. But I think it will be for everyone's benefit," Rabbit said. "It may take some time before people get used to seeing you about the place." She sat at a high desk covered in documents. Behind her, a crescent window overlooked Trivia Place, where the three main roads of Port Knot converged.

"Makes my hair stand on end, walking in the front door," Vince said. "Used to be I had to sneak in through the cellar."

"Those days are behind us," Rabbit said, a touch too quickly. She put on her best politician's smile. "A new start for all of us, Mr Knight. A new start. Now, I hear you've already made your first arrest. It must be a nice change of pace, being on the right side of the law."

"Might get a taste for it. Knocking heads to help people instead of hurting them."

Rabbit cleared her throat. "I hired you to break the gangs in any way you see fit. I suppose I should have known it would involve violence. But you will at least try to bring them to justice, won't you?"

"Course. But if some heads get cracked..."

Rabbit templed her fingers and fixed her faltering smile. "What can I do for you, Mr Knight?"

Vince picked some dirt from under his fingernail. "Found a body last night. Displayed under Quither Pier."

"*Displayed?*" Rabbit narrowed her eyes. "Talking from experience, are we?"

Vince raised his eyebrows. "Really want to know? Can't say for certain but feels almost like the killer left him for someone to find."

She picked up some paper to avoid looking at him. "You don't need to run to me to report every crime in the town."

"Don't intend to. Special case, this."

"Why? Who was it?"

"Don't know yet. But he was a greencoat."

Rabbit tutted and set the paper down. "Damn. The C.T.C. will have to be informed."

"Thought so. Leave that part to you."

Rabbit sighed and balled her fists on the table. "They're

going to want to become involved in the search for the killer."

"Let them," Vince said, shrugging. "Enough on my plate with the gangs."

"I'm afraid I'm going to have to ask one further thing of you, Mr Knight. I intend to stop the C.T.C. from becoming involved in the hunt. And I'm going to have to insist the Watch steers clear of them. You must not enlist their help in finding the culprit."

"Because?"

Rabbit licked her lips. "Can I trust you, Mr Knight?"

Vince crossed his arms. "Seem to be the only one who does."

"I suspect there are those on the council who would like my time as Rabbit to come to an end. And I believe they are making plans for it to come about sooner rather than later. Having to rely on the C.T.C. to find one simple murderer would make the Watch look...inefficient. Having you fail as commander would go quite some ways to making my judge-ment appear flawed. Without me to voice support for you, you would be removed from the Watch before you had time to unpack your belongings. In short, it behoves both of us for you to succeed in this matter. And quickly."

VINCE HAD BEEN slowly pacing the floor of the Watch House for some time when Sorcha arrived.

"Oh, you're here already," she said. "Wait, have you been here since last night?"

"Went to talk to Rabbit, first thing," Vince said. "And someone needed to keep an eye on him."

Walter lay fast asleep in his chair, still manacled to a desk, a line of drool on his chin.

"I forgot he was still here. He can't stay in that chair forever," Sorcha said. "And you need some proper rest."

"Don't need much sleep."

The rest of the Watch arrived soon after, and Vince gathered them around. "Suppose our first order of business should be the body at Quither Pier," he said. "Want everyone keeping an eye and ear out for information."

The Watch exchanged glances with one another.

"What do you mean?" Exeter asked.

"Want to catch who done it."

"I know but who's going to tell us?"

Vince sat in a cracked leather chair and frowned.

Sorcha cleared her throat. "If I may? I believe in your day-to-day life, you must have been privy to all manner of information from the underbelly of the town. The Watch never has been. Is it at all possible you haven't stopped to consider how this new role has cut you off from that sort of information?"

Vince's icy blue eye darted up and down. He would have liked nothing more than to leave the hunt for the killer to the greencoats. He grunted. "Gangs are what I'm here for. Been running the place since I left. Ends now. Killer is probably one of them. First target—the Clockbreakers. Soft. Should be easy enough to take care of. Know how many there are?"

"As far as I know, there's only about a dozen left," Sorcha said.

"Fourteen," Walter said, wiping his mouth. "We've been recruiting."

"So few?" Vince asked.

"A lot of them didn't want to sign up to the new structure," Sorcha said, drawing her thumb across her throat. "They weren't asked twice."

Vince paced over to where Walter sat, stretching and yawning.

"Don't know you," Vince said.

"I, uh, I know you though," Walter said, squirming in his seat. "Or least, I know about you. Flowers recruited me a couple of years ago, before you, uh, abdicated. I've heard stories about you. I hoped I'd never meet you."

The window shattered, scattering glass across the floor which crunched under Vince's boots as he bolted out of the front door. Ten or more people had gathered on the road outside the Watch House. Each one brandished a cudgel of one kind or another—something short, hefty, and easily concealed. In the centre of the group, a man with a horseshoe hairline and red moustache adjusted his spectacles.

"Littletar." Vince raised his fists.

"It is true, then," Littletar said. "You are working with the Watch. When I tell you I never thought I'd see the day, I'm underselling it. The thought never even crossed my mind. It's like finding out King George is pulling pints in the Jack Thistle."

The rest of the Watch filed out onto the street. Ruth swung her mace, Clive grasped his Watch staff in both hands, Frank threw his staff between either hand, and Exeter pulled a knife from his belt.

"Surrender," Vince said.

Littletar stared at him, his mouth open. "You're serious. You think we're just going to hand ourselves over to you?"

"Know what'll happen if you don't." Vince set himself in place, shoulders hunched, fists raised to his face.

Littletar scratched the top of his own head with his fingernail. "Funny, before, I would have known exactly what would happen. But I keep thinking about the eyepatch you've taken to wearing. I keep thinking it means someone got the better of you. I keep thinking that maybe, just maybe, you're not quite the man you used to be." He retreated to the back of the crowd as his people rushed forward.

Ruth swung her mace, connecting to the side of a man's head and sending him clattering to the ground in a quivering heap. Vince swung his fist at the young man advancing on him and missed. The young man laughed, and Vince swung again, and again, missing each time. Clive's staff found the young man's throat and made him stagger backwards, coughing. Vince snarled and defended against his next attacker. He swung out again, this time landing a blow on his attacker's face. And the next.

Exeter slashed furiously with his knife with little regard for who he injured. Indeed, he caught Clive's woollen cloak in one of his arcs, tearing a hole in it. Exeter pranced forward, cutting all around him. "Who else wants some, eh? Come on, then!"

Littletar had scarpered shortly after the fight had begun. Those of his gang who could, now scattered in every direction.

"After them!" Exeter said.

Vince grabbed his arm. "Let them go."

Exeter pulled himself free. "Get off me, you coward!"

"Could be a trap. No idea who else is waiting around the corner."

"I don't care. I'll take them all on!"

Vince leaned over Exeter, letting his shadow engulf him. "No."

Exeter stopped bouncing around on his heels and stood still. "Have it your way...Commander."

On the road, several of Littletar's gang lay unconscious, or bleeding, or both.

"Here we go." Clive helped one up. "Off to the magistrates with you, boy."

"Wait," Vince said. "No sense bringing them there. Magistrates use greencoat guards. Know for a fact some of them are on the take. Bribed more than a few of them myself in my time. Want somewhere we can keep an eye on them."

"What do you suggest?" Sorcha asked.

Vince paced into the Watch House. "Rooms over there, what're they for?"

"It's where I store the Watch records," said Mr Norton. "I have books going back decades."

"Move them," Vince said. "Someone get down to the blacksmiths and order iron bars and good, sturdy doors. Tonight, we're making some cells."

THE CLOSEST SMITHY was a couple of roads away in the area known as Ironworks and had everything Vince needed. Iron rods had a dozen uses in a busy harbour town and were always on hand. He spent a long night putting bars on the window and installing cell doors with help from whichever member of the Watch wasn't out on patrol or guarding the prisoners.

The beadle Norton sat with his nose in his ledger the entire time and didn't lift a finger to help. "We never needed cells before," he said. "We're not a gaolhouse."

After installing Walter as the inaugural occupant, Vince

turned his attention to his desk. He held up his cane to the wall, nodded to himself, then marked two spots with chalk. Over these he placed two metal hooks, driving them into the stone wall with Sorcha's hammer. He took his octopus-handled cane and lay it over the hooks.

Mr Norton tutted. "It's skew-whiff."

Vince grunted at him.

Sorcha locked the cell door behind the injured gang members. "Won't you be needing it to walk with?"

Vince shook his head. "Injured a couple of months ago. Stick was a gift from a friend. Healed now."

"Fair enough. You can always use your staff instead. Have you got yours yet? Every Watch member gets issued with a staff. And a lantern, too. The roads can get very dark at night. And the Entries. Especially the Entries, actually."

"Not one for weapons." Vince held up his fists. "Started life as a boxer."

"Well, in case your hands don't glow in the dark like two fubsy moons, there are spare lanterns in the cupboard over there. And given how you fared against Littletar's Pennymen earlier, you might want to rethink your position on weapons."

Vince scowled at her.

She shrank slightly from him. "I'm just saying—I didn't

expect the great Vince Knight not to land his punches."

Vince sniffed sharply and turned away. "Eyepatch," he said. "Not used to it yet."

CHAPTER FIVE

JUST BEFORE DAWN, the Watch returned from their usual patrols. They gave a general report to Mr Norton who scribbled some notes in his indigo record book. Vince sat at his desk, learning how they all worked.

His mind had been churning all night. When he was in his previous position, he'd never given the Watch much thought. They were to be avoided, yes, but rarely feared. Their numbers waxed and waned like the tide. If there had been a war or a least a serious battle overseas, one could expect the Watch's numbers to swell soon after as injured soldiers sought out some other way to serve their community.

Vince had been raised in an orphanage as his mother had devoted her life to serving the wealthy family she worked for. When Vince was old enough, she sent for him to join the household staff, working first in the kitchens, then in the stables. He had his eyes opened to a whole new world of wealth and privilege. A world so different from his squalid beginnings.

Vince started his criminal career when he was still a young man, no more than a boy, really. Always big, always brawny, he began working for a local thug and soon found he had both a taste and an aptitude for violence. Over the years, he climbed through the ranks, drawing the best–and the worst–people to his side. Collecting strays, as his late husband had once put it. Those Vince couldn't bend to his will, he broke and left as a warning to others. For decades, he ruled the underbelly of the island, amassing enormous power and influence. And in doing so, he became a target. The head of a rival gang murdered Vince's beloved husband, and once Vince had exacted his grim revenge, he sought a way out of the life he'd built.

By that time, he was working with Mr Baxbary Mudge—a wealthy local man with political ambitions. Vince helped him to achieve them, lifting Baxbary Mudge to the role of Fox on

Blackrabbit Council. Mudge used Vince as his personal bodyguard and wasn't averse to wielding Vince's gangs as a weapon to intimidate his rivals. Vince was content to let him until the day at the winter solstice last year when Mudge went too far.

Mudge used Vince and his gangs in his violent bid to overthrow the entire council. Vince turned on Mudge, on his own people, and helped put an end to the attempted coup. When the dust had settled, Mudge was sent to the gaolhouse and Vince walked away from his life. He spent some time working with his mother at the Wolfe-Chase Asylum before being approached by the head of the council with an offer to run the Watch. The council felt the person best suited to stopping the gangs was the one who'd created them.

To Vince's eye, the current Watch looked woefully inadequate to take on the gangs. Exeter was young and healthy and looked like he could fight. Ruth—built strong and sturdy— could clearly take care of herself. Frank and Clive, both former soldiers, were around Vince's age but injured and slow. Their relationship could prove a hindrance. In Vince's experience, the love-struck were often solely concerned for the well-being of one another, to the detriment of all else. And Clive's soft features didn't fill Vince with a lot of confidence in his ferocity on the battlefield. Frank, on the other hand, with his arched eyebrows and thousand-yard stare, might have been a different prospect, once upon a time. However, a musket shot to the hip would slow anyone down.

That left Mr Norton, who never moved from behind his desk until the time came to go home, and Sorcha who appeared to prefer life under pipes. Not exactly a force to be reckoned with, all things considered.

As they were all preparing to leave for home, Sorcha hesitated. "Where will you be living now? You're not planning to stay in here, I take it?"

"Told there were quarters upstairs."

"Oh, there are. I don't know how comfortable they'll be, mind you. Key's in Mr Norton's drawer over there. Door is outside, under the bridge."

Vince left a lantern on for the prisoners, as well as jugs of water and some bread.

"I'll be fine. Don't worry about me," Walter said from his cell. "If I choke on my food, I'll try to die in a corner so I don't make too much of a mess. I'd hate to be an inconvenience."

"Sleeping upstairs," Vince said. "Need help, just shout."

"Shout when I'm choking," Walter said. "I can see why

they put you in charge."

Vince found the door under the arch of Lickbeer Bridge, in the bearded man's throat, as it were. It took a bit of a shove to get it to open fully, and he ducked into the cramped hallway. Some faint blue flecks of paint at the edges of the dusty, carpetless stairs hinted at a more colourful past. At the top of the staircase, a small landing led to a compact parlour. Crabmeat settled onto a threadbare mat in front of the cold fireplace and started snoring almost instantly.

The grubby parlour window looked out to Lickbeer Bridge and the tiered town beyond. Anyone walking up the steps from the road below could see straight into his quarters, not that Vince minded too much. He was far from shy, although he was still getting used to the idea of no longer needing to work in secret.

Upstairs, he found a room with a squeaking bed covered, like everything else, in a thin layer of dust. Overall, the quarters were grimy, basic, and not very well stocked. He didn't think it would matter very much. He only planned to stay a short while.

He stood at the small porthole window set high on the bedroom wall. Too high for most people to look out of but then Vince wasn't like most people. He yanked the window open an inch or so, enough to let some fresh air in. The sun had not long risen, warming up the stuffy room.

Outside the window, tiles rose and fell where chimneys and gables breached the slate sea stretching out before him. Other people talked of loving the place they came from. Vince had never understood the sentiment. Port Knot had never struck him as the sort of place one loved. More like an animal to be tamed or a rival to be defeated.

He took the blanket from the bed and shook the dust from it. Then he kicked off his boots, lay down, and stared at the cobwebs in the peaked ceiling. Port Knot never fell entirely quiet, especially not in the hour after dawn, when the townsfolk were beginning their day. The copper pipes wrapped around every premises rattled, people on the streets shouted and argued, passing horses neighed, and always some business or other clanged and hammered from sunup to sundown. All of which Vince long ago became used to but still he couldn't sleep.

He kept thinking about what Sorcha had said about how he'd assumed the Watch ran much the same way the gangs did. On information. Instead, the Watch appeared to just blunder about, hoping to happen upon a crime. That approach wasn't going to work anymore. Whilst he'd always made sure the gangs were better organised and better equipped than the Watch, something about how the gangs were governed now felt different to him. The divvying up of the town based on skills rather than territory had changed the map entirely. Without proper direction, the Watch would be lost. Without the Watch, he would be lost. With him, Rabbit would be lost.

Sighing, he pulled on his boots and marched downstairs. He donned his tricorne cap and let himself out of his lodgings but not before shaking his head at the snoring Crabmeat. "Some watchdog you are."

He paced the cobbled roads of Port Knot, making his way to the Tangles, the innermost part of the town. The tall, crooked buildings, shoved together like pilchards in a crate, leaned forward over the roads and almost touched one another as they blocked the sky in places. The roads weaved and twisted like snakes in reeds. Little bridges, the curse of Port Knot, popped up everywhere, providing ample hiding places for pickpockets and cutthroats.

Vince stomped down a set of steps and ducked under the low Slaparse Bridge, with its decoration of playful seals. A glint of metal appeared from the shadows. A small knife, held by a sneering woman, thrusting his way. "Give us yer purse!"

Vince took the woman by the arms and carried her out from under the bridge, into the early morning light. He held his chin up and let her get a good, long look at him.

Her eyes bulged wide. "Vince! I...I didn't know you were back."

He set her down and she bolted like a hare from a hunt. He didn't know her name, didn't recognise her face, but he didn't have to. She knew him, who he had been, so her reaction came as no surprise to him. Chasing after her wouldn't do anyone any good. She wasn't part of the gangs but just a hungry, desperate woman pushed to breaking point.

No doubt she'd been approached by the gangs at some point, appraised of her usefulness to them. Had she been skilled enough, she'd have been recruited. Which was how he'd organised the gangs, back when he'd been in charge. He'd found people with potential and encouraged them, trained them where necessary. Instilled loyalty where he could, mortal fear where he could not. They, in turn, were encouraged to seek out their own protégés and repeat the process.

Vince would occasionally meet with those lower down in the pecking order to remind them who was ultimately in charge. The system had worked in Port Knot for decades.

And now he was faced with the daunting task of closing it all down.

A WOMAN WITH hands intricately painted with patterns in black ink opened the door to the cherry house. "We'll have no trouble today, Mr Knight."

"Won't be any from me, Queenie." He hung up his cap. The walls of the wide hallway were painted with a deep, comforting red, the doorframes carved from mahogany, the candelabras subdued enough to be inviting. Before him stood three doorways. Carved into the mantle over the first, a cockerel. Over the second, a hen. Over the third, one of each. He chose the cockerel.

The dimly lit room writhed with the bare flesh of twenty, maybe thirty, men engaged in all manner of sensual activities. The flickering candlelight from the copper lanterns made their shadows dance on damask-patterned walls. To his right, one man lay tied to a bed while another dripped hot candle wax onto his bare flesh. To his left, a hefty, hairy-backed gentleman took strikes from a riding crop across his bare behind.

Vince stood while someone half his age approached and began to kiss and caress his chest, stripping the shirt from him. It fell to the floor. Vince ran his hands through the man's hair while in front of him three more men lay entwined, their breathing heavy, and their voices low. Against one red wall, two men kissed and stroked each other, while against another, a rigid and robust man stood and watched.

The deep shadows and shallow light made it difficult to make out his features clearly but then that was rather the point of this room. Nonetheless, he caught Vince's eye and began to slowly make his way across the floor towards him. Vince moved away from the younger man and picked his way through the throng of bodies.

By the side of a statue of Priapus, they stood face to face, the stranger and him. Vince stroked the smiling man's face, his round cheeks, his smartly pointed beard. He leaned in and they kissed, passionately, deeply, forcefully, even. Given the stranger's bearing and stature—broad in the beam and strong with it—Vince saw no reason to hold back, no reason to play gently. They found a space on a pile of cushions where they lay and made love while all around them the room throbbed with unbridled libidos.

Port Knot used to have four such cherry houses. Though they often formed part of brothels, it was not necessary to purchase any partners for one's time there. They were simply a place for consenting townsfolk to indulge themselves, away from prying—or innocent—eyes. Two of the houses had been closed due to mismanagement and the third had been levelled in the hurricane of the previous year. Now, only this one remained.

A man of large appetites and few inhibitions, Vince had been known to frequent them often. He sometimes favoured the mixed room, where everyone, regardless of gender, could mingle but that night he felt glad to have chosen the gentleman's lounge.

He and the smiling man never exchanged a single word in their time together. Afterwards, they lay on the cushions and the man traced the lines of one of Vince's many tattoos with his finger. His breath warm against Vince's skin, his embrace tight and comforting. Enough to make Vince forget...for a while. Tempted to remain a good deal longer, Vince nonetheless kissed him one last time, dressed, and left.

After a couple of hours spent in the dim light of the cherry house, the bright morning sun stung like a wasp. He ducked into a nearby Entry, grateful for the shade. Two men followed him. Then two more. All with daggers.

"Keep walking," one of them said.

In the confined space of the Entry, Vince didn't fancy his chances of escaping unstabbed so he complied. He walked along, still feeling the strangers kiss upon his lips and wishing he'd stayed in his warm, strong arms. Upon emerging from one Entry into an open square, he stopped in his tracks.

The square sat at the back of several tall, beige dwellings, overlooked by only a few thin windows. Vince knew from experience no one who happened to look out of them would interfere.

Before him, a well-dressed woman with wide, brown eyes, dressed in an amber overcoat, stood and stared. She wore her black hair in tight, locking braids that fell about her shoulders. More people appeared from the other Entries off the square, all brandishing coshs, or clubs, or daggers. He recognised almost every one of the faces. One woman raised her hands and flashed two frogblades at him. They were designed to slash pockets but they could open flesh just as easily.

"Celeste," Vince said. "Fancy seeing you here. Head of the Clockbreakers, I take it?"

Celeste bowed a little. "Who else but the finest thief in

all the Pell Isles?"

"See Merlin hiding back there. Flowers, too. Knew I'd come this way?"

"This is the only cherry house left in town."

Vince suddenly felt very exposed. "Know me so well."

"I know how you think." Celeste pulled a curved dagger from her belt.

"Not that that's saying much," Merlin said. A woman of no more than twenty years, she wore a coat embroidered with stars and crescent moons.

Flowers moved silently around him. A lithe young man with no hair, not even eyebrows, and a crown of daisies tattooed round his head. His bare arms bore inked roses and lilies. He twirled a knife around in his hand. It danced effortlessly across his brown skin, like a swallow in flight.

Vince raised his fists and dropped his stance, ready to fight for his life. He plotted who to attack first, who needed to be put down quickly, who could safely be held off until later. Celeste bared her perfect teeth, a smile or a snarl, he didn't know. Vince spun his head around, trying to count everyone encircling him. A task made much more difficult thanks to his blind left eye. He hadn't been in many scraps since it had been injured. His fight against Littletar's Pennymen had proven how much it encumbered him.

"Relax," Celeste said. "This is just a friendly chat."

"We're not going to hurt you," Merlin said. "Although we could. And I really do want to."

"Not without losing a few limbs in the process," Vince said, raising his fists higher. "Volunteers?"

Flowers stopped and rubbed his thumb across his forefingers.

"Considering it, are you?" Vince asked. "Come on, then."

Flowers laughed as Celeste pointed her dagger at Vince's face. "We know what you're up to, old man," she said. "The new Watch Commander. How very exciting. What a promotion. But you'd do well to stay out of our way. I don't care what you do to the other gangs but you know my lot. You know our faces. You know our names. So stay away from us, and we'll stay away from you. Understand? Show us the same professional courtesy we've shown you today."

"Brave words," Vince said. "Eyes can't lie to me though. Scared. Nervous. Twitchy."

Celeste licked her teeth and pretended not to care. "And, if you'd be so kind, we'd like Walter returned to us with a minimum of fuss. He made a mistake, and he needs to be punished by us, not by you." She nodded at her people and they dispersed, vanishing through the Entries once again until Vince stood alone in the square.

In the distance, a clock tower chimed.

CHAPTER SIX

VINCE SLEPT LATE. Cursing himself, he threw some water in his armpits, pulled on his top shirt, and dashed out of his quarters with Crabmeat in tow. After his time at the cherry house and his confrontation with Celeste, he'd returned to his new bed and fallen into the deepest sleep he'd had in weeks.

As he stormed his way through the packed streets, he ducked and weaved past the townsfolk going about their daily business. He almost collided with a man in a horological wheeled chair crossing a road and stopped himself just in time to avoid being run over by a coach.

He hurried up the steps of the town hall and pushed his

way through the doors. A very unpleasant young man let him into Rabbit's office and gave him funny looks the entire time. It took supreme effort on Vince's part not to snarl at him. Or thump him.

Two large paintings hung on opposing mint-coloured walls of the serene office. One a scene of the Blackrabbit countryside, the other of the harbour laden with tall ships.

Framed by the arched window behind her, Rabbit sat at her desk reading a newspaper. "Ah, Mr Knight, at last. Come in, come in. The man from the C.T.C. will be here any minute. He's blustering about in the records room. He's not impressed at your lateness. Nor am I, come to mention it. Have you seen this?" She thrust the newspaper in front of him.

The first story read "Body Found Under Pier" and detailed the Watch's discovery of the corpse. It went on to describe the new Watch Commander in less than flattering terms. "Ill-bred bull calf...boozed up blunderbuss...the Blight of Blackrabbit?"

"It's what the people think of you," Rabbit said. "We have some ways to go to change their mind."

Before Vince could speak, the doors to the office flung open, and in marched a large, strikingly handsome bearded man with auburn hair, wearing an immaculate emerald-green-

and-white C.T.C. uniform. The silver ring on his little finger clinked against the hilt of his sword as he rested his hand upon it. Following him were four officers, similarly turned out, each with a pained look on their face. They all held various piles of books and files.

"Take this to my cabin," the man said, pointing to one of the stacks. "And this one—all of these—not that, man! What would I want with a history of France? Do you think there's anything in there I don't already know? I've taken a basting in Brest, given a licking in Lyon, and twice been drubbed up the Dordogne!" He noticed Vince and with a swish of his hand, dismissed his attendants from the office. "At last, he arrives!" He spoke with a voice both crystal clear and louder than one would have thought necessary.

Rabbit stood to introduce them. "Mr Invincible Knight, this is the representative from the Chase Trading Company— Captain James Godgrave."

The captain approached him, hand extended. "Invincible, you say? Some names you people have here. Do you know I met a girl last night named Verisimilitude? Verisimilitude! What a mouthful for any child to pronounce. And my own lieutenant is one of you lot. Pertinacity Hancock. We call her Perty for short."

"Vince will do. Just Vince."

"Splendid. Makes things much easier. And since I'm in a good mood, you may call me James. If we're to be working together, we should make it easy on ourselves, don't you agree?"

"Didn't mean to be so late," Vince said.

"Hard night?" James asked with a wink.

The dashing captain had a warm, easy smile. Tall, too, though not approaching Vince's height, and solidly built, with a beer keg for a belly and sturdy legs. He settled himself in a chair next to James's. "Said we'll be working together?" He shot a look to Rabbit.

"It was one of my officers who was killed," James said. "I want to find out who did it." His voice—deep as the ocean and warm as July—rolled up from his barrel chest and filled the whole room.

Though he spoke in the usual clipped English of an officer, Vince detected the faintest hint of another accent in there, too. "Scottish?" he asked. He didn't know why.

"Good ear," James said. "I try to curtail it. Makes things easier in the officer's club. Now, I propose to have a regiment scour the back alleys and public houses for information. These gangs have been running wild for too long. If we kick enough rats' nests, sooner or later the right one will come scurrying out."

"Wouldn't recommend it," Vince said.

"May I ask why not?"

"Go charging in, guns blazing, killer will go to ground. Gangs will close ranks, townspeople will ignore you. Never get answers," Vince said.

"You'll forgive me if I don't take advice from a landlubber. My crew are highly capable. We've turned over better places than this and always got our man."

Vince shrugged and snorted. "Do whatever you want. Your officer, not mine. Rabbit put me here to stop the gangs. Don't care about some drunken sailor on leave."

"A fine attitude to take, I must say," James said. "I'm sure when Rabbit hired you, she intended—"

"Gentlemen, please," Rabbit said. "I didn't invite you here so you could ignore me in plush surroundings."

"My apologies," James said with that smile of his. That stupid, charming smile.

Then the penny dropped. Vince wasn't prone to blushing, but today might have been an exception. He covered his own mouth with his hand, rubbing his neat, snowy white beard. All of a sudden, he didn't know what to do with himself. He felt as though the room had grown smaller, and he had become some grotesque statue within it. Vince studied James closely. The high forehead, the pointed beard, the little mole on his throat—all so familiar. Captain James Godgrave was, he realised, the man he'd met in the early hours of the morning at the cherry house. The man with the firm grip and the skilled tongue.

"Now, Mr Knight, we seem to be at cross purposes," Rabbit said.

Snapping back to his senses, Vince folded his arms and grunted. "Call me Vince."

"*Mr Knight*," Rabbit said, "you are not here solely to curtail the gangs. You are the head of the Port Knot Night Watch. I think it would be good for the people of the town to see you bring this killer to justice. It would help build confidence. Instil some trust in you. You'll need the people of the town on your side if you're going to succeed."

"Wait just a minute." James's voice had turned harder, full of bluster and self-importance. "Spradbery was my officer, and one of my finest, to boot. I should be the one to lead the search for his killer."

"Let him do it," Vince said. "Enough on my plate as it is." He fixed Rabbit with a stare, hoping she would understand the reason for his bluff.

"Look at it this way," Rabbit said. "Isn't it entirely plausible Sergeant Spradbery was done in by a gang member, Mr Knight? Possibly after a night's drinking?"

"Possible, but—"

"And Captain Godgrave, you don't want the killer to escape due to some well-intentioned but unfortunate mishandling of the situation, I'm sure. And don't you agree a delicate and important matter such as this is best dealt with by someone with local knowledge and a deft touch?"

"I certainly do, and I'm sure Mr Knight has the very deftest of touches."

Vince's ears grew hot as beacons, sure to burn themselves into his skull.

"Of course, if you simply allowed my crew to take charge of the situation," James said, "it would make things easier all round. This is the home of the Chase Trading Company, after all. Where better than here to be patrolled by its officers? Who better to welcome us with open arms than the people who have benefitted most from its work?"

"Armed soldiers on their streets are an affront to the people's liberties," Vince said. "Won't stand for it."

"Ridiculous," James said.

"It's true," Rabbit said. "Blackrabbiters are a fiercely independent lot. Whatever the trouble, they will choose their own people over outsiders, no matter whose uniform they wear. You'd do well to remember that, Captain. I must insist you let the Watch carry out their work uninterrupted. As a matter of urgency, I might add."

James's sage-coloured eyes twinkled as he spoke. "I have every faith we're in good hands with you, Vince."

Vince cleared his throat and nodded.

ABOARD THE *LANCELOT Striking,* Captain James Godgrave shoved open the door of his cabin. Behind him, his lieutenant, Perty Hancock, accompanied a seaman carrying a cup and saucer. James swiped the cup and sipped some tea. He threw his hat onto the table, disturbing some papers. His meeting with Rabbit hadn't gone at all the way he'd anticipated.

For starters, he'd expected to attend a meeting of the full council. He had planned to march in, give them all some bluster about honour and duty, and get his own way. It's how things usually went. He thought especially here, on Blackrabbit, people would bend over backwards to please officers of the C.T.C.

Of course, some of them did. The lout, Vince Knight, for one. A bit of a revelation, that one. When James visited the cherry house, he hardly expected to find such a fine specimen. An absolute beast of a man, taller and wider even than him. He felt a stirring in his loins as he remembered the brute's hands on his skin, in his hair. A shame they were set to be at odds, really.

While perfectly prepared to play nicely in front of Rabbit, James doubted the abilities of the Watch. If push came to shove, he would have to exert his authority vociferously and decisively. "Sit down," he said. "What more can you tell me about the incident?"

"Not much, I'm afraid," Perty said. A woman in her late thirties and quite severe-looking, James had always thought. She wore her dark hair tied back as tightly as could be and carried the weight of the world on her shoulders. "After your offer, Spradbery and I decided to go for a drink to talk. It wasn't easy, I'll admit. Harsh words were said, on both sides. Ultimately, we both decided our new roles were more important than any lingering animosity between us."

"So everything was patched up between you two?"

"No. No, we both know...we both knew...it would take time, but..." Perty's voice broke, just a little. "We were starting to make headway." She blinked hard and cleared her throat. "Sergeant Tresome arrived and joined us for a while. We left Spradbery in the company of some comely local maiden or other in the early hours of the morning and returned to the ship. It was the last I saw of him. I take it we are to go into town and investigate further?"

"Rabbit has decided against it," James said, shaking his head. "She wants to leave it to the local Watch."

"Surely they're not equipped for this?"

"She has faith in her man, Mr Vince Knight. What an extraordinary person he is. Whatever possessed Rabbit to hire someone like him?"

Perty's eyes widened. "*That's* who's running the Watch?"

"You know him?"

"I've heard about him my whole life."

James leaned in. "Well? Don't keep me in suspense."

Perty rubbed her cheek. "When I was a girl, my friends used to tell stories about him. We were all terrified of him, used to frighten each other every time we went past an Entry.

We'd push each other in and run off, leaving them at the *mercy of Vince*. He was supposed to hold all of the criminals in Port Knot in the palm of his hand. I didn't believe he was real until I grew older and started to hear other adults telling stories about him. I was chatting to someone in the tavern last night and they said he's turned over a new leaf of late."

"After a lifetime of crime? What prompted such a sea change?"

"Until recently, he and a former council member ran the gangs on the island. The old gangs, that is. There wasn't anyone who wasn't under their thumb. He was the enforcer, the one who kept everyone in line, by any means necessary. After Vince's abdication, the old gangs fell to in-fighting. The survivors organised themselves into the current structure. I'm not sure exactly what that structure is, but it appears highly efficient. The Watch was struggling to cope and needed someone to take over, show them how it's done."

"But surely there must have been other options? The man's a scoundrel! He should be in the gaolhouse himself, not sending other people there."

"Who better to tear down the new gangs than the man who built the old ones? He knows them, how they think, how they operate. From what I understand, he recruited most of them into a life of crime in the first place."

James leaned back and crossed his arms. "A criminal of some renown. And Rabbit thinks he's a suitable person to head the Watch? Quite a lapse in judgement. I wonder what the rest of the council think. I must make a point of asking them. What makes Rabbit so sure he isn't still working for the gangs?"

"Last Midwinter, Councillor Baxbary Mudge tried to stage a coup d'état. He was thwarted only thanks to help from Mr Knight."

"Oh yes, I read about it in the papers. I can't recall Mr Knight's name being mentioned. I suppose it must have earned him a significant amount of favour in Rabbit's eyes. I wonder how far that favour will stretch?"

CHAPTER SEVEN

SORCHA WRAPPED AN old rag around a leaking joint, pulling it as tightly as she could. She had been at the Watch House since well before sunset. She'd come in before her shift had started so she wouldn't have to listen to her sister Orla's complaining. She whacked a copper pipe with a spanner. The water inside gurgled. She gave it another thump before twisting some bolts.

Mr Norton had his face buried in his ledger. "Keep it down in there!"

Sorcha jumped to her feet and charged to the door. "C'mere to me now, Mr Norton. If you know of a quiet way to fix a leaking pipe, I'd love to hear it! Come on, then! Out with it."

"Watch your tongue, you."

"Or what? You're no longer in charge, Mr Norton, or had that escaped your notice?"

"I'm still the beadle. I still say who's on the Watch roster and who isn't!"

"And who'll fix the pipes if not me? Who'll keep the carts rolling? Who'll stop the front door from sticking? Who'll keep Clive's leg ticking? If you want to try, be my guest." She held the spanner out.

Mr Norton pushed his spectacles up. "Just...try to hit things more softly."

Sorcha huffed and went back to her work. She had wanted to go out on patrol with the rest of the Watch, but the pipes had made a convincing plea for her to remain at the Watch House. She hadn't joined up to be a handywoman, but she'd fallen into the role fairly quickly.

She had been testy all day. She'd seen a dead body before, seen quite a few of them, actually, yet still she found herself beached on the memory of the body under Quither Pier. Perhaps it was simply because the poor man wasn't much older than her. Investigating murder wasn't something the

Watch did often, but every once in a while, a relative of a victim would come to them seeking help in finding justice. Regrettably, the Watch's success rate was low. Port Knot was a rough town and if people didn't want to talk, they wouldn't, and no amount of persuasion would convince them otherwise.

Of course, that could all change now. Vince had very persuasive methods, Sorcha was sure. If there was any information to be scared out of the woodwork, Vince would be the one to do it.

She yelped when Vince suddenly dropped into a chair behind her and threw his legs up to the table.

"You frightened me half to death," she said, with her hand splayed open on her chest. "How does a man your size make so little noise? You look like an elephant, but you move like a cat."

Vince raised his eyebrows and sharpened his stare.

"Sorry. Sorry. You just gave me a fright," she said. "Your meeting didn't go well I take it?"

"C.T.C. want to investigate."

"Makes sense, I suppose. The victim was one of theirs." She approached his desk slowly, as though she were creeping up on a sleeping guard dog.

"Rabbit wants us to do it. Quickly."

"Oh. We know who he is, by the way. Frank and Clive asked around. His name was—"

"Spradbery," Vince said. "Captain Godgrave mentioned it. At the meeting."

"Frank and Clive checked all the usual places, but it turns out Spradbery was drinking in the Star We Sail By."

"Off the beaten path."

"Very. It's not the closest alehouse to the docks. He had some friends with him who left him in the company of noted bedworker, Ms Ataraxy Crimp."

"Spoken to her?"

"That's the other thing. Ms Crimp hasn't been seen since."

"More to worry about," Vince said with a tut. He thrust himself out of the chair and slapped his meaty hand against the door to Walter's cell. The iron bars rattled, and Walter jumped away with a little shriek. Vince took the key and opened it.

Sorcha stood with her hands on her hips. "Here, what are you doing?"

"No sense keeping him locked up," Vince said.

Walter tentatively crept to the door and poked his head

out. He took a few steps out from the cell and paused like a rabbit from a burrow, checking for eagles.

"Celeste wants him back," Vince said. "Can't risk her coming here to get him."

Walter stopped in his tracks. His back stiffened, his eyes widened, and he ran back to the cell, pulling the door closed behind him.

"What are you at now, ye eejit?" Sorcha asked.

"I'm safer in here with you than I am out there with her," Walter said.

"Too bad." Vince pulled the door open again. "Can't stay here. Not an inn. Get out."

"Please, Mr Knight, have a heart! Let me stay. If Celeste gets me, she'll have my hands broken."

"Crabmeat, get him out," Vince said.

Crabmeat plodded over towards the cell, licking his lips.

Walter started to sweat. "No, wait, please. Look, what if...what if I told you where the Clockbreakers were going to hit next?"

Vince clicked his thick fingers. Crabmeat sat on the floor.

"A new family has moved into a mansion on Barley Hill," Walter said. "Word is there's a safe just waiting to be picked clean."

"When?" Vince asked, slamming his hands against the cell bars.

Walter nearly jumped out of his skin. "Tonight. It's tonight. Definitely tonight."

SORCHA HAD SPENT long enough cooped up in the Watch House and insisted on going with the rest of the Watch. All of the houses in Barley Hill were mansions with their own lush gardens and high fences. The most affluent area of the town, it lay just a stone's throw from the overcrowded townhouses but still a world away.

She and Alfie Exeter hid in the shadows of a gatehouse. Farther up the road on the other side, Ruth hid behind some bushes. Somewhere out of sight entirely, Frank and Clive had sequestered themselves.

Alfie Exeter squirmed, like a cat ready to pounce. "I don't care what the commander says—I'm not letting them go this time."

"There aren't Pennymen," Sorcha said. "They're just

Clockbreakers."

"Gang's a gang. We've been too soft on them for too long, and look where it's gotten us. You want to give them time to make a new Vince Knight? We have to make them afraid of us, afraid of being caught. It's the only way."

"I don't want to believe that," Sorcha said quietly.

"We've both heard the stories of how Vince operates. He isn't going to take a gentle approach. Maybe now's the right time for you to get out."

"Sometimes I think I'd like to get away, to see more of the world but I can't. Not yet."

"Because of your sister?"

She sighed and thought about it. "I'm all she has. She gave up everything to protect us both, what am I supposed to do, just say—thanks! See you, now! I'm off to live a better life without you! I can't do that. I can't just run away and abandon her. It's bad enough I'm out with you lot every night. She doesn't like it; she thinks I'll come to a bad end."

"She might be right."

"Ah, she worries too much."

He put his hand on her shoulder, and her mouth instantly turned dry. "If it helps, I'm glad you joined up. Let's be honest, you'd feel guilty if you left Blackrabbit," he said.

"And I'd miss you."

Ahead of them, the great edifice of Hearthstone Manor loomed. The moon hung high and bright, and every window of the house danced with candlelight. Sorcha strained her eyes to catch any movement in the night. "There," she said in a whisper and pointed to the westward side.

Three figures in black slinked through the hedges and up to a window. In the moonlight, a glinting of metal betrayed the Clockbreakers' activities. They pushed a Ticking Ginny against the sash window. A horological device the size of a saddlebag, it produced two thin plates which slid out and pushed themselves under the window frame. A flick of a lever caused the plates to start rising by themselves, popping the lock and forcing the window open. One of the Clockbreakers shoved the window sash all the way up while the others packed away the device and leaned it against the wall. Then all three slipped inside the mansion.

Sorcha and Alfie Exeter quickly scurried across the lawn to the window. They were, as planned, joined by Ruth, who had watched for their movements, and then Frank and Clive, who had been watching hers.

Sorcha peeked inside. The Clockbreakers had already left the room. She went in through the window first. Clive tried twice to heave his metal leg up the windowsill. Frank grabbed it and tried to help, earning them both a withering stare from Alfie.

"Useless codgers," he said in a hiss.

Clive jabbed his finger towards him. "You watch your tongue!"

"Keep your damn voice down!" Alfie said. "Wait out there, in case they get past us. You might actually be useful, for once."

Sorcha checked the hallway was clear but before she could lead them from the study, Ruth marched out, mace in hand. In the hall, candles burned in their sconces. A rustling from a couple of doors down told them the Clockbreakers were already in the room with the safe.

Ruth rapped her mace against the wall. "Oi! Come out, you lot!"

The three young Clockbreakers rushed out of the room, aghast. They faced Ruth and the Watch in the hallway, fidgeting and squirming, uncertain what to do.

One of them, the biggest of the bunch, dredged up some courage and put his fists up. "Think you can take me, do ya?"

Ruth tutted. "I do, as it happens." She pointed her mace behind him. "But I think he wants first crack at you."

The Clockbreaker turned to find Vince filling the hallway. In his eyepatch and tricorne, he looked ten times the villain the poor housebreaker could ever hope to be. Still, he was game, Sorcha had to give him that. He balled his fist tightly and swung at Vince's jaw. He missed. Vince grabbed him by the face and shoved him backwards into the wall. The Clockbreaker crumpled to the floor like a doll.

Another Clockbreaker threw off his cap to reveal his bald head, tattooed with a crown of daisies.

"Flowers," Vince said. "Safe must be worth a lot if you're here."

With one hand, Flowers pulled a dagger from his belt and lashed out at Vince. With the other, he drew a small tube. He flicked a miniature striker on the top. The little horological device sparked and smoke began billowing from the tube, filling the hallway in seconds. Sorcha dropped low and crept closer towards Vince, trying to see through the smoke.

Flowers dropped the tube and again slashed his knife at Vince, who swerved and landed a swift punch to his side. Flowers wheezed and slashed his dagger again. While Vince ducked away, a frogblade shot from Flowers's sleeve, catching Vince on the cheek and drawing a thread of blood. Coughing in the smoke, Vince grabbed wildly, catching Flowers by the arm and swinging him hard. Something crunched when Flowers slammed into the doorframe.

The last of the Clockbreakers struck out at Ruth, who dodged the clumsy attack. Alfie pulled his knife and charged at the Clockbreaker. The two wrestled. Alfie took a kick to the leg before being head-butted. The Clockbreaker broke free and lunged farther into the smoke. He returned a moment later, whimpering and crawling on the carpeted floor. Vince emerged coughing and rested his foot on the man's back, pushing him flat.

Alfie raised his boot, preparing to kick the Clockbreaker in the face.

"I give up! Stop!"

Vince shoved Alfie back against the wall. "Man's down! Leave him be."

Alfie squared up to Vince, teeth bared. He barely came up to Vince's shoulder. Vince didn't say another word, just stared into Alfie's eyes. Sorcha wondered if it came to it, how they would stop Vince from killing him. Should Vince decide to turn on them all, they wouldn't stand a chance against him.

"Alfie, leave it," she said. "Please."

The owners, who had been told to hide, crept downstairs when the smoke reached them, fearful their new home had caught fire. They were starting to question their decision to move to Port Knot, but Sorcha reassured them they'd have no more trouble. She helped them open some windows to clear the house of the Clockbreakers' smoke weapon.

Vince had elected to be the one to hide in the house to await the thieves. Sorcha still wasn't sure what to make of him, but he was no coward; that much was certain. They marched Flowers and his associate out of the mansion where they met Frank and Clive. Clive carried the Ticking Ginny under his arm. Vince heaved the unconscious third Clockbreaker over his shoulder.

"You didn't have to slam the poor lad quite so hard, you know," Sorcha said. The man was starting to come round, thankfully.

"Had to make sure he didn't get any ideas."

She took a handkerchief from her pocket and handed it to Vince. "For your face."

He took it and dabbed his cheek. "Only a scratch. Gone by morning."

"If we're going to round up every gang member one by one, we really need to get a horse," Sorcha said.

"Cart wouldn't hurt either."

"Oh, we've got a cart. Just no horse to pull it. I keep it in good order though. In case we ever do get one. I suppose you want to keep this lot locked up at the Watch House too?"

Vince nodded. A victory like this could only be good for him, and the Watch as a whole. When she'd been told who was coming to take command of them, she almost fell out of her seat. It was like putting a hungry wolf in charge of a flock of sheep.

"Why did you take this role?" she asked. "If you don't mind me asking? I mean, I suppose I can understand the thinking behind it. You know the gang members better than anybody, you know the town, and you know the people. But why turn your back on the gangs, after all this time?"

Vince stopped and thought about it for a moment. He glared at her as if deciding between answering her or biting her. "Orphanage taught me to always clean up my own mess."

CHAPTER EIGHT

JAMES HAD BEEN offered very plush accommodation in town for the duration of his stay, but he preferred to remain on board his ship, the *Lancelot Striking*. He always felt it set the crew at odds when the captain slept ashore and they didn't. And it wasn't as if he were swinging in a hammock below decks. His cabin had been fitted to the highest standards. Still, he looked forward to the first morning he awoke in his own bed, in his own house, surrounded by open fields and melodious birdsong. Instead of the endless boiling of the sea and the cackling of gulls.

He stood by the portside window of his cabin as the

harbour wound down for the day. The great lifting cranes which swivelled from sunup to sundown were still, the traders who littered the docklands had packed away their wares, and the bedworkers had begun their nightly promenade for trade. They walked along the docklands, keeping away from the waterline and hugging the walls. Each carried a little lantern, enough to keep them safe in the night.

One of them, a sturdy lad with hair the colour of straw, caught James's eye but he thought better of it. C.T.C. regulations forbade crew from bringing people on board for the purposes of sex, and the prospect of a quick rut against an old boatshed didn't excite him the way it used to.

He picked up a book but it didn't hold his interest for long. Instead, he pulled on his uniform coat and took himself down the gangplank to the shoreline. His boots crunched where he walked, leaving deep prints in the shingles.

He really didn't want to do away with Vince Knight. If it came to it, he would, but he'd feel remorseful about the deed. He wondered if perhaps Vince might be amenable to remaining as head of the Watch under James's command. Not that there would be any need for a Watch once the C.T.C. was given jurisdiction over the whole town. James had plans to place regiments throughout the town and beyond, into the countryside. He saw no reason why the C.T.C. shouldn't patrol the entire island.

In fact, such was the impression he'd gotten from his meeting with Swan. There were a handful of small villages dotted about the island, nothing close to the size or difficulty of Port Knot. As Swan had told him, where Port Knot led, the rest of Blackrabbit would follow. He was perfectly prepared to assume responsibility for the whole island. And perfectly prepared to remove anyone who stood in his way.

IN THE BEND of a road called Bibbler's Brook on the east side of town nestled a tiny alehouse named the Star We Sail By. The prow of a sailboat extended above the doorway, complete with an old masthead shaped like a portly gentleman wrapped in only a single ribbon of diaphanous silk which left nothing to the imagination. The wooden nude looked longingly to the grubby stained-glass star clasped in his outstretched hands. Some bedworkers leaned on the bulwark of the sailboat balcony and waved to Vince, beckoning him to join them. On any other day, he might well have done.

He let himself in through the double doors. Gregory Diamond, the landlord of the Star, froze in place, spilling some of the ale he'd been pouring onto the counter.

"Not here for you," Vince said, nodding brusquely to him. "Watch business." Spotting his target, Vince made a beeline through the tobacco smoke for a man with a wispy beard, drinking alone by the little dilapidated stage at the back of the room. He plonked himself down on a stool in front of the man and glowered at him. "Evening, Dick."

"Vince," Dick said, lifting his tankard an inch off the table. "We haven't seen you around much of late."

"Busy," Vince said. "Greencoat sergeant in here a few nights ago. Dead now."

"Crying shame, that is," Dick said, taking a sip.

Vince stared at him. The tankard started to quiver, just a bit. Just enough.

"What makes you think I—"

Vince slammed his open palm on the table. "Here every night."

Dick set his tankard down and wiped foam from his lip. "Two greencoat officers came in that night. Both in uniform. The man—a sergeant, he was—had loose hair to his shoulders.

It looked like straw. The lieutenant was a woman. She wore her dark hair tied back tightly as could be. They had some drinks at the bar."

"And?"

"And they talked to one another. Not to anyone else. Hushed, like. They didn't look right in each other's company. Like two children forced to play together. She couldn't wait to get away. You could see it on her face."

"And Crimp?" Vince asked.

"Ms Crimp was here all evening. She turned away potential customers like she was waiting for someone in particular. A while after the two greencoats arrived, Crimp approached the sergeant with the straw-like hair. She was all over him. He was loving it; you could see it in his face. And in his breeches. The lieutenant didn't look too impressed. She just sat there like a gooseberry while Crimp and the sergeant ignored her. Another woman came into the bar later, another greencoat. She sat with the lieutenant for a while. Crimp and the man were getting cosy so the lieutenant and the newcomer left them to it. They walked out and didn't come back."

"Jealous, you think?"

"No, I don't think so. The second woman, she didn't pay the sergeant much attention. And I don't think the lieutenant liked him very much."

"Not uncommon to start that way," Vince said.

"Anyway, Crimp and him left about an hour or so later. That's the last I saw of either of them. You heard what the greencoats have been up to of late? They're building something new in their headquarters, but nobody can say what. Weapon of some kind, I reckon. It must be something big. Maybe big enough to kill for."

Vince scrutinised Dick's deeply wrinkled face. He would know if Dick were lying or holding anything back. Vince leaned in. "Hear anything about Crimp, come tell me straight away."

Dick avoided looking at him, beads of sweat gathering on the bridge of his long, blotchy nose. He just nodded.

Vince stood, scraping the legs of the stool on the shabby wooden floor. On his way out, he passed by frame after frame of torn and faded playbills. Memorials to the Star We Sail By's past as a playhouse. Gregory Diamond mopped up a spillage with a rag and avoided looking at him. Vince left without speaking to anyone else. If Dick didn't see it happen, then nobody did. He walked to the harbour, to Quither Pier. He imagined Spradbery and Ms Crimp arriving, arm in arm. They stopped at the barrels, kissed, caressed, maybe more.

Spradbery is stabbed in the back. By Ms Crimp? Or by someone else? If by someone else, perhaps Crimp escaped and went into hiding, fearing for her life. She was the key to it. He needed to find her. Unless she was dead too, of course.

He felt out of his element, however much he didn't want to admit it. He was used to causing crime, not solving it. If the Watch couldn't find this killer, Rabbit would be powerless to stop the C.T.C. from taking over. Or Captain James Godgrave would grow tired of waiting and take the matter into his own hands.

He didn't seem like the patient type. And if he took over, the public would never get on the Watch's side. The murder of a gang member meant less than nothing to the townsfolk but a greencoat? And a sergeant, no less? The people of the town might not want armed soldiers on patrol, but if the Watch couldn't satisfy their thirst for justice, they'd flock to the side of anyone who could. And this whole experiment would crumble. What would he be left with, then?

He leaned on the rotten barrels under the pier. Barrels, he knew from experience, which were easily big enough to hold a body. Spradbery had been a small man, slight in build. It wouldn't have been so much work to put his body into one. He would have been found eventually, but the longer his body remained hidden, the better, surely? The killer could have been disturbed before they could hide the body, but Vince was no stranger to the theatre of violence, and to him it really felt like the body of Spradbery had been left where it could be found. And then he started to wonder if that was the whole point.

"Penny for your thoughts?"

Vince spun on his heels to find James Godgrave approaching across the sand.

"Careful," Vince said. "Don't want to get your nice coat all wet."

The damp sand clung to James's shiny black boots. "Don't worry," he said, "I won't be the one who has to clean it."

"Come to check up on me?"

"Not at all, I didn't know you'd be here. I found it hard to sleep. It's much too warm, so I thought I'd take a little stroll." He leaned against one of the barrels.

"Too warm to sleep but not too warm for a coat."

James brushed the shoulder of his emerald overcoat. "It's never warm enough to led standards slip, my good man."

"People see the Watch and the C.T.C. conspiring in the moonlight, they might start to talk," Vince said.

"Quite right," James said. "Let's have a drink. Somewhere bright and conspicuous with lots of witnesses."

The nearest alehouse was the Jack Thistle tavern, along the seafront. James ordered a bottle of the local whiskey and they took a seat by the window. James wasn't the only green-coat in attendance and two drunken men saluted him.

"Crew?" Vince asked.

"No, not mine, at least," James said. "Local boys, I would guess, from the looks of them. No crewmen of mine would be allowed out with their uniforms in such a state."

"C.T.C. headquarters is just down the beach," Vince said, pointing. "Big draughting office. Warehouses. Probably came from there. Working on a new weapon. Something hush-hush."

James's eyebrows shot up and he laughed. "Not so hush-hush it escaped your cauliflowered ears."

Vince touched one of his own little jug ears and frowned.

"I didn't mean it in a bad way." James lowered his voice to a purr. "They taste better than they look."

Vince grunted with surprise. "Do remember me, then?"

James's eyes twinkled like stars. "Oh, yes. As soon as I saw you in Rabbit's office, I recognised you. There aren't many men built like you, on this island or anywhere else. A silver bull in a tricorne. Also, there's the eyepatch. Even in the subdued light of a cherry house, one couldn't miss it.

"Oh," Vince said. "Forgot about that."

"I do wonder what's underneath."

"Lost treasure," Vince said.

"You haven't had it long, have you?"

Vince ran his finger along the bottom of the leather patch as he spoke. "Couple of months."

"Dare I ask what happened?"

"Let my guard down."

James sat up straighter and laughed a little. His whole frame jiggled. His eyes became upturned crescent moons. "I cannot tell if you're joking or not, so I'm just going to assume you are until I hear otherwise. It makes you appear delightful instead of exasperatingly enigmatic." He lifted his glass and sniffed it, crinkling his nose up. He took a sip and winced. "Ghastly. You Pellans have no business making this; you don't know your arse from your elbows." He tilted the bottle and squinted at the label. "You can't even spell the word correctly. Every Scotsman knows there's no 'e' in whisky."

"Gets you drunk the same."

James leaned in, sharpening his words. "It very much does not, my good man. Too many glasses of this stuff and you'll wake up with a splitting head and melted teeth. Scottish whisky carries you away on a gentle amber tide. This stuff drowns you in a muddy maelstrom."

Vince took a long drink from his own glass and stared at James the entire time.

"If anything," James said, "I didn't think you had recognised me in Rabbit's office."

"Took me a minute."

"I'm hurt," James said with a little laugh. "Are there so many men in your life that I simply number one among dozens?"

Vince took another sip of his drink. "Can't blame me. Spent most of the time with my face in a pillow."

James settled back in his seat and grinned. "So, the new commander of the Night Watch. What is your grand stratagem for ridding the town of the gangs, hmm?"

Vince shrugged. "Bust open every gin house in town. Crack any heads that need cracking."

"We are indeed kindred spirits!" James toyed with the silver ring on his own little finger, rubbing his thumb across the pacing wolf engraved upon it. "Have you found anything out about Sergeant Spradbery's death?"

"Someone might have seen what happened. Gone

missing though.”

“Any idea where to find them?”

“Some.”

James raised his eyebrows again and wobbled his head, waiting for more information.

“Let you know what I find,” Vince said.

“If you told me their name, I might be able to help, you know.”

“Don’t need help,” Vince said. “Rabbit doesn’t want C.T.C. involved.”

“And you always abide by the rules, do you?” James asked.

“Only when it suits.”

James shook his head and laughed, flashing his pearly white teeth. He really was the most wretchedly dashing man Vince had seen in a good long while. Vince drained his glass and stood. “Will say this, though—feels like it might not have been about Spradbery. Feels like one way or another, some-one was going to end up dead under the pier. Thanks for the drink.”

James’s gaze wandered from the tip of Vince’s boots to the top of his head. “I’ll see you again soon, I hope.”

Vince grunted and left the tavern.

CHAPTER NINE

VINCE LICKED HIS square thumb and ran it across a scuff on his boot. Before he could clean it off entirely, a young boy, around ten or eleven years old, ran into the Watch House. He turned this way and that before spotting Vince and slapping a piece of paper on his desk.

Vince nodded at the lad and flicked a farthing to him which he snatched out of the air and slipped into his pocket before running back outside again.

Mr Norton pointed his quill at the door. "And just who was that boy?"

"Brendan," Vince said. "Knew him when he was living

on the rooftops of Gull's Reach last year. Good lad. Poor family. Thought I could help him earn some honest coin."

"Another impressionable mind corrupted." Mr Norton returned to his note-making. "You just can't help yourself, can you?"

Vince ignored him and traced his finger down the page until he stopped and jabbed. "There's one. Everyone, grab your gear."

"Where are we going now?" Ruth asked.

"Home, I should think," Clive said.

Ruth yawned and stretched her arms. "Been up all bleddy night."

Vince pushed them out of the door. "Sleep later. Walk now."

The sun had risen and stirred a mist from the sea. Clouds gathered overhead. He hurried them down towards the docks.

"I hope this heat breaks soon," Ruth said. "You could have drowned a puppy in my pits yesterday."

"Why would anyone want to?" Clive asked.

"I'm not saying they would. But they could. If they had to."

Vince shushed them and braced himself against a wall to

get a good view of the ships. He leaned out and squinted. A tap on his shoulder. Sorcha, Exeter, and Frank had arrived. Sorcha produced a small spyglass from her pocket and held it out to him. He grunted and took it, holding it to his good eye.

"We saw you all running out of the Watch House," she said in a whisper. "What are you looking for?"

"There. *Dancer of Belgrade*." He pointed to an unassuming clipper docked nearby. Its crew was unloading cargo. A cart approached and two men started lifting some of the crates. "Come on."

He ran across the harbour with the Watch in tow. With a tremendous yell, he grabbed one of the men and shoved him to the ground. The other, startled, dropped the crate he was carrying. Some of the clipper's crew rushed to the man's aid, shouting all the while.

"*Back away!*" Vince bellowed at the top of his voice. "Port Knot Watch."

"I don't care who you are," said one of the crew. "Put him down."

"What are you doing?" Sorcha asked.

"Check the crate," Vince said, still holding the man by his lapels.

The crate had cracked open where the other man had dropped it. Sorcha pulled at the broken wood. "Pistols."

"Mr Peter Finch. Purveyor of stolen goods. Need something without a lot of questions asked, Peter can get it for you. Part of the Pennymen now, yes? Going to sell these on to the one of the gangs? Gunbrides, perhaps?"

"It's true, then," Peter said. "You have turned."

Vince let go of Peter's lapels and gave him a light slap on the cheek. "Bad news for you." He turned to the crew of the *Dancer of Belgrade*. "Back to work, you lot. Watch will pretend you didn't know you were smuggling weapons."

The crew shuffled off while Sorcha took Vince aside. "Shouldn't we do something about the crew?"

"Not enough of us to... Wait." He straightened up when he spotted a group of eight or nine people coming towards them. In a flash, the group had pulled clubs and sticks from their clothing. They darted towards the Watch. Vince pummelled one, two, three of them, but more were approaching from the dockside.

Frank and Clive were putting up little resistance, but Ruth clobbered one of the gang over the head with her mace and kicked the ankle of another. Two of the gang were trying to scoop up the crates of weapons but the horse, panicked by the scuffle, reared up and threw off the cart.

Vince took a punch to the face. He swiftly recovered, grabbed his assailant by the throat, and punched him square in the mouth—twice. The man's lip exploded and he fell to the ground. Two women grabbed Vince's arm, two men took his other, and someone else started smacking his stomach with a club. He growled and shouted.

Frank lay on the ground, not moving. Sorcha fought with her staff, fending off two men with knives. Exeter and Clive were surrounded. In a moment of clarity, Vince saw how it would all end. He cursed his stupidity, rushing in without a thought. He'd been too used to getting his own way, too used to people cowering when he barked at them. Those days were gone, and now the Watch would pay the price for his arrogance.

A musket shot cracked the air and heralded the arrival of a troop of C.T.C. officers, and in a flash, the dockside was filled with emerald green uniforms. With bayonets levelled, they rushed into the gang and pulled them away from the Watch, beating and punching as they went. They herded most of the gang into a corner while others scarpered back towards the town.

Vince leaned against the cart to catch his breath. Sorcha

tended to Frank, who had come round. Ruth checked her own nose wasn't broken.

"Nasty business, all this," said a smiling James Godgrave. "Got me out of bed. You're lucky we heard the commotion."

"Had it in hand."

James's laugh was too warm to be a sneer. "It didn't look that way to me." He leaned on the cart, right beside Vince. Unnecessarily close. Their arms touched. "How did you know about the weapons? Ah. Wait. You knew the ship from your time as chief criminal, didn't you? Not so very long ago, you'd have been the one taking delivery. What did they call you, back then? Commander in Crime? The King of Thieves? The Blight of Blackrabbit?"

James must have read the story about him in the Blackrabbit Courant. "Was either going to be muskets or opium."

"The Watch isn't equipped to deal with something on this scale."

Vince tapped the crate with his boot. "Better equipped now."

"Oh, no, you're not keeping those," James said. "No, they belong to the C.T.C. now. As do these fine folks." He swept his hand towards the gang members being held at bayonet point. "A quick jaunt to the magistrates and then—"

"No." Vince stood in front of James and tried to stare him down. Tall though he was, James still had to look up to a fully extended Vince.

James's smile grew a touch wider. "No?"

"Coming with me." Rabbit would be furious when she found out the greencoats had come to the rescue of the Watch. Vince couldn't do anything about it now, but he could stop them from interfering any further. "Don't expect you to understand. New here. Don't know how things work."

"You are quite correct," James said. "Well, would you at least allow my people to escort them to the Watch House? Your Watch is still, I believe, outnumbered."

Vince did a quick headcount and paused before reluctantly nodding his approval. He instructed Exeter and Clive to collect the crates of pistols and ammunition. They calmed the horse, loaded the cart, and followed the procession of prisoners all the way into town. Townsfolk lined the roads to jeer at the captives.

"This is going to make you a lot of friends," James said.

"Few more enemies too."

JAMES WRINKLED HIS nose at the onslaught of odours as he passed along a slender road that meandered and undulated like a stony stream. He walked under the malodorous arch of a bridge, shaped to resemble the open mouth of a bearded man, and found the Watch House on the other side. He and his troops took the gang members inside while Watchmen Exeter and Clive took the horse and cart to the back.

As grimy inside as out, the walls were a displeasing mustard colour, the air hung thick with dust and old tobacco, and the furniture was riddled with woodworm. "And where shall we be putting them?"

Across the untidy room, Vince flung open some cell doors. The gang members were marched inside and the doors locked behind them.

Someone already locked up—a young hairless chap with a band of daisies tattooed round his head—gripped the bars and called out to the new inmates. "Welcome, everyone. Make yourselves at home. Walter's been here for a while, he can show you the ropes. Like how snitching gets you special privileges."

"I didn't tell them about you lot!" Walter said. "How could I?"

With the new prisoners safely ensconced, James ordered Perty to take his troops back to the *Lancelot Striking*. Vince had the pistol crates brought in and locked away in a cell on their own.

James grabbed the cell door and rattled it. "This seems sturdy enough."

"Should be," Vince said. "Built it myself." He took his tricorne off and hung it on a hook. He ran a meaty hand across his snowy hair, fixing it into place. James wanted to run his own hand through it, to once again feel its silken strands between his fingers as he kissed Vince's thick neck.

As the Watch tended to their various injuries, James sat on the edge of Vince's desk. He ran a finger along it and left behind a channel in the dust. "Charming little place you've got here."

Vince paused in the lighting of his pipe and frowned. "Glad you approve."

James tried not to laugh. How easy it was to get under this big man's skin. He wondered if anyone could do it or if he, because of their connection, found himself specially placed. He almost considered it a unique position to be in, but then there had been nothing unusual about his trip to the cherry house. Nor Vince's, he suspected. Certainly, neither had been out of place or uncomfortable there. Though he found it hard to imagine how Vince felt comfortable anywhere. The story in the Blackrabbit Courant failed to convey Vince's presence. A massive man, in breadth and height, who ducked through every doorway and dominated every space, making other men seem as boys in his wake. A frigate in a world of sloops. "What do you plan to do now?"

"Haven't made up my mind."

Apparently, Vince didn't trust him yet. Shrewd. James had given him no reason to. "Do you anticipate trouble from the rest of their gang? Will they come to free their compatriots?"

Vince puffed on his pipe and blew a cloud of smoke into the air. "Maybe. Regret it if they do. Cells don't mean I have to take prisoners."

"You're a man after my own heart," James said, grinning. "I believe the best way to deal with crime is to crush it beneath our heel."

Vince snorted and grumbled under his breath, "Quickest

way, at least."

"I must admit I don't quite understand how it all works. This lot, what do you call them?"

"Pennymen," Vince said. "Not the brains though. Recognise most of them. Brawlers. Boxers. Fighters."

"The foot soldiers, then?" James asked.

"Sorcha's hovering," Vince said. "Thinks I don't notice. Easier if she explains."

"You don't like to say much, do you?"

"Not like you."

James laughed. "That's fine, the world needs listeners. Otherwise, who would we talkers talk to?"

Sorcha, with her hands behind her back, sidled up. A pretty young girl, not at all the sort of person James expected to find serving with the Watch. She dressed the part, though, in her striped shirt and trousers.

"I wasn't exactly hovering; it's more like I was keeping myself available should you or..." She rotated her hand.

James chuckled and bowed his head slightly. "Captain Godgrave."

"Should you or Captain Godgrave here need anything," she said.

"Tell me about this lot, then."

"If the gangs—or anyone else, really—steal anything not immediately useful to them, they sell it to the Pennymen," she said. "Fences, smugglers, and counterfeiters. They're the ones who move stolen goods around. If you need anything, they can find it for you. If you need to get rid of anything, they can help you there too.

"Most of this lot are low in the pecking order. They work in shops and stalls and serve as foot soldiers, I suppose, like you said. Though they're not all men, obviously. When the gangs reorganised, all the criminals with actual skills and brains got snapped up. The ones that were left became the infantry of the Pennymen. Mostly because Fortitude Littletar can afford to pay for them."

"You already had some prisoners. Who are they?" James asked.

"They are part of the Clockbreakers," Sorcha said. "Robbers, housebreakers, pickpockets, and shoplifters. Not often violent, though mistakes have been made during muggings."

"And this is all the gangs are? Some burglars and a handful of shopkeepers?"

"Oh, no, no, there's more than just them," Sorcha said. "After Vince's...change of heart and Councillor Mudge's incarceration last Midwinter, the gangs who had been under their control started fighting for dominance. The more ambitious among them did away with their competitors fairly quickly and brutally. That was a horrible time, let me tell you. We were stumbling across brawls every other night, finding bodies left, right, and centre. When the dust settled, four gangs remained—the Clockbreakers, the Pennymen, the Gunbrides, and the Cream.

"The Gunbrides are where robbers go for more excitement. They hide in the countryside and ambush travellers at musket point, and frequently with fatal results. They've been growing bolder lately, moving closer to town. We don't know who's in charge of them yet."

"One of my favourites, most likely," Vince said.

James's eyebrows shot up. "Of course. These are all your recruits. All making their way in the world you left for them."

Vince sank farther into his chair and puffed on his pipe a little harder.

"The fourth gang are the ones the others are all afraid of," Sorcha said. "Referred to as the Cream, because they rose to the top. It's rumoured they take a percentage of all the other gang's takings, as well as protection money from every business in the rougher side of town. We don't know who's running them yet. No one will tell us anything. I'm right, aren't

I, Walter? Going to tell us about them now, are ye?"

Walter looked sheepishly at his cellmates and shook his head.

"So this fourth gang, they're the new Vince?" James asked.

"You might say as much," Sorcha said.

Vince puffed on his pipe. "Rather you didn't."

"You should be flattered," James said. "It took a whole gang of people to replace you. I suppose these Pennymen have the most to lose if you're successful. The Clockbreakers and Gunbrides can both carry on robbing people but the Pennymen depend on the other gangs for business."

"Exactly," Sorcha said. "Which is why they have the most enforcers. The most foot soldiers."

"Tell me this, young lady—if these gangs have their territory all worked out, why all the hubbub?"

"Not everyone who breaks the law is in a gang," Sorcha said. "Some people are just opportunists, or they've fallen on hard times and are trying to feed themselves or their family. And skirmishes between the gangs are common. Big egos and short fuses are a volatile mix. All too often, it's the ordinary people of the town who are caught in the middle."

James stood and fixed his cap into place. "I see. Well,

should you require any more reinforcements, you know where to find me. My door is always open for you." He winked at Vince, causing him to snort on his pipe. It might have been a laugh. It might have been a choke. Whatever the case, James took it as a victory.

CHAPTER TEN

SORCHA TOSSED AND turned in her bed, fighting a losing battle. One thing she didn't like about working with the Watch was the hours one had to keep. Starting work at sunset and returning home at sunrise put one at odds with the wider world. Giving up, she plodded downstairs to the sewing room.

Her sister, Orla, sat working on the hem of a robe à la polonaise in rose and lemon stripes. Unlike Sorcha, Orla had sandy hair and a penchant for floral gowns, as evidenced by her current garment which had been crafted from several shades of lilac.

She had a mouthful of pins and a well-rehearsed scowl.

"Can't sleep?"

"Too much noise outside. I swear you ask all the coach-men in the quarter to come down our road on purpose."

The windowless sewing room sat at the rear of the shop, permanently lit by candelabra and several lanterns. Orla had wanted to work from the shop floor, with its tall, bright windows but the activity drew attention, which drew customers, and so she'd never been able to get anything done. The peace and quiet of the sewing room were, she often said, worth a little eye strain.

"I heard about the murder," Orla said.

"Did you? How?"

"Word travels fast." She tapped a newspaper on the table.

The Blackrabbit Courant had one story about the body of an officer of the Chase Trading Company being found under a pier. It also had yet another scathing article about the new head of the Port Knot Night Watch.

"Is it true? All that business about Mr Knight?"

Sorcha ran her finger down the paper. "Ah, most of it would be, now, yes. Now, this part is unfair. He doesn't snarl like a tiger. He grunts like a bull. And, if anything, they're understating how big he is. He's as tall as a house and wide as a horse."

"I really don't want you working with that man."

Sorcha rolled up the newspaper and slapped Orla on the head with it. "You just don't want me working where you can't see me."

Orla took the pins from her mouth. "It's only a matter of time before the people he used to work with come looking for revenge. Do you want to die protecting someone like him?"

"I don't want to die at all."

"Then stay here, where the only imminent threat to your life is Mrs Maunder finding out her dress isn't ready yet. She sent word she wants the sleeves shorted which meant I had to draw it all out again."

Sorcha lifted a brass sewer. "I'll never understand why you don't use this." She turned a key on the top of the horological device. A needle held at the end moved up and down.

"Because I'm faster without it. Just because something is new doesn't mean it's better."

Sorcha set the sewer down. It clicked and rattled on the table top, trying in vain to sew, until Sorcha slapped it silent. "You could always hire more people, you know."

"I wouldn't need to if—"

"Yes, yes, if I just worked here. I know, I know." She

smacked her on the head again.

The bell above the shop door tinkled. "Ms Fontaine, are you in?"

Orla sighed and looked to the clock on the wall. "She's early." She pushed the pins into a red velvet cushion and straightened her clothes, then put on her best smile and went to the shop floor.

Every wall in the Quick Tailoring shop held long shelves made of dark walnut and filled with roll after roll of fabric. Examples of hats in varying styles hung from beams overhead. The customer stood framed by the floor-to-ceiling bay windows on either side of the front door.

"Mrs Maunder, so good to see you," Orla said. "I have your dress design right here."

"Oh, splendid, you received my note."

"Yes." Orla guided Mrs Maunder to a Bergere chair by the window. "The one you sent last night. And the one you sent this morning."

Sorcha wandered out from the sewing room, still reading the newspaper. She leaned on the shop counter.

"Now, Sorcha, when are you going to accept the offer of courtship from my Apricate?"

She didn't look up from the paper. "From who?"

"Apricate. My youngest. He's ever so fond of you, you know."

"And it's not like you have any other offers," Orla said.

Sorcha tutted loudly and held up the paper. "This isn't what happened at all."

"What's that, dear?" Mrs Maunder asked.

"The Watch was *not plucked from the jaws of certain doom* by the heroic soldiers of the Chase Trading Company. Who is this Hawksmoor person, and where is she getting her information from?"

"It's what I heard happened," Orla said. "Everyone was talking about it yesterday. Marjory Winkleigh told everyone in the market about it in great detail. Apparently, her husband saw the whole thing."

"I heard the Watch were on their knees before the C.T.C. arrived," Mrs Maunder said. "A little longer in the sleeves, I think, my dear. The weather is turning."

Orla rolled her eyes.

"We weren't on our knees," Sorcha said, throwing the paper onto the counter. "Sure, you can't believe a word they print."

"Why ever not, dear?"

"Because the Chase family owns it! They won't print

anything that makes them or their company look bad. We had things well in hand. Vince would have sorted them all out in no time."

Mrs Maunder's eyes lit up. "What is he like? I hear he's an awful brute. Ten feet tall with arms like tree trunks. Face all beaten and bent from a lifetime of fighting. Tattooed from head to toe without an inch of his flesh left unpainted, and strong as a bull with the passion to match." She took a faraway look in her eye.

"Um, well, I don't know about any of that, and frankly I hope I never do, but he's not as bad at this rag makes out. And the greencoats have no business meddling in Watch affairs."

"I don't know where the Watch would be without them," Orla said. "I dread to think what would have happened to you if they hadn't been there."

"The Watch wouldn't have let anything happen to me."

"They might not have had much say in the matter," Mrs Maunder said. "What do we think about duck egg blue for the trim?"

"I think it would clash with the rose," Orla said. "We should just let them take over looking after the town."

"Who?" Sorcha asked.

"The greencoats," Orla said.

"Thank you for the endorsement," Sorcha said.

"She has a point, dear," Mrs Maunder said. "The C.T.C. are better at this sort of thing. They fight battles all the time."

"At sea! Not in the middle of a busy town! Are you saying you'd be happy to see uniformed soldiers with rifles marching through the streets?"

"If that's what it takes in the immediate future to get the gangs under control. As a temporary measure, of course."

"But it wouldn't *be* temporary," Sorcha said, throwing her hands in the air. "Once you let weapons like that onto the streets, you'll never get rid of them. They have rifles so the criminals will start carrying rifles. Then every shop owner thinks they need a rifle. Then people start thinking they need a rifle at home. Then they start thinking they need to carry rifles when they go out. Before you know it, we'll have running gun battles in the streets."

"I think you're exaggerating, my dear," Mrs Maunder said. "Now, tell me, what do you think of lemon twill?"

IN A PRIVATE part of the Frost & Thaw tearoom, Agatha Samble sat with her back to an ornate rice-paper screen painted with lemon trees. On the other side of it lay the public part of Port Knot's most vibrant entertainment venue, humming with people enjoying their evening out on the town.

Around her table, the council members and their guests chatted about the business of the day, while on stage a band played some dreadful modern music.

"I can ask them to play a different tune," her husband said.

She laid her hand on his leg. "They must be due for a break soon. Besides, once he arrives, we'll hear little else."

All about the place were dotted horolistic animals in fantastic colours, calling and singing and performing for a largely indifferent audience. The whirring and ticking of their mechanisms drowned out by the well-to-do of Port Knot society dining and chatting amongst themselves.

Agatha became aware of a growing racket over the general din of the crowd. The server working the door of the tearoom arrived with Captain Godgrave and one of his lieutenants in tow. The Captain's voice rolled across the room like cannon fire. On a shelf overhead, a clockwork penguin flapped its tin wings and squawked from an opening beak.

"Penguins don't sound anything like that," Captain God-grave said to his lieutenant. "Not unless they've been shot, at least. Perty, do you remember the one I picked off in Angola? Two hundred yards if it was an inch."

The server nodded to let him know his statement had been heard and entirely disregarded. Captain Godgrave straightened the cuffs of his best uniform coat and made sure his auburn hair was perfect. It was. As far as Agatha could tell, it always was.

He took his seat, smiling broadly at the other guests. "I didn't realise we were late."

"You're not," Agatha said. "We just wanted a chance to talk about you before you arrived."

His lieutenant sat next to him. They'd met a handful of times since Captain Godgrave's arrival on the island, and Rabbit had always found her difficult to read. She had a look of mild fright in her eyes at all times. Rabbit supposed being around Captain Godgrave all day would do that to anyone. The man could purr like a kitten or roar like a lion and give no warning as to which way he was leaning.

Still, there was something more to Lieutenant Hancock. Ah, that was it. Hancock. She must be part of the Hancock family from the Tangles. She kicked herself for not seeing it sooner. She had the soft brow, those shallow cheekbones of her infamous father. She didn't appear glad to be back on home soil, but then sailors rarely did. They spent their time at sea dreaming of the land and their time on land dreaming of the sea.

Agatha introduced them both to Magpie, the minister for trade. A tall fellow with a dimpled smile and a cutthroat approach to business. Next came Badger, the minister for agriculture, effortlessly approachable and congenial. Their host, Fox, also happened to be the owner of the tearoom and the vibrant heart of Port Knot's social life. "And I believe you already know Swan, Mrs Dorothea Chase."

"Of course, we've met a handful of times," Captain Godgrave said. "Good to see you, Councillor Chase. Sorry, I mean Swan."

It always pleased Agatha when mainlanders followed the proper protocol for addressing a member of the Blackrabbit council. There were some traditions she would remain forever immovable on.

Fox's companion, the dapper Mr Noss Quaintance, introduced himself before returning to his conversation with Agatha's husband. The first course consisted of boiled mutton which Agatha found slightly too tough. Fox—Ms Clementine

Frost—could always be counted on to provide wonderful company and she regaled them all with delightfully salacious stories about her clientele. Agatha turned positively pink at one tale involving a trouserless gin merchant, a musket ball, and an ill-advised wager.

Thanks to the glass walls of the tearoom, the harbour and the sea were in full view at all times. As the stars appeared in the clean autumn sky, Agatha's head bubbled from the wine which was constantly being refilled. Her husband, Aldo, spotted the signs and refused further refills on her behalf. Courtesy prevented her from doing so herself, and she quietly thanked him for his intervention.

Fox swigged from a great goblet of the finest cut glass. She'd had as much as anyone else but it didn't appear to affect her whatsoever. "We heard about your scuffle at the docks yesterday, Captain Godgrave. Quite the exciting event, I must say."

"Poor old Vince and his Watch were somewhat outclassed," Badger said. A wildly handsome man with long limbs and enchanting brown eyes, he'd caught James's attention. That much was obvious.

"I'm certain Mr Knight would have handled the situation in time," Agatha said.

"I cannot say I got the same impression," Captain God-grave said. He smiled at Agatha as he spoke, his eyes turning to crescent moons and his whiskers bristling. "If my troops hadn't pitched in, things could have turned quite nasty indeed." He used the last word in his sentences like daggers to stab his point into the listener. They were sharpened and driven with enough force to crack bone.

"What's the sense in having a boorish lout on the payroll if he can't even fight properly?" Badger asked.

Magpie pushed his empty plate forward. "We're just lucky he didn't help the smugglers."

Agatha had expected Magpie, the youngest of the council, to be most in favour of her gamble with Vince.

"Vince helped himself to their wares," Captain Godgrave said.

"What do you mean?" Agatha asked.

"Didn't he tell you?"

"Mr Knight has authority in these matters. He doesn't report every little thing to me."

The table positively groaned under the bowls of fruit and sweets laid upon it. Captain Godgrave plucked a sugared almond and popped it into his mouth. "I wouldn't call crates of muskets and ammunition in the hands of a man like Vince

Knight a *little thing.*"

The council exchanged weighted glances with one another. Agatha set down her wine glass and stared at him. He hadn't stopped smiling for the entire meal. Rabbit didn't trust people who smiled all the time. It showed a flagrant lack of understanding about the world around them.

Swan, in her purple silk brocade dress, stood and raised her voice so everyone at the table could hear. "In light of the events at the docks, it's the decision of the Chase Trading Company that our soldiers shall patrol the town during the hours of daylight. In recent weeks and months, we've seen the town slide into chaos, and I, for one, will not stand by and allow it to slide any further. Port Knot can ill afford to suffer from any more of the Watch's failures. Captain Godgrave, I should like you to take command of this endeavour."

He raised his glass to her. "I'd be delighted."

Agatha's wine-soaked mind raced. How very neat it all was.

"Do the rest of the council agree?" Swan asked.

"I wasn't aware this was an official meeting," Rabbit said. "And I without my mask."

"Oh, it isn't," Swan said. "But then, it doesn't need to be. The C.T.C. does not require Council approval to form its own Watch, especially considering it will operate only during daylight hours and thus will not interfere in the business of the Night Watch. Nonetheless, courtesy insists I at least ask my colleagues for their approval."

Badger and Magpie nodded their answer.

Agatha turned to their host. "Well, Fox? What say you?"

"If this were an official meeting, I should be obliged to point out the people will likely resist attempts to patrol their streets and monitor their activities in this manner," Fox said. "However, speaking as a private citizen, I would be grateful for a more robust show of force against the criminals who treat this town as their playground."

Over dessert, guests moved about and mingled among themselves. Captain Godgrave held court, boasting about some sea battle against the French to anyone who would listen.

Agatha slid over to Swan. "Fortunate that Captain Godgrave happened to be in attendance so you could appoint him as the head of the...what shall we call it? The Day Watch?"

Swan cut into a slice of strawberry tart with her fork. "Sometimes events conspire to aid one."

"I can't help but wonder why he is here at all. On Blackrabbit, I mean."

Swan laughed a little, not very convincingly. "There are plenty of C.T.C. captains in Port Knot at any given moment."

"Precisely my point. You had plenty to choose from. What makes this one so special? Why did you summon him here?"

"Whatever makes you think I did?" She popped the fork into her mouth.

"Experience," Agatha said.

Swan swallowed her food and dabbed her mouth with a napkin. "Captain Godgrave is here to brief the C.T.C. command about the rumoured sinking of a pirate stronghold in the Atlantic. We know a crew of pirates is sailing the *Ivy*, a stolen C.T.C. ship close to the heart of our organisation, and one Captain Godgrave served on many years ago. He attended the aftermath of the sinking, hoping to find some clues to the *Ivy's* whereabouts."

"And did he find anything?"

"If you must know, he did not. Is there anything else you'd like to know, Rabbit? Perhaps you'd like me to run down the expenditure of the captain's journey? A full crew manifest, perhaps?"

"That won't be necessary."

"I'm so glad to hear it. Isn't this tart exquisite?"

CHAPTER ELEVEN

SORCHA HAD BEEN tasked with repairing some of the spare striker-lanterns. The delicate mechanisms had become jammed, and she carefully took them apart and laid them out before her. She wore about her head a band from which hung a magnifying glass. "I hear the council are having some fancy dinner in Frost & Thaw tonight."

"No doubt we'll read all about it in the newspaper tomorrow," Mr Norton said. He sat at his high stool, nose in his record book.

"Why would you want to?"

"Because it makes a change from reading about the

gangs." Mr Norton directed his comment at Vince before leaving to relieve himself in the water closet.

"Not one for subtlety." Vince sat beneath his silver octopus-handled cane, legs up on his desk, frowning as usual.

"He almost hit the ceiling when we were told you were going to take over," Sorcha said, examining a cog. "He's been the de facto commander of the Watch for years."

"Soldier, I take it?"

Sorcha removed the magnifying glass and set it next to a pile of gears. "How did you know?"

"Can spot them a mile off."

She drew closer, lowering her voice. "He'd been with the Chase Trading Company for years before an injury confined him to the land. We get a lot of former soldiers in the Watch. It's something close to a military life, I suppose. All regimented hours and being told what to do."

"Certain folk thrive on routine."

Sorcha pulled her chair close to Vince's desk. "Mr Norton said there were no gangs in Port Knot before you appeared."

"Plenty of gangs back then," Vince said. "More than there are today. But smaller. Worked differently. The town was carved up, backalong. North was one gang, the south another. East, west, centre, docklands, the Reach. Lots of little pockets. Under Jack Kneebone, I brought them together."

"Who's Jack Kneebone?"

"Crook. Before your time. Mudge came along after Kneebone died. Had plans and wanted my help to realise them. Two of us had the town in the palm of our hands for years."

"We always thought you were the brains behind the gangs. But you worked for Kneebone and then Mudge?"

Vince waggled a finger in the air. "With. Not for. Provided a service. Want to ship goods, go to the C.T.C. Want to commit crime, come to me. No different."

Sorcha tried not to laugh. "Well, now, come on, it's a bit different. Shipping a load of tin to the Continent doesn't usually involve breaking anyone's legs."

"All changed now though. Never known gangs to work like this before."

"It might have something to do with the fourth gang. The Cream. We've never seen them, mind. The ones working in the background, keeping everyone in line. I don't suppose you have any ideas who they could be?"

"Some."

"Well, by all means, be mysterious about it," Sorcha said.

"No point saying anything until I know more."

"I know the Pennymen have the numbers, but honestly, it's the Gunbrides who worry me the most. Ah, they went very strange, very quickly, so they did. Do you know why they call themselves Gunbrides? They actually have little handfasting ceremonies where they marry their guns." Sorcha shook her head. "I've never heard the likes of it. Absolutely out of their minds, the lot of them. Apparently, they think it strengthens the bond between them and their weapon. Although quite how bonded a person needs to be to a flintlock pistol is beyond me. They have one spouse—their pepper-box muskets with all the extra barrels—and then their children are ordinary flintlocks."

"*Children?*"

"Out of their minds. I told you. That's what those pistols we took from the *Dancer of Belgrade* were destined to be."

"Made them orphans," Vince said.

It might have been a joke. Sorcha found it hard to tell with Vince. "I was terrified of you, you know," she said. "I'd never seen you before the day you walked through our door, but you haunted my life—all our lives, really. We picked up after you. Your people would brawl in the streets, and we'd have to try to stop it from getting too out of hand. You'd have someone beaten to a pulp, and we'd have to make sure they got to a doctor. The people who worked for you talked about you like you were a force of nature. The man upstairs. That's what they called you when you started working from the library bar at the Lion Lies Waiting."

"Heard that, did you?"

"And we knew you were working from the Dogtooth pub in Gull's Reach for years before that."

"Never came after me." Vince didn't look at her.

"What would have been the point? To make it easier for you to snap our necks? Sure, we'd never have gotten near you."

"True."

Sorcha played the braces over her shoulders. "Did you ever... Were you ever worried about us? About the Watch?"

"Not for a second."

"I'll give you a moment to think about it and break it to me gently," she said.

"Worried about the greencoats. Why we bribed them."

She scrunched up her face. "You never bribed us."

"No need."

"Again, take all the time you need to answer."

Mr Norton returned and took his seat. As he was about

to speak, a great peal of thunder broke overhead. From the night sky, rain fell in sheets, drenching the road outside.

"At last," Mr Norton said. "The storm should clear the heat. The Watch will be back for their coats soon enough."

Sorcha stood by the door as water dripped from the gable overhead. "I used to hate this place when it rained. The town, I mean. There were always plenty of bridges to sleep under, but the water flowed like a river beneath them."

"Slept on the streets?" Vince asked.

"For a while. When we first got here. When I was about ten or eleven, meself and Orla ran away from our mother and her family in Dublin. They were...not kind to us. Orla sneaked us onto a boat, and we came here."

"Don't seem like an obvious fit for the Watch."

Sorcha's gaze flicked to Mr Norton, who had donned his little spectacles and returned to his note-making. "We spent the first month sleeping under Rumbath Bridge," she said. "It has these huge lobsters carved on either side of the arch, and their claws touched at the capstone. I always thought they looked like guards at a castle gate. They made me feel safe, I suppose. Orla knew how to sew, and she did it well. She's as fast as anything at it. Fingers move like lightning. She managed to get some work at a local tailor. The owner, Mrs Quick, took a shine to both of us and gave us a little room to live in, barely more than a pantry, really, but better than nothing. She gave us meals too. She even let Orla make clothes for us from whatever scraps were left over at the end of the day. I started fixing leaks around the shop, got a taste for working with my hands like that.

"One day, Mrs Quick was stopped on her way home from the market by three robbers. They took whatever coin she had on her, the food she'd bought, her shoes. She didn't fight them; she just did what they asked. And then they slashed her cheek open. Just like that. For no reason. No one helped her. She hobbled home, bleeding and crying, and no one helped her. That's not right. That's not the way the world is supposed to be."

Vince faced her, still frowning.

"She passed away a couple of years ago and left the business to us," Sorcha said. "Well, to Orla, really. I'm not much of a seamstress. I haven't the patience for it. Besides, I thought my time would be better spent here."

Vince nodded and grunted his agreement.

Every time she thought about Mrs Quick coming into the shop in distress, it upset her. She could still see the blood stains on her pretty periwinkle gown. The look of terror on her face. She quickly wiped her eyes.

Vince drummed his sausage fingers on the desk. "Time to arrange a meeting." He bolted from his chair, grabbed his tricorne and coat and dashed out into the rain.

Sorcha took her coat and raced after him. They picked their way along a slick road, ignoring the stench of discarded vegetables lying in the gutters. The rain showed no signs of easing up and tiny streams raced over the cobbles, back to the sea.

Sorcha pulled her collar up. "How are you going to find them?"

"Don't need to. Only need to get word to them."

"By finding someone from a gang? We've got plenty of those in the Watch House cells."

Vince grunted. "Not about to let any of them out. Probably don't even know where the Cream are."

"So we're just going to walk around until we find trouble?" She hopped over an overflowing gutter and under a sloping roof.

Vince led her down an Entry and pointed to an unmarked door in a damp stone wall. "Always know where trouble is. Means it can't sneak up on you."

The wooden door, already infected with rot, crumbled

when Vince kicked it. He barged into the little gin house and grabbed the first person he saw. He slammed the man over a table and pointed at his face.

"Get word to the Cream. Want a meeting. Tomorrow night."

The man, slack-jawed and sweating, nodded. Vince let him go and surveyed the room. Sorcha, staff in hand, stood behind him. A bar no longer than a man's leg stood at the back of the room and held some bottles. Behind it, a woman wearing an apron gawped. Not a single person made a move against him. No one objected. No one so much as whispered. Half a dozen people in the room and they all watched him and held their breath. Half a dozen people all frozen in place, wide-eyed. Vince snorted and left.

When they were far enough away, Sorcha dropped her shoulders. "I had no idea there was a gin house there."

"First rule of gang recruiting—know where all the best troublemakers drink."

"I think you made the poor fella wet himself."

"Better have," Vince said. "Else I'm losing my touch." He stopped suddenly and spoke quietly. "Going to be trouble soon. Can smell it in the air. Need to ask you a favour."

A BLINK OF lightning lit the room as thunder rolled in from the sea, chased by sheets of rain. The town became roofed in clouds the colour of old chicken bones. The masts of ships docked in the harbour rattled and shook. Rainwater poured from guttering and gathered first as puddles, then as ponds. In a matter of minutes, the roads of Port Knot turned to brooks.

Agatha Samble stood by the crescent window in her office. Rain ran down the glass, obscuring her view but doing nothing to stop the surge of petrichor. She breathed deeply of it. While she had been the first to complain about the unseasonal heat of previous weeks, she didn't relish the approach of this delayed autumn weather. After a showery night, a fairly dry morning had given way to another brutally thunderous lashing. Ever since the hurricane of the previous year, people in the Pell Isles became skittish with the onset of any storm.

On the other side of her office doors, her assistant, Mr Uglow, raised his voice. "Sir, please you can't just..."

"Think you can stop me?" The doors banged open, and Vince Knight barged in, red-faced and ready for a fight. He held up a copy of the morning newspaper. "Can't do this."

Rabbit sat down and composed herself. She set her jaw, absolutely determined not to show any fear. "I know how it sounds, Mr Knight, but—"

"Ridiculous! Hobbled, we are. Hobbled!"

"You can go, Mr Uglow. Please, Mr Knight, sit down and take some water. You look fit to burst."

He rubbed his huge hand over his mouth, flattening his snowy white beard. The laces of his shirt were undone, revealing a slice of his brawny chest and the tattoos thereon. His trousers—not breeches made from thick linen as befitted a worker—were rumpled. Evidently, he'd come straight to her office from his shift with the Watch. He likely hadn't even slept yet.

"Greencoats patrolling in the day makes the Watch look weak. Like we're not up to the task."

"From what I hear, you needed Captain Godgrave's forces at the docks the other day."

"Would have taken care of it ourselves." He paced the floor, jostling the paper every now and then as though trying to shake loose the words printed upon it.

"But you didn't," Agatha said. "And the public knows you didn't."

"Thought you didn't want us working with the green-coats?"

"I don't."

"But you don't mind them having their own Watch?"

"You are the Night Watch. The clue is in the name. If the C.T.C. wants to patrol during the daytime, there's nothing you or I can do about it. It's their money, their time, their resources. Anyone is free to enforce the peace in the town. You're just lucky up until now no one else has wanted to." She took a deep breath. "Look here, Mr Knight, I am no happier than you are about the situation. But it does confirm my suspicion that Swan is vying for control of the council."

"Swan wants your position?"

"I believe so, yes. I believe she arranged all this in advance. I believe it's the sole reason Captain Godgrave is on Blackrabbit. And I believe he's here to stay."

He stopped pacing for a moment, considering his options. His heavy brow knotted, his eye darting. Agatha wondered if the eye covered by the patch moved with it? Did it move at all? Was there even any eye present?

"Opening salvo, then," he said. "Give them the town

during the day. Make my Watch look weak. Swoop in and take over our duties."

"We see it the same way, Mr Knight. Once the C.T.C. controls law and order in the town, it strengthens Swan's position. She'll garner greater public support, and support from the rest of the council."

He stopped and tutted. "People won't stand for it," he said. "Armed soldiers on the streets? Watching their every movement? Be riots."

"At the moment, their choice is armed soldiers or armed gangs," Agatha said. "Which would you prefer? On second thoughts, don't answer. I'd rather not know. I put you in charge because I thought you could convince the gangs to stand down. Or at least would know how to bust them. It appears I was wrong. Have you even tried talking to them?"

"Have a meeting with the leaders tonight."

"Make it count, Mr Knight. For all our sakes."

He threw the newspaper onto her desk and marched out, brushing past Agatha's husband.

"Was that...?"

Agatha nodded and greeted him with a kiss on the cheek. The tip of his waxed moustache tickled her.

"He's so big!" Aldo said. "He had to duck on the way

out. How did he go about the town for decades without being seen?"

"I dread to think," Agatha said.

Aldo sat at her desk and took the newspaper. "Word has gotten out, then."

Agatha sighed and sat in her leather chair. Rain slashed against the window. "I hoped we'd get another day or two to prepare."

"You'll be fine," Aldo said, taking her hand. "You've been Rabbit for a long time. The people support you."

"For now." Agatha squeezed his warm hand. "Sooner or later, every tide must turn."

CHAPTER TWELVE

VINCE STUMBLED OUT through the town hall gates and stood on the empty road. He took his tricorne cap in his hand, tilted his head back, and let the rain cool his skin. He breathed heavily. He had always preferred Port Knot in the rain. The gloomy weather fit the town better than bright, hazy sunshine.

He knew better than to go into Rabbit's office, shouting the odds but he couldn't stop himself. Something of a worry in itself, actually. He'd worked hard to control his temper over the years, to keep a level head. Without it, he'd have been dead a dozen times over. When one is the focus of ire for a gaggle of the most dangerous people on the island, one cannot afford to go off half-cocked.

He plodded through puddles on his way back to the Watch House, where he stood and peered in through the window. Since the cells were filled with Pennymen, the Watch had to take shifts during the day to keep an eye on them. Frank lay on the floor with a blanket over himself, fast asleep. *Better than nothing,* Vince thought.

Under the little bridge with its carved bearded face, he let himself into his quarters. Crabmeat greeted him at the door, wagging his tail furiously. Vince scratched his ear before heading upstairs.

On his bed, he found a folded piece of paper. He flipped it open. *One Pitfolk Lane. Midnight.* The threadbare curtain by the porthole window fluttered in the breeze. He stomped out of his room. "Nice work protecting the place!"

Crabmeat ran upstairs and jumped up on his leg, licking his lips. Vince huffed and petted him, over and over. "Just glad they didn't hurt you, boy."

VINCE TOLD NO one about the note. Mr Norton laid out the assignments for the evening.

Vince had only one addition. "Want Sorcha to go out with Frank and Clive."

"But those lanterns still need fixing."

Vince stared at Mr Norton, who rolled his eyes and scratched Sorcha's name on his record book. "Whatever our commander wants, our commander gets."

Sorcha took Vince to one side. "Did you not hear back from the Cream? Do you not want me to come with you to—" She stopped when he glowered at her.

He lowered his voice. "Need you to keep them busy. Fewer people who know about the meeting, the better."

Her voice turned to a whisper. "Oh, right. I understand." She winked at him and tapped the side of her nose. She grabbed a staff and a working lantern. "Come on, boys. Crime won't stop itself. Ah, but wouldn't it be great if it did though? Think of the time we'd save."

Before midnight, Vince took his cap and overcoat from the hooks on the wall. He didn't say a word to Mr Norton, and Mr Norton didn't ask any questions. Mostly, Vince assumed, because he didn't care what Vince got up to. He took a circuitous route from the Watch House to ensure he wasn't followed by Sorcha. It seemed to Vince like the sort of thing she might do.

One could always spot the oldest places of the town as they all had names from the days when Port Knot had been a mining village named Stonewarren. Number One, Pitfolk Lane turned out to be a former foundry. Generally, the townsfolk preferred to sweep away old buildings, tearing them down to make way for new ones. However, working in the oldest parts of town became more and more difficult over time and so many were simply left to rot. These forsaken places often found new life as gang hives.

Vince found the door already open. He steeled himself. He probably should have taken a weapon but he always did his best fighting barehanded, and even his new eyepatch hadn't truly shaken his faith in his fists.

Given he'd been invited, he saw little point in subtlety. He barged through the open door and into the foundry. Moonlight fell in shards through the broken skylight above. The foundry lay empty, save for a ruined cart and a handful of broken tea crates. A mouse ran along a nearby, cobweb-infested beam strung with garlands of rusted chains.

Ahead of him, three figures stood, shrouded in shadow.

"Thought we should talk," Vince said. "Face to face.

Greencoats are going to start patrolling the streets. In daytime. Going to be a lot of unrest. Can be made worse by you lot. Or better. Hoping you'll see sense. Help keep things calm."

One of the figures stepped forward into the moonlight. A woman with a cloud of black hair and dressed in amber.

Vince furrowed his brow. "Celeste?"

She nodded. "And I believe you know Mr Fortitude Littletar, of the Pennymen."

The moustachioed Fortitude Littletar stepped forward, his thumbs hooked into the pockets of his striped waistcoat.

"And—"

"Hugo Lambshead," Vince said.

Athletic in build and cocksure in demeanour, the last of the three wore his black hair peaked in the centre, like the crest of a parrot. Though the nights had turned colder, he wore no shirt but had on a long, plum-coloured coat with shiny silver buttons over his black breeches and black leather boots. On his belt, a holster. The handle of his multi-barrelled pepper-box musket stood proud from it. On his bare chest, a tattoo—two muskets crossed.

"Heard about your strange ritual," Vince said. "Knew it had to be you running the Gunbrides."

Hugo Lambshead lifted his pepper-box musket from its

holster. Its stock had been carved like a mermaid, with long hair curled up around the barrels. He kissed it, running his tongue along to the small hatchet bayonet at the end. "Strange," he said. "I'll tell you what's strange—how anyone could lay eyes on Summersong here and not fall in love with her." He pointed the weapon at Vince. "Hah! He didn't even flinch. Same old Vince. Only, no, you're not really the same anymore, are you, old man? Time was you'd be standing here with us. But now you're a filthy turncoat. I should shoot you right here."

"That's not what we agreed." Littletar placed his hand on the end of Summersong and pushed down.

Lambshead snapped at him, his eyes wide and manic. "Don't you touch her. Don't you ever touch her."

"Didn't bring me here to kill me," Vince said. "No such thing as a fourth gang, then?"

Celeste held her hands up. "You got us," she said with a little laugh. "We knew first-hand the power of a figurehead. We saw how you kept the ordinary rank and file in line. But having one person in charge led to the chaos of last Midwinter. So we got our heads together and decided to form our own little shadow council, as it were. Things are more stable now."

"Or they were until you came back," Hugo Lambshead said. "Taking the established gang members off the street will make space for new criminals, ones who don't know the ropes, ones who don't know where to draw the line. There will always be crime in Port Knot. It can either be chaotic and unpredictable, or organised. Civilised."

"How?"

Fortitude Littletar pushed his spectacles up. "It seems to us that where people keep getting hurt is when they run counter to our intentions. For example, your recent interference with the Pennymen operation at the docks. If you'd simply turned a blind eye—pardon the expression—we would have been and gone in a matter of minutes without anyone knowing we were there."

"You could have let my Clockbreakers open the safe in Hearthstone Manor. The family is wealthy enough to replace whatever they lost," Celeste said.

Vince lay a thumb over his forefinger and cracked a knuckle. "Should just let the Gunbrides shoot anyone they want?"

"Of course not," Littletar said. "But if you were to spread the word that cooperation was a wiser course of action than resistance, wouldn't it make things easier on everyone?"

"Watch is just to be a mouthpiece for the gangs? Tell us what you want the public to know, we pass it on, like good little boys and girls?"

Celeste put her hands on her hips. "There are always the petty vandals, the drunkards, the thieves who don't measure up to our standards. Plenty to keep you occupied, well into retirement. We're also going to have to ask you to keep the greencoats out of our hair."

"Can't do it. Got no say over what they do."

"But you do speak with them, no? You do have a rough idea of their plans? It would be no trouble at all for you to send word to us? Let us know the places we should avoid?"

"Want me as a spy."

Fortitude Littletar tutted. "A vulgar word for what is essentially a favour to some old friends."

"Say I don't?"

"We'll burn down the Watch House," Hugo Lambshead said. "And the house of every Watch member. And their families. And their families' businesses. We'll burn everything, Vince. We'll burn it all."

"Not making this sound good."

Celeste approached him, slowly, her hands open. "There is no good option here, Vince. There's only compromise.

We're not going away. Neither are you. Out of respect, we've left you alive this long. Out of respect, we're giving you a chance to save face, and to keep your new role."

"Respect? Fear, more like."

Hugo Lambshead turned red in the face. "Fear? You seriously think we're still afraid of you? With your one good eye and your little team of layabouts? It didn't take you long to replace us, did it?"

"Jealous that daddy has a new family?"

"Don't you dare, you condescending swine." Lambshead shook Summersong at Vince again. "Don't you bloody dare. We were children when you got your hooks into us. We looked up to you, and you walked away, left us to scrabble in the mess you and Mudge left behind. We could have your whole Watch in the ground by sunrise."

"Like you did your real parents?" Vince asked. "Remember the day I found you, covered with blood and soot. Shot them both. Mother by accident. Father on purpose. Just to see what happened."

Hugo Lambshead closed his eyes and ran his musket along his own face. "I could have ended up in gaol that day. Or the orphanage. But you took me under your wing, put me with a new family, nurtured my talent."

"We all owe you a debt to one extent or another," Fortitude Littletar said. "You bought out my family's debts. Saved them from ignominy and imprisonment, saved me from a short life of poverty. You gave all of us the opportunity to be more than we were. The chance of a better life, just as you'd done a hundred times before. And in turn, we took in new blood, passed on what you taught us. Generation after generation of criminal in Port Knot, all carrying on your teachings."

Vince's brow furrowed, and the blood pumped in his ears. He balled his fists.

Celeste laid her hand on his shoulder. "But it wasn't just you lifting us, was it? We gave you a reason to live. You passed on your knowledge, your skills. Hugo is right; we did look up to you. But now, you've turned your back on us. Did you really think there wouldn't be consequences?"

"Didn't...didn't abandon you," Vince said. "Wanted a better life."

"For yourself," Celeste said. "Not for us. You never gave us a second thought. If you continue to cross us, we'll have no choice but to retaliate. You might survive; you have a knack for it, but the people around you? Will they survive? And what will you be left with then, old man? What will you be without the Watch? What will you be without any of us?"

CHAPTER THIRTEEN

AFTER THE NIGHT Watch shift had ended, Vince ordered Mr Norton to take over keeping an eye on the prisoners.

Mr Norton had grumbled but accepted it needed to be done. "They can't stay locked up here forever though."

He was right, of course. The Watch House made a poor substitute for the Blackrabbit Gaolhouse and lacked the facilities needed to house prisoners for any real length of time. The Pennymen had only been there for a couple of days, but Walter had been locked up for longer. Not that he showed any intentions of leaving, mind you. Crabmeat had taken a liking to him and often slept by his cell while Vince worked.

Vince washed in his quarters. He threw on a clean shirt, and ten minutes later, he knocked on the blood-red door of the cherry house. Queenie answered it, giving him the customary knowing look. He'd had one brawl there, about five years ago, and she'd never let him forget it. Well, two brawls. But they were kind of the same, really. One sort of ran into the other. He'd paid for the damage, which was the only reason she hadn't banned him for life.

He shook the rain from his cap and coat, hung them up to dry, and entered the cockerel room. In the low lighting, he stripped his clothes off and threw them in a corner. He heaved his heavy shoulders, stretched his arms, and breathed. One day, he realised, he'd have to try to figure out why he only ever felt truly relaxed in places like this. Not today though.

He stood aside to let a naked man in a wheeled chair go past with his strapping companion. Barely ten men occupied the room, most lounging and chatting in the buff. A far cry from the last visit when he'd met—

"Vince?"

He turned to find a nude James leaning against a wall with a muscular gentleman on his arm.

"Not meant to use names in here," Vince said. "Bad form." He walked away. James left his muscular companion and followed.

"You're right, of course." James kept his voice deep and purring. "I forgot myself in the excitement of the moment." He set his hand low on Vince's back as they walked, just above his buttocks.

To his mild annoyance, the sensation of James's hand on his skin stirred Vince's loins. Something which did not escape James's attention.

"Been here all night?" Vince asked.

"A few hours, at least. A bit of a celebration, you might call it."

Vince grunted and sat on a bench. "Heard your news."

"And you came to celebrate it too? How decent of you." James went to sit next to him but stopped and moved when he realised he'd be on Vince's blind side.

"Came to drown my sorrows between someone's legs."

James laughed a little. "I know it's not the outcome you were hoping for, but surely you can see it's good news for the town?"

"Armed soldiers aren't good news for anyone."

"Tell that to a besieged colony." James took a bottle from

a nearby shelf and poured two tumblers of gin. He handed one to Vince.

Groans of pleasure from a nearby bed distracted them both momentarily. James slid his hand across the tattoo of a shark on Vince's round stomach, and then slowly down between his legs. He gently stroked Vince's member.

"Leave the gangs to me." Vince sipped some gin. It could have stripped blood from a carpet.

"I couldn't if I wanted to," James said. "They're the whole reason I have a Watch of my own in the first place."

Two elderly gentlemen passed by, hand-in-hand, and winked at James, who raised his glass to them.

"Got plans to deal with them?" Vince asked. "Gangs, I mean."

"We're going to round up every single gang member. And any who try to act up will be put in the ground."

Vince vigorously shook his head. "Can't do that. Don't deserve it."

"I very much beg to differ. I think it's the absolute least they deserve. And you've changed your tune. I thought you were all for a tough approach?"

Vince slammed his tumbler on the bench, stood, and turned away. He squeezed his hands tightly and opened them again, over and over.

James crossed his legs. "Weren't you the one who planned to call into every gin house in town and break any heads you recognised?"

"Before. Not now." Vince's blood was up, and his voice went with it, drawing stares from the other patrons.

"Whyever not?" James asked. "Could it be because I'll be the one to do it instead of you?"

"*Yes!* No... I..."

A slender man wearing only blue sapphire earrings and a high collar studded with jewels approached them. "Excuse me, but you seem to have forgotten that other people are present. Perhaps you boys would be better off in a private room?"

"Quite right," James said, rising to his feet. "Shall we?"

Vince ignored him.

The man in the collar cocked his hip and played with an earring. "Or perhaps I should fetch Queenie, and see what she thinks?"

Vince sighed and followed James through an archway at the back of the room. It led to a domed hallway lined with looking-glass panels, even on the ceiling. James found an empty room and stood back. He squeezed Vince's bare behind as he passed by, then he shut the door behind them.

The little private room had one large bed covered in cushions. Overhead, several lanterns fitted with red glass hung from gold chains.

"There now," James said. "You're free to be as contradictory and hypocritical as you like."

Vince stared at him and pursed his lips. "Infuriating man."

"Yes, you are," James said. His smile refused to budge but his voice turned sharper. "Look, what is the matter with you? We both want to stop the gangs, and we're both prepared to do anything to achieve it!"

Vince pointed at him. "*No!* Not anything! Not anymore."

"Whyever not, man? What's changed?"

Vince turned away and slapped his hands on the lavishly papered wall. The lanterns overhead wobbled on the end of their chains.

James slid over to one side of the bed and patted his hand on it. "Have you gotten it all out of your system? Good. Come over. Sit."

After a moment, Vince did as he was told. "Met with... the Cream." He saw no reason to let James know about the shadow council. Not yet. "Made me see things...differently."

James's smile finally disappeared. "In what way?"

"Thought I could come here and get rid of the gangs. Break them apart. But it's not so simple. Gangs aren't just criminals working together. More to it. Almost like...families."

James tutted. "Hogwash."

"Brought most of them into this life. Taught them how to survive. Whole world was happy to let them rot but not me. Then I left. Abandoned them. Didn't give a second thought to what it would do to them." He squeezed his hands together between his knees. "And the Gunbrides. Something wrong with them. Lambshead has twisted their minds. Don't deserve to be killed for what they can't control."

"They don't deserve to be left to run wild either. They're dangerous to everyone around them."

Vince studied his rugged face. He wanted to ask if James knew of Swan's plan to replace Rabbit as head of the council. He wanted to ask if James knew he was helping her to do so or if he was just a pawn in her game.

Vince chose to help Rabbit because it kept him in employment, yes, but also out of loyalty. Rabbit had been the one who kept him out of gaol after Mudge's failed coup d'état. Rabbit had given him the Watch. But he couldn't escape the fact that he simply didn't want Swan to be in charge of the council. He'd been at loggerheads with the C.T.C. for most of his life; he didn't want them controlling the council or patrolling the streets. "Your new watch. Going to be around long, is it?"

"Just until the gangs are quashed," James said with a shrug. "I have no doubt we'll be successful, in time. Once things have quietened down, we'll step aside. Until then, I've been looking at buying a house in the countryside. Something with a grand garden. You'll have to come and visit when I've settled in." He grinned then, and his eyes turned to little up-turned crescent moons, twinkling in the lantern light. He lay back and rested on his side, casually running his fingers through his own chest hair.

He could be lying to my face. If James knew of Swan's plan, he might be actively helping her—he might be knowingly working against Vince. He might be planning to take over Vince's Watch, eventually. But there he lay, playing it all down.

"Don't hurt them. Gang members. Please."

"I can't make any promises." James used his thumb to turn the ring on his finger. "If they attack my people, my people have a right to defend themselves."

"Don't provoke them, then. Don't rush in, guns blazing."

James's smile made a triumphant return. "Fine. For you.

As a favour. Now, I wonder what you might do for me?" James ran his hand up Vince's inner thigh.

Despite himself, Vince's response was immediate and unmistakable. While James busied himself between Vince's legs, Vince sighed and growled, just a touch. He ran his hands through James's coiffed hair, ruffling it just because he knew it would annoy him.

James knelt on the bed and hugged Vince close, kissing his neck, his cheek, his lips. In the candlelight, his sage-green eyes sparkled more than ever. He squeezed Vince hard, as if testing how rough he could be, how much pressure he could apply before Vince broke. He would have to squeeze a good deal harder than that.

They lay on the bed kissing and caressing before James turned to the wall and pulled Vince in close behind him. Vince slipped his hand first over James's ample stomach then down to clamp on his wide, pale thigh. James groaned and was caught breathless when Vince pushed hard against him. Neither man was in any great hurry to finish, and they remained in the little private room at the back of the cherry house until the clock tower chimed at noon.

CHAPTER FOURTEEN

THE LITTLE BRASS clock on the bookshelf weakly tinged the hour. James stood by the arched window as crowds gathered outside the council building. Despite what the Blackrabbit Courant had reported, the mood of the townsfolk had yet to shift in favour of the C.T.C. patrols. Indeed, it had taken just two days for the people of Port Knot to take to the streets to voice their concerns over the armed soldiers on their streets during daylight hours. "I just don't understand what they're so worked up about."

Rabbit's ceremonial mask failed to hide the rolling of her eyes. "Mr Knight and I did warn you, Captain Godgrave. I'm surprised at Swan pushing ahead with this. She ought to have known better."

"Can't these blithering nincompoops see we're trying to help?"

"All they see is more weapons on their streets."

James's blood was up. "There's a world of difference between a musket in the hands of a C.T.C. officer and a pistol in the grubby hands of a highwayman! Why don't you go out and talk to them?"

"I already tried. There's only so much I can do. I can't force them to accept you. Nobody likes to feel as though they're constantly being monitored."

The newspaper on Rabbit's desk had article after article about how the public was throwing their support behind the C.T.C. soldiers and welcoming them with open arms. The truth was somewhat different. A good many patrols had been either forcibly removed from premises or denied entry altogether. Some townspeople were even tipping their chamber pots onto patrols from high windows. One such occurrence led to several injuries.

One soldier reported how she'd been pelted with rotten cabbages for trying to find out where a barrel of rum in someone's front parlour had come from. None of these stories had been printed thanks to the C.T.C's influence over the paper. Though with the growing discord, James wondered how much longer the deception could be maintained and vowed to do something—anything—to prolong it.

The shouts from outside grew louder as more people arrived.

"You can't just sit there while a baying mob gathers at your door."

Sighing, Rabbit stood, and left her office. James followed her to a balcony overlooking the road in front of the town hall. The gates to the town hall grounds had been closed and two guards posted. The shouting grew louder when the crowd spotted them.

James thought there was something primal about the sight of this woman standing above the crowd in her simple gown and her animal mask made of feathers. Something ancient.

Rabbit raised her hands to silence the rabble. It almost worked. "People of Port Knot, please, I understand your anger."

"Then why did you let it happen?" one voice called out.

"Get rid of them!" shouted another. "No greencoats on our streets!"

Rabbit held her hands open as she spoke. "The presence of armed C.T.C. officers in our town is temporary. Until the situation with the gangs is under control, we need—"

"We have a Watch—let them take care of it!"

"I agree that our Watch is doing their very best, but these are unprecedented times and they call for unprecedented measures. Captain Godgrave here may not be a Blackrabbit native but I can assure you he is one of us in spirit. He wants only the best for our town. Isn't that so, Captain?"

James squared his shoulders and spoke in his very loudest voice. "Absolutely. My officers are the most highly trained, the most skilled, and the most disciplined in the entire Chase Trading Company. They will keep you safe from the ruffians and cutthroats."

A chorus of booing erupted from the mob. One woman, eyes full of tears, shouted up to him. "Then how do you explain what happened in Gull's Reach this morning? Your lot strong-armed their way into our building, broke down our doors, and dragged my cousin away in tears!"

"If my officers entered a premises, I can assure you they had a very good—"

"They had no reason, and they had no right!"

"They had every damn right!" James struck the balcony

wall with his fist. His face had flushed red; he could feel it. "They're trying to keep you safe, you ungrateful wretch, can't you see that?"

The booing and jeering grew louder.

Rabbit crossed her arms. "Temper, Captain. You are not at sea now, and these are not your crew."

"If I didn't know better," James said, "I'd say you were enjoying this."

"Captain Godgrave! I'm affronted beyond belief."

James grabbed his cap from the table and marched out of the office. He hurried downstairs, muttering under his breath the entire time. In the hall, he paused at the front door, waiting for it to be opened.

"Captain, I think it might be safer if you were to leave through the rear doors."

James stared at the doorwoman. "Young lady, I do not leave establishments through the rear doors like some trades-man. Open. Up."

The doorwoman gulped and did as she was told. She waved to the guards at the gate. James strode out into the still-booing crowd. Someone reached for him, but he slapped their hand away and bellowed in his very best sea voice. "If a single one of you bath-shy miscreants lays a finger on me, I'll have you all thrown in the gaolhouse!"

The crowd backed away enough for him to reach his carriage. The door carried the seal of the Chase Trading Company—a letter *C* entwined within a ship's wheel. Someone had smeared something foul across it and the handle. He walked to the other side of the carriage, climbed in, and sat, breathing heavily. The ungracious mob of Port Knot would soon be put to heel—he would make sure of it.

The carriage left Trivia Place, pulled out onto Quarrier's Run, and followed the winding road to the docklands. They passed the C.T.C. draughting office and stopped outside a whitewashed building on the harbour's edge. James composed himself and disembarked.

Perty Hancock welcomed him inside. "It's all ready, sir."

"Some good news, at last."

The main entrance led to a bright mezzanine overlooking the floor below. He leaned on a railing. Below him, a number of desks were occupied by some of his soldiers. Before him, a great curving turret of glass and iron ran from the roof to the sea below and offered the chance to survey the piers and curving sweep of the docklands.

"Swan sent word she'll be arriving this afternoon to speak with you," Perty said. "We should have everything ready by then. There is a small dock underneath, at the base of the glass turret. Carved out of the rocks. Or there might have already been a cave there. I didn't ask. We can load and sail a jolly from right inside the building if we need to."

"And the cells?"

"Ready and waiting to be filled." Perty kept her voice low. "In fact, they were ready before I arrived. So very good of Swan to provide all this for us. She must have been planning this for a while."

James smiled and raised his eyebrows. "She may well have been." He rapped his knuckles on the railing, drawing the attention of everyone on the floor. He stood straight and addressed his people. "Today starts a new chapter in the story of Port Knot. No longer will these streets be overrun by rogues and ne'er-do-wells. Today, they will face the wrath of you—my Blackrabbit Sentinels."

VINCE SAT STUDYING a map of the town, running his finger along the roads and lanes he knew so well when young

Brendan ran into the Watch House. "Ms Fontaine says you're to come to Gull's Reach right away, sir."

Vince grabbed his tricorne and hailed a coach. On the swift ride to Gull's Reach, he couldn't help but notice the number of people hurriedly walking away from the area. He found Sorcha and Exeter standing in a shop doorway.

"The Gunbrides are up to something." Sorcha led him closer to River Walk. "They've posted sentries on Bezzle Bridge. They're not letting anyone in or out."

A little island connected to the town by a single, great stone bridge over the slender river Lowena, Gull's Reach had always been of a law unto itself. The Reach consisted of a collection of tall, flat-roofed tenement buildings shot through with arcades and had been Vince's base of operations until the hurricane of last summer.

"Looking for new blood?" Vince asked as they hid from view.

"Conscripting, you mean," Exeter said.

"No. I don't think so, anyway," Sorcha said. "This doesn't feel right. They've never been so brazen before. I spoke to someone who sneaked out before they blocked the bridge, a man named Arthur. He said the Gunbrides were putting their people on the roofs and spreading them throughout the buildings. They brought supplies with them. Food, water, ammunition."

"Here to stay, then," Vince said. "Can't barge in and knock their heads; they'll pick us off from the windows."

"And civilians might be caught in the crossfire," Exeter said. "I hate to say it but I think we should get the greencoats. We're going to need serious armament to put this lot down."

Vince just grunted. Holding his hands up, he stepped out to where the sentries could clearly see him.

"What are you doing, ye mad eejit?" Sorcha asked in a hiss.

"Going to talk to them," Vince said. "No need for anyone to die."

Leaping dolphins held wide, flat Bezzle Bridge on their backs as it spanned the narrow river which divided Gull's Reach from the rest of the town. He slowly walked towards the four sentries—seasoned Gunbrides, all, with steady hands. He knew them by name. He'd personally recruited two of them. They all steadied their pepper-box muskets at his chest. Each weapon had been decorated in a unique way. Painted trees adorned one, stormy clouds another.

He stopped at the boundary and called out to them. "Get him."

The sentries exchanged glances before sending the youngest to the nearest tenement. After a few minutes, she returned with Hugo Lambshead in tow. He still wore his plum coat over his bare chest.

Vince raised his voice. "Got an explanation?"

Lambshead held his musket up. "It has been decided that Gull's Reach is ours. Leave."

"Can't." Vince slowly lowered his hands.

"The people here want us to protect them."

"From what?"

"The greencoats, in part, but mainly you," Lambshead said. "The Watch used to be there just to break up bar fights and deter thieves. Useful, in a pinch, but hardly essential. Now you're in charge, the people don't feel safe knowing you can legally, and with the backing of the council and magistrates, have anyone who crosses you thrown in gaol, or worse. The people of the Reach know you better than most. You took a special interest in this part of town. You recruited from here. So you'll have to forgive them if they don't feel like you have their best interests at heart. The people want us, Vince. Not you. They don't trust you."

Vince shuffled about where he stood. He found it a hard point to argue. While not many knew his face, most everyone knew his reputation. "Speak for them?"

"You can come and ask them yourself if you like," Lambshead said, stepping aside.

Sorcha rushed from her hiding spot. "You can't!"

Vince turned and winked at her. "Don't worry." Only as he walked across the bridge did he realise how winking while wearing an eyepatch just looked a lot like blinking.

He walked with Lambshead to the closest tenement. A cheerless, flat-roofed lump of red brick many stories high.

On the empty stairs, Vince stopped and took Lambshead by the elbow. A move that earned him a glancing blow to the head from Summersong. "Listen. *Listen.*" He looked about himself, making certain they were alone. "Just stop. Risked my life when I left the gangs. Had people come after me because of it. Try to kill me. Did this to me." He touched his patch. "Doesn't have to be that way for you. Or the rest of the shadow council. Only been a year but the town has changed. Have a unique chance to get out now. All of you."

"Rabbit wants us all behind bars."

"Rabbit hired me to stop the gangs. Doesn't care how I do it. Wind down your operations. Lay fallow until people forget. Dismantle it all and none of you need face repercussions. None of you need see the inside of the gaolhouse. Or worse."

Lambshead raised his chin. "Are you threatening me?"

"Think the greencoats will be lenient towards you? Because they want the town. Want to take it from the Watch. So long as I'm around, I can protect you all."

"Hah, where have I heard that before? And let's suppose we did all pack up and go home. What's to stop someone else from taking our place?"

Vince straightened his back. "Me."

Lambshead snorted an ugly laugh. "You overestimate your importance, old man. But you are right about one thing. The town has changed. It's no longer going to listen to you. Time was, we all jumped when you clicked your fingers. Time was, we followed where you lead. Those days are gone. The town no longer needs you." He looked Vince up and down. "Frankly, I'd be surprised if anywhere does."

CHAPTER FIFTEEN

VINCE FOLLOWED LAMBSHEAD upstairs to a dank living room with torn wallpaper and a fusty odour. A group of residents sat around a small table, muttering amongst themselves. They stopped when they saw him.

"Mrs Damerell, isn't it?" Vince asked. "Speaking for the Reach?"

"As much as anyone can." A young woman of slight build and little presence made up for by a formidable determination in her brown eyes. She wore a simple grey gown and tiny, plain earrings. She bade him to sit.

Lambshead took a chair opposite him.

"Gunbrides didn't take the Reach by force, did they?" Vince asked.

"They didn't have to," Mrs Damerell said. "Look at you. Walking in here, bold as brass. You've some bleddy cheek."

"Doesn't have to be any trouble here."

"There isn't going to be," Mrs Damerell said. "Now that the people who were made homeless by the hurricane have been rehoused, the council has gone back to ignoring the Reach."

"Could have taken one of the new houses over in Ironworks," Vince said.

"I didn't want one," Mrs Damerell said. "The people of the Reach were good to me and my family when we lost our home in that storm. They took us in, helped us as best they could, fed us when they could barely feed themselves, when the rest of the town wanted nothing to do with us.

"For years, the Reach has been left to fend for ourselves while criminals run rampant through our streets, our arcades. Then we hear Vince Knight himself has been given the full backing of the council! The man who terrorised us for years, the man who sent his gangs in to recruit our children—"

"Wasn't—"

"Our *children* to fight in his little army of miscreants, and thieves, and cutthroats. You didn't do much recruiting from Barley Hill, did you, Vince? You weren't combing the houses of the wealthy and influential looking for pickpockets to train. No, it was here, it was to the Reach you came prowling. You swept in and took anyone you wanted."

Vince thumped his fist on his knee, over and over.

"You got your claws into my husband too," she said. "Do you even remember him? My Arthur? He took up arms for you and Councillor Mudge last Midwinter, swallowed what you were selling him hook, line, and sinker." She bared her teeth when she spoke, her eyes wide and burning with hatred for him. "Arthur left the Reach when he saw what we were planning. The Gunbrides came to us with a proposition. Let them in without a fuss, and they'd protect us from the greencoats. And from you."

"Didn't need to do that. Not out to hurt anyone. Not anymore."

"And what possible reason would we have to believe you?"

"Have my word. What makes it worth less than his?" Vince pointed to Lambshead. "Think he won't turn on you? People I helped recruit ended up with him and those like him. Pistol thrust in their hand and pushed out into the world."

"On whose orders?"

"Baxbary Mudge's." Vince all but spat the name out. "Worked with Mudge. Carried out Mudge's vision. Followed Mudge's plans."

"And you were just a wide-eyed innocent caught up in his machinations?"

"Not exactly."

"Not remotely," Mrs Damerell said. "You used your knowledge of the Reach to further his cause. But more, you gave him ideas, didn't you? You helped him, Vince. He couldn't have done any of it without you. You. Helped. Him."

Vince hung his head and rubbed his nose. "Won't lie to you. Done horrible things. Unforgivable things. Trying to be better now. Watch is...is my way of making it up to the town. To the people."

Mrs Damerell bit her lip. "It's not enough, Vince. It won't ever be enough. How could it be? Should you live to be a hundred years old, you couldn't possibly make up for all the damage you've done, all the lives you've ruined. My sister worked the Tangles for one of your pickpockets. She was caught once by a group of sailors and beaten to within an inch of her life. She lost the hearing in one ear because of it."

She pointed to a man across the table. "Fred's father owed you money and couldn't pay. You had his legs broken. He never worked again. Claire's mother worked in a bank for a while. One of your people coerced her into giving them a key, said they'd kill her elderly parents if she refused. Her employer found out and let her go, put the word around about what she'd done. She couldn't find decent work again. And that's just the start of it. We all have stories about you, Vince. About the people who worked for you. There's not a life in Gull's Reach that hasn't been tainted by your fetid touch."

The blood pumped in Vince's ears. He closed his eyes and breathed deeply. The chair creaked beneath him. "Tell me what you want."

"Leave us in peace," she said. "Let the Gunbrides worry about the Reach. Your duty ends at the bridge. And you can tell the greencoats the same."

"Can't do it. Greencoats won't allow it. Council neither."

"The council only cares about us when we kick up a fuss. When we're an embarrassment. Just this morning, a squad of greencoats barged in and took Troth Bisbrow away. They held his mother up against the wall by her throat. They hit his father with the butt of a rifle. That's what life in Gull's Reach is now. We're not even worth talking to. Just come in and drag us off to the magistrates without a word of explanation."

"Greencoats shouldn't have done that, but you're not thinking clearly," Vince said, shaking his head. "Let a gang like the Gunbrides in, you'll never be rid of them."

Mrs Damerell leaned forward and rested her elbows on the table. "From where I'm sitting, the only difference between Mr Lambshead's gang and yours is that his is trying to help us."

"Watch isn't a gang. It's..."

"It's what?"

"Official. Sanctioned."

"Not by us. Not by the Reach. Not any longer. Any Watch member or greencoat who tries to cross Bezzle Bridge will be shot on sight."

Vince shook his head again. "Madness. Never going to work."

"Then make it work," Lambshead said. "You can speak to Rabbit any time you want. To the council. Go and talk to them. Make them understand."

Vince jerked to his feet, knocking his chair away, and clenched his fists. Lambshead flinched and aimed his pepperbox musket. What they wanted was completely unworkable, but arguing would get someone killed. Vince nodded his acceptance. It took every ounce of self-control for him not to punch Lambshead's face until it turned to a sticky jelly there and then. Instead, he balled his fists and stormed out.

On the stairs, he passed more Gunbrides. Younger than Lambshead and the other members he knew. He stopped a redheaded girl with freckled cheeks in her tracks and pointed to her weapon. "Don't all get pepper-boxes?"

The girl stared up at him, a lump in her throat. She put on a brave face when she spoke. "We have to earn our spouses."

"Not been with the Gunbrides long, then?"

She shook her head. "They recruited me a month ago. I couldn't believe my...luck." She stood with her common flint-lock held away from her body.

"Not used to it yet," Vince said. "Afraid of it."

"No!" the girl said. "No, not afraid. Never fear the kiss of a musket. It's an honour for a bride to be kissed by her spouse on the day of her handfasting. I have my pepper-box picked out already. His name is Pickstich. He can lift a button from a shirt at thirty paces. On our wedding day, he'll be fired at me, and I'll know what it is to be kissed by my true love."

She ran up the stairs leaving Vince alone. He knew of gang initiations though he'd never approved of them. A person should prove their worth through their actions, not through some nonsensical ritual. That girl could not have been more than fifteen years old, and Lambshead had convinced her that being shot was a good thing.

He crossed Bezzle Bridge to find the assembled crowd silent. They stood back to let him through.

Sorcha and Exeter greeted him. Sorcha breathed out, her shoulders slumped. She even smiled at him. "Thought sure you were coming out of there in a box."

A woman in a wheeled chair pushed through the crowd. "Good meeting with the Gunbrides, Mr Knight? Are you working to stop them or to aid them, I wonder?"

Vince glared over his shoulder at her and carried on back to the Watch House.

CHAPTER SIXTEEN

IT TOOK A day to arrange a meeting of the council. Rabbit had assured Vince they were taking his request seriously but stressed nothing could be done until the full council was available. Which meant waiting for Badger to return from his trip to Little Acorn on the south of the island.

On the morning of the meeting, Vince sat in the council chamber and drummed his sausage fingers on the oval table.

Rabbit couldn't understand what she'd been told. "You're saying Gull's Reach wants the Gunbrides to act as, what, their own Watch?"

"Essentially," Vince said.

Magpie fussed with his mask. "As if that place isn't bad enough."

"Did once say anyone was free to set up a Watch," Vince said.

"I meant a respectable organisation of civic-minded citizens," Rabbit said. "Not lunatics who wed their muskets."

Captain James Godgrave threw open the doors to the council chamber, shouting at Mr Uglow, the clerk. "Yes, yes, I know the way. I'm not an ignoramus. Get me some tea, will you? Decent stuff, not the floral muck you gave me last time. Ah, council members, how delightful to see you again. And in your splendid masks."

Rabbit tensed up when he spoke. His way of assuming everyone in any given room had just been sitting around waiting for him to arrive irked her to no end. That it happened to be true in most cases came as no balm. "Captain. Please take a seat."

"Mr Knight, I wasn't expecting to see you here, but it's always a pleasure. Now, what is so urgent I had to come to this meeting in the middle of my luncheon? Have you finally discovered the murderer of poor Sergeant Spradbery?"

"Not yet," Vince said.

"It's war," Badger said. "The people of Gull's Reach have

declared war on the town."

"Now, you're being a little extreme," Magpie said. "We're talking about a few armed troublemakers and their supporters. I'm sure Captain Godgrave's Sentinels can—"

Rabbit sat up even straighter. "If we send more soldiers in there, people are going to be killed."

"If that's what it takes..." Magpie said. "All this is bad for the town's reputation. We've seen how it's affected trade already."

Swan nodded her head. "Ships are already starting to avoid us. If we don't nip this in the bud, it will hit the town coffers severely. Which is, I believe, why you were hired in the first place, Mr Knight. To stop the situation in this town from degrading any further?"

"Couldn't have known this would happen," Vince said. "Greencoats are making a bad situation worse."

James coughed and blustered. "Now, I object very strongly to your accusation. My officers never act in anything but the most professional manner. If the situation in the town is worsening, it's because the namby-pamby approach the Watch has been taking to these gangs has allowed them to blossom. Criminals are a weed—they must be thoroughly uprooted."

Vince grunted and crossed his arms. "Seen where head-strong tactics lead."

"What do you suggest?" Rabbit asked.

"Take them off the streets," Vince said. "Greencoats. Sentinels. Whatever they're calling themselves."

"Absolutely not," Swan said.

"Not on your life," James said, eyebrows arched and smile broadening.

"Take them off until things calm down."

"And how long will it take?" Swan asked. "How many ships will avoid the port until then? How much money will be lost?"

"More important things to worry about than money."

Swan laughed and licked her lips.

"See why the Reach wants nothing to do with you," Vince said. "Don't care a damn about them. About the people."

Swan tutted. "Of course we do; don't be so childish. We can't be held to ransom every time someone has an outland-ish demand. The whole island depends on us, not just the people of Gull's Reach."

"People of the Reach are desperate," Vince said. "Scared. Because of the greencoats. But more because of me. Feel like they don't have any choice."

"Well, we can solve half of that problem right now," Swan said.

Fox cleared her throat. "Are we certain the idea is so unworkable? It's no secret the Reach attracts a...certain kind of resident. The Watch has its hands full every time there's a sporting event, or a new gin house opens. It would lessen the burden on them, and on the rest of the town, if there were some alternative. If the people of the Reach feel their needs are better met by the Gunbrides, ought we not give them a chance to prove it?"

"Gang gets bed in, they'll never leave," Vince said. "Not entirely."

"You'd know better than anyone," Magpie said.

Rabbit raised her hand before anyone else could speak. "Do you have a plan, Mr Knight?"

Vince grunted again. "Course."

"Then I suggest you carry it out as soon as possible."

WITH HIS PIECE said, James promptly left the council

meeting. Nothing further of value would be decided with or without him present. He spotted Vince fixing his tricorne cap in place and leaving the town hall. The rain had started again, and James braced himself as he called out after him. He pulled his overcoat closed and dashed after Vince, calling all the while.

Finally, Vince stopped, and they took shelter under a jettying overhang. "Well?"

"That's not very polite," James said, laughing. "I haven't seen you for a couple of days. I wanted to talk to you."

"About?"

James stood with his hands on his hips before he noticed his elbow was getting dripped on. "I wanted to know how you were."

Vince shrugged. "Fine. Same as ever."

James tilted his head as he spoke. "Are you? Because you don't look fine to me. You look as though you've hardly slept."

"Lot going on."

"True, true. And on that note, I just wanted to say my Sentinels stand ready to assist you with fighting the insurgence in Gull's Reach."

"Won't be necessary," Vince said, still avoiding his gaze.

"Won't be any fighting."

"Do you really think you'll be able to talk them down?"

Vince just growled a little, some deep murmur from the back of his throat.

"Oh, come now, you really don't want to tell me your plan? We want the same thing—the Gunbrides out of Gull's Reach."

"Difference is I want them out alive." Vince shook his head as he walked away.

That afternoon, James sat in the officers' club of the Chase Trading Company headquarters. Overlooking the docklands, the club stood head and shoulders above any other establishment he'd visited in town. The bar was oak, the furniture leather, and the carpet woollen and overlaid with a smattering of rugs in the Ottoman style.

He swirled a brandy as a fire crackled in a nearby hearth, filling the air with the comforting aroma of peat. It reminded him of home. When he had his house in the countryside, he vowed, he would always have a fire on the go. The halls would fill with the aroma of peat. It would seep into the bones of the place.

On a side table lay some copies of the latest edition of the Blackrabbit Courant. The masthead featured a rabbit being chased by a swan, a badger, a magpie, and a fox. He lifted a copy.

The first article spoke of the Gunbrides' takeover of Gull's Reach and how it spelt disaster for the town. It lamented the feeble efforts of the Watch in general and even speculated on Vince Knight's possible involvement with the takeover, as he had been spotted crossing the bridge and conspiring with the Gunbrides' leader.

James wondered how much truth there was to the story. Vince had softened in his approach to the gangs. And he had indeed been going back and forth from Gull's Reach. Perhaps they'd gotten to him? Either by appealing to their shared history or by blackmail?

An officious older woman approached him and bowed slightly as she spoke. "Captain Godgrave, a visitor." Behind her came a dark-skinned young woman in a wheeled chair powered by a shiny horological engine underneath the seat.

"Ah, at last," James said, rising to his feet. "I thought perhaps you'd gotten lost."

"I had some trouble convincing the doorman to let me in," she said, shaking his hand. "Ms Emmeline Hawksmoor. A pleasure."

"Something to drink, Ms Hawksmoor?" James asked.

"Some stout would be lovely, thank you." She manipu-lated a little lever on the arm of her chair and rolled it so she sat facing him.

James laughed a little as he spoke. "You don't look like a stout drinker to me."

She took a notebook from her satchel. "Someone has to do it. Now, Captain Godgrave, thank you for meeting with me today."

"Not at all. It's a pleasure."

"It's also mandated by the admiralty of the C.T.C."

"It can be two things, can it not?" James said with a chuckle. "I was perusing your publication before you arrived."

"What did you think?"

"I think it's very impressive work. I also think it's highly complimentary of my organisation."

"Quite the coincidence considering the C.T.C. pays for it," she said, all but rolling her bright eyes. "Your name, God-grave. I don't think I've ever heard it before."

"It's an old Scottish name, from the time of the Illumination. Family lore has it my ancestors were instrumental in driving the adherents of the Roman religion out of the Highlands a thousand years ago. They took great delight in ridding themselves of its scourge and took the name

Godgrave in celebration.”

She scribbled some notes on the page. Her amaranthine dress showed signs of wear around the bust and sleeves. Clearly not someone overly concerned with appearance.

“You are unattached, yes?”

“I can’t see how that would be of any interest to your readers?”

“Oh, believe me, anytime a handsome man in uniform struts down Quarrier’s Run, there’s interest. You’ve made quite an impression in your short time here. In more ways than one.”

“There’s nothing worse than a wallflower,” James said. “If one wants to get ahead in this world, one has to make one’s voice *heard.*” He deliberately put some extra thunder in his voice, to really drive home his point.

“I wonder what you make of the demonstrations outside the town hall? The people of Gull’s Reach, in particular, were certainly making their voices heard.”

“A lot of fuss about nothing. I spoke to my officers. The man they arrested, Bisbrown, was seen fleeing from a serious assault. He refused to go along with them, and so some force was necessary to extricate him.”

“I heard he lost a tooth.”

"The man he assaulted lost more than that."

"He admitted his part in it, then?"

James twisted the silver ring on his little finger. "He will in time. I know seeing armed C.T.C. soldiers has been something of a shock, but it really is for the best. Without Blackrabbit, there would be no Chase Trading Company. We owe this island and its people a great debt. All we ask is a chance to repay it. And I should very much like your help to do so."

"In what way?"

"If I may speak frankly and privately?"

Ms Hawksmoor clasped her hands over her notes.

"It's clear there are some teething problems with my Sentinels to which the public cannot long be blinded," James said. "Your publication has done sterling work in trying to get the townspeople on our side, and I should like you to continue to do so, not out of pressure from above but rather because you truly believe it.

"I'm certain a few kind words from you could help the townsfolk see past the greencoat uniforms to the people inside. Dedicated, professional individuals who only want to help the people of Port Knot, and all of Blackrabbit, really. And surely a bright young woman like yourself can see how my Sentinels are best poised to deal with not only the situation in Gull's Reach but the wider issue of the town's criminal gangs?" He leaned forward and flashed his warmest smile, absolutely certain he'd won Ms Hawksmoor over.

CHAPTER SEVENTEEN

VINCE REGRETTED THE way he'd brushed James aside but doubted James had taken it personally. He struck Vince as a man with particularly thick skin and unshakable faith in his own allure.

He would have liked nothing more than to take James to the Jack Thistle, get a bottle of whiskey, and figure out what to do about the Gunbrides. But he still couldn't trust James. Not completely. Not yet. James's ambition meant he'd always be working on some other angle. Always be looking for a way to win.

Despite his assurances to the council, Vince did not, in

fact, have a plan. To avoid dwelling on it, he took an empty grain bag and shovel and walked to a quiet part of the beach. There he pushed the shovel into the dry sand, tipping it into the bag. When he'd filled it, he tied the bag closed and heaved it over his shoulder. People cleared a path for him as he lugged it the whole way through town, to the back of the Watch House.

By the time he arrived, he'd already worked up a sweat. He stripped his shirt off and hung it over the handles of the cart they'd taken from the Pennymen. The horse shuffled about, nervously, and he laid his hand on its chestnut muzzle to calm it down.

He took a length of thick rope and tied it to the bag. He threw the other end over a beam in the lean-to and heaved the bag of sand into position. He steadied himself and tapped the bag lightly with his fists, testing its worth. He closed his eyes for a moment, his body instinctively dropping into a fighting stance.

He raised his fists and thumped the bag. It swayed. He jabbed left, right, left again, each time falling short of where he expected to hit. He used to have a dependable, devastating left hook but now with his left eye ruined he missed the mark almost every time.

This sort of training was the next best thing to the cherry house when it came to clearing his mind. When he lost himself in his boxing, everything else drained away. Colours dimmed, the world pulled away from him, and the little voice in the back of his head detailing every mistake he'd ever made fell mercifully silent.

He walked around the little yard and shook his hands out before trying again. He lashed out, harder and harder each time. His punches landed wildly. He paused, adjusting his stance and began to hammer it again. The bag shook and shuddered under his onslaught. His muscles tightened, his hands throbbed but he jabbed and bashed with every ounce of fury within him. Sweat pooled at the small of his back and glossed his armpits. A light drizzle fell on him, cooling his bare, inked skin, and still he struck. He gritted his teeth and growled, the growl became a roar, his fists blurred where they pummelled, the beam above him creaked, the bag wobbled, the rope began to fray, he shouted and stopped suddenly, grabbing the bag close, halting its swing.

Sorcha held out a cup of water. "Thought you might be wanting something to drink."

His breathing had become heavy, and he wiped the sweat from his brow. "Prefer an ale."

"I can get some. I think Mr Norton has some hidden out in the sheds."

Vince waved his hand and shook his head.

"Fine, never mind," Sorcha said. "Your meeting with the Council went well, I take it?"

He grunted a response.

"The Council was never going to agree to let the Gunbrides take over the Reach," Sorcha said. "Lambshead must have known as much."

"Still insisted I ask."

"Because it makes him look like he's acting in good faith, I suppose. He can tell the people of the Reach he did all he could. He reached out to the Council, and it was the Council who rejected him, instead of the other way around."

"Good way to keep the public support."

"Exactly. Now that avenue is closed, they're left with no choice but to be the brave protectors of Gull's Reach." She hopped up onto a barrel under the lean-to, keeping out of the rain. "So, let's assume that was their plan all along. The next part is you."

"Lambshead's no fool. Knew I'd come after him."

"He might have guessed in your new role, you'd have to try some diplomacy first."

"Knew it wouldn't work too."

"Which makes it look like you're not up to the task."

Vince bristled at that. "Wants to discredit me. Make me look weak."

"I'd say there's more to it. I'd say he wants to keep you on a tight leash. To give you orders instead of taking them, for a change. How far is he willing to push it, do you think?"

Vince didn't answer.

"How did it go with the Cream?"

Vince took his shirt and pulled it on over his head. "No fourth gang. Just Celeste, Littletar, and Lambshead working together behind the scenes. Shadow council, they called it."

"Ah, right, I thought that might be the case." Sorcha kicked lightly at the hanging bag of sand. "Most of the higher-ranking criminals are dead or in gaol. There isn't anyone else it could have been, really."

Vince shrugged and took a drink of water. He wiped his wet moustache on the back of his hand. "Shadow council want me to pass information to them about the Sentinels."

"Spy on them?" Sorcha hissed in her conspiratorial voice.

"Said if I don't they'll...make me sorry. Told them no anyway."

"What did they threaten you with, exactly?"

Vince considered making something up. "Said they'd take it out on the Watch. And our families."

"A risky thing to do, no? Threatening you? What makes them think you won't just snap their necks?"

Vince sighed and cracked a knuckle.

"Oh!" Sorcha eyes widened. "You won't do it, will you? You won't hurt them now."

Vince frowned at her. "Has to be a better way. Has to be."

"I reckon they're testing you. They want information on the greencoats, so let's suppose for a second you provide some. What happens then?"

"Gangs avoid the Sentinels. Avoid getting caught."

Sorcha held her hands open. "Or they get lead into a trap."

Vince considered it for a moment. "Too many of them. Watch couldn't catch them all."

"Not alone, no, but maybe with the help of the Sentinels?"

Vince balled his hands on his hips. "Not them."

"Be reasonable, Commander. They've got the numbers; they've got the weapons; they've got the training;

they've got—"

"James."

Sorcha cocked her head to one side. "Who?"

"Captain Godgrave."

"Oh, him. You don't trust him?"

Vince kicked at a little stone on the ground. "Never trust the overtly ambitious. Usually just looking for the next back to stab."

"I thought you were on good terms with him?"

"Doesn't mean I trust him. Can't be sure he won't take the opportunity to sweep the Watch off the board. Let us take the first hits in battle. Nice, neat way to do away with us."

"You have a very low opinion of the man. He seemed pleasant enough to me. Can't you just talk to him, at least? You're not running a criminal empire now, you know. You're going to have to start trusting other people eventually. Besides me, I mean."

Vince snorted and lightly thumped the bag one last time.

JAMES OPENED HIS leather satchel and carefully set into it the brass compass which had been a gift from his mother to celebrate his captaincy. Next came the last of his notebooks. He lifted one to thumb through it when there came a knocking on his cabin door. "Enter and be quick about it!"

Mr Hamlyn opened the door and nodded. Behind him, Vince removed his tricorne cap before ducking inside the cabin.

"Ah, Mr Knight, this is a pleasant surprise." James waved Mr Hamlyn away.

Vince sat heavily in a chair, placing his cap on one knee.

"Yes, well, let's not stand on ceremony," James said. "Do take a seat."

With the flat of his mammoth palm, Vince smoothed down his scruffy, snowy white hair. Parted at one side in an unconvincing nod to convention, it made him look like a schoolboy trying to make himself presentable after running around with his chums all morning. "Hate being on boats," he said. "Too damn small for me."

"Ship, my good man. You are on a ship."

Vince scanned round the room with his solitary eye. "Packing up?"

"I won't be captain of the *Lancelot* for much longer, now

the Sentinel building is ready. What can I do for you?"

Vince cleared his throat. "Have a proposition."

"Now I really am all ears." James's eyebrows arched even higher and his grin grew wider by the second.

"Spoke to the gang leaders a few nights ago," Vince said. "Asked me to spy on you for them."

"The gall! The audacity!"

Vince toyed with the brim of his tricorne cap. "Thought we could concoct something between us."

"I think I see what you mean. Lure them into a trap."

"Need to make sure we get them all at once. Threats have been made. Not idle ones."

"Of course, of course. I must say, this is quite a turna-round given our conversation this morning."

"Spoke to someone about it. Suggested I be more...trust-ing."

"I should thank them," James said.

Vince fixed him with a steely glare. "Can't let anyone know the Watch and Sentinels are working together. Rabbit's orders. Trusting you with this, James," he said. "Don't let me down."

Big, powerful Vince sitting there—his shoulders slumped, his voice gentler than ever, cap literally in hand—made him look so much softer than James had ever seen him. There was no angle Vince was working. It wasn't a scheme or a ploy of any kind. Vince was simply and honestly asking for help.

"I'm sure we can come up with something," James said.

CHAPTER EIGHTEEN

JAMES LIFTED A tea crate full of identical indigo-coloured books from a chair and set it on the floor next to a rocking horse. "Hiding away in a little room together wasn't entirely what I had in mind," he said. "Though I can't say I'm not enjoying it. But do you ever sleep?" He dragged the chair across bare floorboards to the window.

Vince leaned against a wall and hid behind a mustard curtain, glancing down at the street below. "Don't need much."

"How can you be certain they'll pick this shop?"

"Saw their conditions in Gull's Reach," Vince said. "Need provisions. Told them your lot were patrolling east and north of the town today. Best place to get flour this close to the Reach is that shop. Know how they think."

James sat with his legs spread wide, a hand on each knee. "And you're certain they won't simply buy some?"

"Might do," Vince said. "Either way, we'll know they trust my information. Gunbrides haven't set foot on this side of Bezzle Bridge since they took over the Reach. Know they'll be lifted on sight."

"Why wouldn't they just wait until nightfall? They know my Sentinels can only patrol until sunset."

"Lambshead needs to make a point," Vince said. "Needs to demonstrate he's not afraid of you."

"A show of strength," James said. "I suppose there's little to be gained by besting the Watch."

He'd hoped for some reaction from Vince, some bristling, some grunt, but Vince gave him none. Perhaps the big man had finally caught on to James's ways. "How long will we have to wait? I should have brought a cushion."

"Plenty of padding in your posterior as is," Vince said.

James laughed and leaned forward. "Was that a joke? An actual joke from the lips of Invincible Knight?"

Vince's face didn't shift an inch. He slipped off his overcoat and flung it onto the bed.

"Whose house is this?" James asked.

"Mr Norton, Beadle for the Watch. Told him I needed to use it."

James dropped his voice to a whisper. "He isn't home, is he?"

Vince shook his head. "Told him I'd need a couple of hours. Don't need Rabbit finding out we're working together."

"He reports to her?"

Vince shrugged. "Might do. Can't take the chance."

"Someone else you don't trust." He lifted one of the books from the nearest crate and paged through it, reading name after name. "These are the Watch records?"

"Mr Norton has them going back years."

The crates were stacked high in rows two or three deep. "Decades, more like," James said.

Vince rolled up the sleeves of his top shirt, revealing thick forearms painted in black, green, and blue ink, all under a dusting of white hair. On his left arm, a mermaid lay seductively on some rocks, on his right a merman did the same. A fin-backed sea serpent wound its way from his elbow to his wrist, its jaws wide and ready to strike.

Vince asked if during all his travels at sea James had ever

seen a real mermaid. Stifling a little laugh, James said he hadn't.

"Sailor showed me one," Vince said, quite seriously. "Dead, though. Years back, it was. Having a drink with him in the Star We Sail By. Pulled out this little bundle from his coat. Opened it up and showed me her remains. Little dried up torso with a stiff fish tail."

"And did he charge you to see the body, by any chance?"

"Only a halfpenny," Vince said, frowning.

James smiled at him again. What Vince had actually seen was most likely the top half a monkey sewn to the bottom half of a fish. A trick played by sailors to earn themselves a little extra coin while in port. "I've never seen so many tattoos on a landlubber."

"Like them," Vince said.

"I can see that. Know many sailors who would take umbrage at you having an anchor." James had noticed the anchor on Vince's upper arm during their time in the cherry house.

"None who'll say it to my face."

"Not if they have any sense. Though I can't say I've ever seen one quite like that, with the spindle in the crown."

Vince touched his shoulder. "Dad's symbol," Vince said. And nothing more.

"Do the rest mean anything?"

"Some of them." He pulled at the plunging collar of his shirt and tapped the octopus beneath. Its tentacles wriggled out, diving beneath the water and emerging to attack the ship above his other nipple. "Got the body done years back, when I started making headway in the town. Eight other people in my way, backalong. Eight gang leaders. Each time I got rid of one, I got a tentacle added. Thought it would take years to complete."

"How long did it take?"

"An autumn."

James laughed again. "So efficient, Mr Knight."

"Not the word people normally use."

"I can't imagine there was much left of them when you were done."

Vince didn't answer. He covered his chest. "Been staring at the rocking horse since you came in."

"Have I?"

"Not sure it'll hold your weight, to be honest."

James faked a smirk. "They always remind me of my son."

Vince finally turned his attention from the window. His brow furrowed, and his hands fell to his sides.

"Silly, really," James said, "but you know how sentimental sailors can be."

Vince took another chair and put it by the window, close to James. He sat without saying a word.

"I was married once. A lifetime ago," James said. "My husband and I took a home in a village in Scotland. A little cottage with trees and bushes, and a river at the end of the garden. We ended up adopting a child—a boy named Robert—from a family nearby. They had fallen ill and were unable to care for him. He was only a couple of weeks old when he came to live with us. We loved him immediately, of course. How could we not? His parents passed away shortly afterwards, and we raised him as our own.

"He grew to be a fine boy, with the blondest hair you've ever seen. He loved to be outside, made friends with everyone. My husband made a rocking horse for him, which he loved more than anything. He used to climb onto it every night before bedtime, and when he'd start to nod off, I'd carry him to his bed.

"One day, when he was five years old, he had two friends call on him. They played in the garden, as they'd done a hundred times before. He loved to climb trees, especially the one stretching out over the river. I had tied a rope to a branch and we used it to swing out over the water. I always took it down afterwards and hid it. But Robert must have known where I kept it because that day he and his friends put it back up without my knowing.

"I'd received a letter and was reading it in my kitchen when the two boys ran in, shouting. Robert had been swinging from the rope and gone into the freezing cold river. He'd been swept downstream. They couldn't see him."

Vince placed his hand on James's knee.

"I went out with them to look," James said. "We called after him. I found him caught in some reeds. I waded into the river to pull him out." He rubbed his face and sat up straighter. "My father used to say calm seas carry no ships. To experience peaks and troughs is to know one is alive. I had never experienced a trough like it, before or since. It felt as though someone had pulled the heart from my chest and tossed it aside."

James swallowed hard. "I've faced the Spanish armada, I've been caught in squalls I thought would never end, and I've stared down the barrels of more muskets than I care to count...but I've never been more frightened than I was that day."

Vince didn't speak but his expression had changed into

something altogether new. His gaze soft but all-encompassing.

"It happened on Midwinter's Eve," James said. "There's a special kind of cruelty in grieving while the rest of the world celebrates. Not long after, my husband and I parted ways for good, and I returned to sea."

Vince squeezed James's leg, just a little. Just enough.

James sniffed and wiped his face again, trying to smile. "Sorry, hah, sorry."

"Don't be," Vince said. "Grief needs no apology."

James took Vince's hand. How warm it felt. How solid.

On the street below, people shouted. Four Gunbrides drew up to a shop in a horse and cart. They quickly drew their weapons and ran inside.

"This doesn't feel right," James said. "Just letting this happen."

"Part of the plan," Vince said.

"Do the shopkeepers know that?"

In a matter of minutes, the Gunbrides returned to the road and threw bags onto the cart before racing away.

"Now what?" James asked.

Vince gathered his overcoat from the bed. "Back to the Reach. Talk to Lambshead."

James stepped closer to him. "I don't like the thought of

you going alone."

Vince turned up the collar of his coat. "Worried about me?"

"A little bit. Perhaps. Your luck will run out eventually, you know."

"Not luck. Know these people. How they think."

James squinted at him. "You may know this lot intimately but not the next generation. Or the one after that. Sooner or later you'll find yourself left behind. Ignorant of their ways. And then they'll get the better of you. It is the nature of the young to sweep away the old. They can't help it. They are the crashing waves, and you are but a shell on the sands."

"Won't come to that. Don't plan to do this forever. Need to clean up the mess I made. Then it's someone else's problem."

Vince slid his hand around James's waist.

"We're supposed to be working," James said with a grin. He leaned in and kissed Vince on the lips. With his free hand, Vince cupped James's crotch. James groaned and kissed him harder. Had they not been in someone else's home, James would have pushed Vince onto the bed.

"When will I see you again?" James asked.

CHAPTER NINETEEN

VINCE COMPOSED HIMSELF and knocked on the door.

"About time," Sorcha said. She let him into her tailor shop. "You're cutting it fine. Take your shirt off and help yourself to the oil on the counter."

Vince lifted the bottle next to the comb and sniffed it.

"It's for your hair!" Sorcha called from the sewing room.

He cupped his hand and poured a little of the oil into it. He spread it onto his head and combed it through. Though he kept his beard short, he touched a little of the oil into it.

Sorcha appeared from the sewing room, shirt in hand. She set it on the counter. "Bend down. Come on." She took the comb and tidied his hair. "It's like you've never used oil before."

He stripped off his old linen shirt and tried on the new one Sorcha had made for him. It fit perfectly. "Not wearing this."

"Commander..."

He held up his arms. The sleeves had been made from yard after yard of soft, thin cotton and the frilled lace cuffs wafted like lions' manes. Worst of all, the collar with its rolling cascade of ruffles ran down his chest like a river breaking over rocks. "Feel like a peacock."

"Don't exaggerate. You've got a nice shirt and tidy hair. You're not King Louis." She pointed at his trousers. "Are those the best you have? Have you no breeches? Are they clean, at least?"

"'Course! Know how to wash my clothes."

Sorcha ducked her head and raised her shoulders. "Sorry, sorry, but you can never be sure with men like you. You look the type to regard cleanliness as a moral failing. I haven't time to run you up a new pair, and I definitely don't have any in your size. You could moor boats to those thighs." She pulled his braces up over his shoulders. "Now, I found a nice waistcoat and let it out a bit for you. And before you start about not needing one, you do. You're going to Rabbit's home. Silver Hope. One of the seven great houses of Blackrabbit. You have to look nice. Or at least nicer."

"Didn't know you cared."

"Yes, well, you're my commander and if you look bad it'll reflect poorly on the Watch. And also if you get this wrong I might be out of work. Brush those dog hairs off your lap before you go. Where is that animal of yours? You're not bringing him with you."

"Left him at the Watch House. Taken a shine to Walter."

"Lucky him."

She thrust his overcoat into his hand and began to shove him out of the shop. "Now, get in a carriage, be polite, and try not to grunt at anyone."

HE PULLED AT his collar the whole way. He never usually wore shirts so tight. Mostly because his bull neck wouldn't allow it, but he preferred to wear them open. He found it more comfortable.

The carriage rattled along Miner's Rest and out of town. It would still be some hours before sunset, but he kept his eyes peeled for highwayfolk. The Gunbrides had been known to prey on travellers in the countryside under the cover of darkness and with them all currently ensconced in Gull's Reach, it paved the way for enterprising upstarts to take the reins. Nonetheless, the carriage passed along unmolested and soon raced through the high, round gates of Silver Hope.

Vince paid the driver to stay. "Hopefully won't be here long."

The driver nodded and took his carriage to the stables courtyard where he joined the other waiting coachmen. The great house sat alone on a cliff edge to the east of the island. The roof of Wolfe-Chase Asylum sat solemnly in the distance, across rolling fields and barren hills.

Footmen-and-women waited on the steps to provide assistance. Inside the grand entrance hall, Vince took a glass of wine from a silver tray. About him, the great and the good of Blackrabbit society halted their mingling long enough to stare at him and whisper. He growled under his breath.

"It's all a bit much, isn't it?"

James approached him, descending from the sweeping

staircase as though he owned the place. Dressed in ivory silk shirt and breeches, with a white woollen coat embroidered with silver thread, he cut a fine figure.

"Dressed for it," Vince said. The Samble family had made their money from silver mining. "Not sure I've seen you out of uniform before."

James raised his eyebrows and sipped his wine. "Oh, I'm fairly certain you have."

Vince glared at him, causing James to laugh.

"If I may say, I am surprised to see you here."

Vince hooked a finger into his collar to loosen it. "Not the sort of place I'm used to."

"You surprise me."

Vince had to hand it to Sorcha; she knew what she was talking about. His frilly shirt blended in perfectly with the general garb of the gathering. If anything, it wasn't quite frilly enough. Badger—in his salmon-pink stockings, ruffled shirt, and silken frock coat—looked as though he were attending the court of the Sun King. Vince had never cared for the excesses of fashion. Though if anything could change his mind on the matter, it might well be the sight of James in all his finery. His auburn hair and beard had been trimmed to perfection, the ends of his moustache swept up just the right amount, and his suit hugged him in all the best places. "Never thought I'd see the inside of this house."

James's grin widened. "Not by invitation, at least."

A troupe of footwomen arrived, carrying lanterns. Each took a handful of people with them through to the next high-ceilinged room. It contained no lights and the windows had been shuttered. Half a dozen concave tables stood, waist height, around which the guests were urged to gather. Vince and James had one to themselves. Once every table had been occupied, a gong sounded.

In the middle of the room, a striker-lantern flared to life, illuminating the figure of Rabbit herself.

"Guests. Friends. Thank you all for coming. Silver Hope was built here to enjoy the spectacular sights of our beautiful island. But why go outside in the bracing cold when the sights can be brought in?" She raised her hand, and in seconds, the white bowls of the concave table flooded with light from above and began to move. Waves blasted against chalk-white cliffs, birds flew across rolling countryside, carriages rattled along laneways, and finally, the town of Port Knot shimmered into view, full of life and movement.

Guests gasped and squealed with delight. Some reached into the bowl to touch the illusions, only to have their hands become home to a darting rabbit or diving gull.

Vince craned his neck to get a better look at the mechanism in the ceiling. A copper box above where Rabbit stood fed pipes over each table. Around the cornicing, a clockwork device ran slowly on a rail.

"It's connected to a rotating turret on the roof," James said. "The images come from outside, through lenses and looking glasses, and then into each bowl. I've seen these sorts of camera obscura before, though never on this scale, I must admit."

The crowd clapped and cheered at the spectacle. As the panorama turned, the sky began to dim. The projection halted over the sea as the clouds turned first to a hearty orange, then melted to a cheerful pink. The light warmed James's face, enlivening the auburn tones in his ducktail beard. Vince laid his hand on the table, next to James's. James stretched his little finger out to delicately touch Vince's, his silver wolf ring all but glowing from the projection. A tingle raced through Vince's arm. He slid his hand closer just as the doors to the room were flung open, allowing light from the hall to flood in. The projections turned murky before fading from sight altogether. Silhouetted in the doorway, Fox stood with her companion, Mr Noss Quaintance.

"Oops," Fox said. "Hope we didn't spoil the moment?"

TO VINCE'S IMMENSE disappointment, chatter at the dinner table danced between the price of fish, how best to improve the older piers, and the difficulties in transporting rocks from the quarries through an ever-expanding town. Not once did anyone mention the Gunbrides.

James leaned in, keeping his voice to a whisper. "You're still brooding. You are at a party. You might try to act like it."

Vince dabbed his mouth on his napkin. "Feels wrong, this. Celebrating while Gull's Reach is—"

"Occupied?"

"In distress."

"There's nothing to be done about it at the moment, so why not simply relax and enjoy yourself?"

Magpie of the council caught Vince's attention from across the table. His dimpled smile widened when he spoke. "It's quite a thrill to have you here, Mr Knight. I never imagined I'd be sharing a table with your sort."

Vince's fork paused halfway between plate and mouth.

Magpie laughed, awkwardly. "Well, you know what I mean. The criminal class. I never understood it, myself. This innate need some people are born with to cause strife, to become larcenists, say, to set themselves so thoroughly outside of society." He laughed again. "It quite boggles the mind." He looked around the table for some support and found more than Vince would have liked.

He set his fork down and wiped his mouth. "Wonder why they steal? Sitting here with gold candlesticks while people freeze and starve."

"And that justifies their crimes?"

"More explanation than justification."

Magpie laughed again as if being interrogated by a child. "Are we to be blamed for the circumstances of our birth?"

"Are they?"

As he ate, Vince became aware of a growing sense of unease within himself—a vague notion his presence was nothing more than a part of Rabbit's entertainment for the evening. A curiosity for her guests to gawp at. Every now and then, his little jug ears picked up talk of his past, of his crimes.

Swan commented on how, by rights, he ought to be behind bars. He not only felt out of place, he looked it too. So much larger was he than anyone else present, even James, a space had to be cleared in order to make room for him at the table. A fact which did not go uncommented upon.

He made a point of resting his massive forearms on the table, daring anyone to draw him on the point. If he had to take up room, then he would take up as much room as he possibly could. After all, it's not as though the tiny portions they were being served needed it.

Rabbit pointed to the ring on James's little finger. A silver band engraved with a snarling, pacing wolf. "That's an unusual choice for a nautical man."

"It was a gift," James said. "A long time ago. A reminder."

"Of?"

James took a deep breath and turned the stem of his wine glass between his fingers. "The importance of vigilance," he said. "Many moons ago, I was a lieutenant serving aboard a ship named the *Ivy*. We were near Tortuga and rescued a woman from a tiny atoll. She said she'd been shipwrecked and had swum to safety but we all knew what really happened. She was a pirate, and she'd been marooned there by her crew. Left to die in the sun. The captain wanted to lock her up until we found out who she was, but I argued against it. She was a hard worker and keen to start a new life for herself. The captain released her to my charge.

"She pitched in wherever she could, swabbed the decks, worked the rigging. Might have been the best sailor on the ship, and I include myself in that. Everyone kept telling me to watch my back. The quartermaster, in particular, a German fellow, bent my ear about her any chance he got.

"Anyway, after about a month at sea, I was roused from my bunk by a call of fire. We were besieged by a pirate ship. Our new recruit had gotten word to her old crew that she had a C.T.C. ship ripe for the plucking. She used it as a way to get back into their good books. I tried to convince her to side with us, but she'd made up her mind. There was a fight and our captain was killed by her crew. She left with them, and that was that.

"I was terribly guilt-ridden, of course. And I thought my career with the C.T.C. was over. The crew agreed the pirate had them all fooled. They had started to see her as one of them. A week or so later, the quartermaster called me into his cabin. He presented me with this ring he'd made from the sword which felled our captain. And he said these words: 'Feed the wolves in winter and be eaten in the spring'. I found it to be a valuable lesson, and so when I took command of the *Lancelot Striking*, my first ship as captain, I had copies of the ring made for all my lieutenants and sergeants."

Rabbit locked eyes with Vince for just a moment before tasting her wine. Oblivious to all others around them, Fox and Mr Quaintance laughed and made merry. Mr Noss Quaintance, a graceful man with golden-brown skin, wore an ostentatious suit better suited to a royal court than a dinner. The material of his pewter frock coat comprised of thousands of tiny lilies embroidered along the cuffs, lapels, and pockets with large peach-coloured flowers emerging from a bank of green-and-yellow bushes. His silken waistcoat showed similar florals, giving the man the appearance of being nothing less than the spirit of spring itself come to dine in the depths of autumn.

His moustache, slim. His eyes, enchanting. His manners, impeccable. Though not aristocracy by birth, Mr Noss Quaintance could give any one of them a run for their money. He also, Vince knew from experience, could be absolutely ruthless. They had met several times before, and each time Vince had to fight the urge to snap the man's neck. Every time Mr Quaintance opened his mouth, the blood boiled in Vince's ears.

"I once attended a show in Paris," Mr Quaintance said. "They had all manner of acrobats and dancers breathing fire.

At the climax of the show, they brought out a child's chair and table and set upon it a teapot, cups, and the daintiest little cakes you ever did see. Then they brought out a mangy dancing bear to sit at the table. I never laughed so much as I did at the sight of the animal trying to lift the cup and saucer. It was as though the shabby beast thought it were a real person!"

"It sounds delightful," Fox said. "When was this?"

"Oh, years ago," Mr Quaintance said, just loud enough for everyone at the table to hear. "I cannot think why the memory of it came to me this evening. I say, Mr Knight, you do know that particular fork was meant for the fish course?"

A murmur of amusement rippled along the table.

Vince skewered a piece of venison and held it up. "Fork doesn't know that." He shoved the meat into his mouth, maintaining eye contact all the while.

Mr Quaintance turned and spoke some words to Fox, who giggled. Under the tablecloth, James lay his hand on Vince's thigh and squeezed. "Take a deep breath," he said. "And more sensible bites."

CHAPTER TWENTY

THE DESSERT COURSE made several guests gasp. A sugar work centrepiece depicting Blackrabbit Lighthouse on its craggy outcrop provided the backdrop for a plethora of individual bowls of fresh and sugared fruits, jellies, jams, and creams.

Some of the guests had started to wander about the room, eating their desserts and admiring the paintings. Others, including James, had taken themselves off to the water closets.

Rabbit moved to James's chair and spoke quietly to Vince. She thanked him for coming, and for keeping his cool. "You and Captain Godgrave seem to be getting along well."

Vince cleared his throat a little. "Just being polite. Have a lot to talk about."

Rabbit sipped from her glass. "Mm, well, don't get too cosy with him. Remember who he works for."

Vince fiddled with his collar again. "Still not sure why you invited me here."

Rabbit laughed. "I thought this might be a good opportunity for the council and the other important people of the town to see you in a less formal setting."

Vince raised his eyebrows at her. "Think this is less formal?"

Rabbit lifted her glass. "We don't take wine at the council meetings," she said. "No matter how often Fox suggests it. You may have to get used to this sort of evening, depending on how long you remain with the Watch. How goes the search for Sergeant Spradbery's killer?"

"Slowly."

"I hear there may have been a witness?"

Vince stared at her.

"Word gets around," she said softly. "I keep my ears open."

"Ms Crimp. Haven't found her yet. Worried about her. Good woman."

"A bedworker, I believe?" Rabbit asked. "My Aldo speaks fondly of her. He used to be in the trade, you know."

"Remember him," Vince said. "Long time ago now. Used to work Pudding Quarter of an evening."

"It's where I met him." Rabbit glanced over to where her husband held court with Fox and Mr Quaintance. A dashing bald man with deep-set eyes and an easy smile. "My friends all said I was a fool. They told me a bedworker's skill lay in making their clients believe there was no one else in all the world they wanted to see. But with Aldo it was true."

Their affair had turned heads, but more due to the difference in family than occupation. When she and Aldo had been handfasted, he had taken her family name. "I've always had a knack for seeing people as they are, Mr Knight." Her eyes flickered to the far end of the table, where Swan sat conversing with her bored-looking husband.

James returned and insisted Rabbit remain in his chair. Rabbit thanked him but moved on to the next cluster of guests. Her role on the council meant never staying still for too long.

James pulled his chair a little closer to Vince. He kept his smile but lowered his voice. "What were you two conspiring about?"

Vince studied James's face for a moment. Everyone else at the table was deep in conversation. His head felt light from the wine. A different glass with every course and more besides. "Rabbit believes Swan wants to be the head of the council. More, she thinks Swan is actively trying...to... Already knew, didn't you?"

"Yes. Don't make a scene."

Vince's ears flushed, his words hissed from his gritted teeth like steam from a kettle. "Helping her do it, aren't you?"

"We can discuss it tomor— Where are you going?"

Vince shoved back his chair and rushed out of the dining room, clawing at his frilly collar as he went. He passed painting after painting of the Blackrabbit countryside, the cliffs, the hills, and even some of the other Pell Isles.

James hurried along behind him. "Wait, dammit, wait." He reached out and grabbed Vince's arm. Vince shook him off but stopped, nonetheless.

"Look, will you just...?" James stopped, looking around the empty hallway and lowering his voice. "Will you let me explain?"

"Don't need to explain yourself to me. Quite clear what you've been up to. Working behind the scenes to ruin my chances!"

"Please, just... Look, come in here. Come on." James grabbed the nearest door handle and turned it.

Vince followed him inside. James turned the knob on a striker-lantern, lighting the narrow room. The walls held star charts and astronomical devices in cases. On a cramped desk, a paper detailing the discovery of a new planet by a man named Herschel. The thin room ended in a small glass conservatory jutting out over the cliffs. There, a telescope stood alone, pointing to the skies.

James sat on a thin, creaking chaise longue. "Swan asked me to come to Blackrabbit. When I arrived, she told me she wanted me to set up a rival Watch."

Vince stood with his arms folded, shaking his head. "Before we ever met, you knew you'd be working to get rid of me."

"I had no idea who you were at the time. No one had even mentioned your name at that point. In subsequent meetings, it became clear Swan had other plans in motion. She wanted to replace the Watch with my Sentinels and use us to bolster her public support for when she eventually made a move against Rabbit. That's all."

Vince threw his hands in the air and let them slap against his sides when they fell. "Oh, should have said so sooner.

Were only trying to ruin my life in two different ways! Going to get rid of me when your Sentinels replaced my Watch or going to get rid of me when your employer replaced Rabbit. Much clearer. Should thank you, really."

James's eyes had turned as sharp as his words. "It isn't that simple!"

"Sounds it to me."

"I didn't know you back then! For pity's sake, man, it's not even been two weeks since I arrived here!"

"Answer me this—scheming to replace me when we met in the cherry house the first time, were you? Trying to soften me up?"

James stood and tried to take Vince's hand, but Vince shook him off. "No, Vince, look at me. No. I didn't know who you were in the cherry house. The first time I heard your name was later that day when Rabbit introduced us in her office, but I didn't truly know who you were until Perty told me about you. And then there was the article in the blasted Courant."

Vince stood in the narrow conservatory and rubbed the back of his hand across his mouth. Far below, the waves rumbled in darkness. "Always knew you were going to take over from me, didn't you? Even when we shared a bed."

"Once I knew who you were," James said, "who you had been, I was even more determined to get rid of you."

Vince shot him a look.

James gripped the lapels of his own white waistcoat. "You wanted me to be honest. I found you attractive, certainly, but I wasn't about to let my libido scupper my chances of success. If it came down to it, I would have removed you from the Watch by force. I want this town, Vince. I want this island. I want my Sentinels."

Vince laid his hand on the telescope. "At any cost?"

James took a deep breath. "Not any cost. Not any longer. But I meant what I said about not letting my libido stand in my way. I won't stand aside just because I want you in my bed. I truly believe my Sentinels are better suited to ensuring the safety of my town than your Watch is. And the safety of the town is what matters most."

Vince walked slowly to where James stood, forcing him to move back flat against the wall. He leaned in close and placed his hands on either side of James's face. He closed his eyes and rested his forehead against James's. His voice rumbled like waves outside. "Don't want to have to fight you too, James."

James spoke softly, his lips so close to Vince's own. "We

want the same thing. I am not your enemy, Vince."

Vince pressed his lips to James's forehead and held them there for a moment. Then he stepped back and without another word, he left the narrow observatory and walked out through the front doors of Silver Hope.

CHAPTER TWENTY-ONE

TEN MINUTES AFTER walking into the Jack Thistle tavern, Vince was slurping the broth in his fish stew and wiping the excess from his moustache. He hadn't eaten as well as he'd liked the previous night at Silver Hope, and his rumbling stomach had woken him early. The food in the tavern could hardly be described as first-rate but it did the job.

He didn't know his way around a kitchen. When he'd been working at the asylum, his meals had been provided. Before that, local businesses had been falling over themselves to provide food for him in a bid to earn his favour. For a time, he'd had someone taste the food before he ate it. Better safe than sorry.

The tavern didn't object to his presence. Located so close to the docklands, the clientele consisted mostly of visiting sailors looking to make the most of their brief shore leave. They were wont to overdo it, and fights were common. The tavern keeper said it helped to avoid trouble to have the Watch Commander eat there.

When he finished his food, he asked for a quill pen and some paper. He was still sketching on it when young Brendan arrived. "Find this. Quick as you can. Two crowns in it for you." He folded the paper and handed it to him, sending the lad on his way.

Vince's sleeping had been erratic. Between working in the Watch House at night and keeping an eye on the Gunbrides by day, he hardly had time to get his head down. So when word whipped round the tavern about how the C.T.C. headquarters was under attack, he didn't quite know what to make of it.

He slapped a coin on the table, grabbed his tricorne, and rushed outside. Sure enough, from farther down the docklands, screams and shouts could be heard. Then the occasional crack of a musket shot. By the time he ran there, the fighting had ended. He found James's lieutenant, Hancock, in the confusion of soldiers and smoke.

"The Gunbrides," she said. "Raided C.T.C. headquarters in broad daylight."

"Why?" Vince asked.

"Weapons and ammunition," she said. "Presumably to make up for the cache you intercepted at the docks last week. We're regrouping and then we're going after them. It's not as if we don't know where to find them."

"Not yet," Vince said. "Need to talk to Lambshead first."

"Sun's up," Lieutenant Hancock said. "That means its Sentinel business."

"Tell James I asked him to wait," Vince said, hurrying off towards town.

"He won't listen!"

"*Tell him!*"

He bounded up Quarrier's Run and outside the theatre with the opera-playing automata, he jumped into an empty carriage, much to the annoyance of the driver.

"Oi, you can't just—"

"Gull's Reach! Go! *Now!*"

The driver did as he was told, taking Vince west along the twisting roads to Bezzle Bridge. From the moment the Gunbrides had installed sentries on the bridge, a crowd had gathered across the road to watch them. Bodies came and went, but its numbers rarely dwindled below thirty or so.

Without breaking his stride, Vince marched past the sentries, over the bridge. Ahead, the people of the Reach were cheering for their returning heroes. He forced his way through them and into the first tenement. "Lost your damn minds!"

In the staid gloom of the stairwell, Lambshead turned, barely looking at him. "Well, since you intercepted our delivery from the *Dancer of Belgrade*, you didn't leave us much choice."

Mrs Damerell put her arm out, blocking his way. "Go home, Vince," she said. "This isn't your concern."

"Raiding the greencoats? Think they'll ignore that?"

"You'd better hope they do," Lambshead said.

The blood pumped in Vince's ears. He clenched his fists and closed his eyes, trying to calm himself. He clamped his teeth so tightly he thought they would shatter in his skull.

He flinched at the first gunshot. Another volley followed, all close by and coming from the direction of the bridge. Lambshead squinted at him and quickly drew Summersong. Mrs Damerell fled with the other residents deeper into the tenement. Vince grabbed the muzzle of Lambshead's weapon and twisted. The pepper-box pistol fired. Smoke filled the room. Vince's ears rang from the shot. Someone screamed. Vince punched Lambshead in the stomach, sending him to the floor. Vince still held the pistol. He rushed to the doorway of the tenement just as James Godgrave and his Sentinels charged across Bezzle Bridge, past the prone bodies of the sentries.

From the floor, Lambshead shouted at him. "This was your plan! To distract us while your greencoat friends approached!"

"No friends of mine," Vince said, helping him to his feet.

Lambshead shoved Vince and ran farther inside the building. From his blind side, the red-haired girl with the freckled face snatched Summersong from his hand and darted upstairs. Vince hesitated before bolting after Lambshead, swiftly followed by the Sentinels in their emerald-green uniforms. They shouted at Vince to stop, but he ignored them.

He ran through squalid room after squalid room, batting at hanging clothes and stumbling over discarded shoes. He emerged into one of the many arcades which tunnelled the length of the tenement blocks. This one had been built to house shops but all stood empty, most boarded up. Leaks poured from the ceiling, forming puddles for Lambshead's boots to splash in as he ran full tilt along the passageway, pursued by Vince.

Lambshead skidded to a halt when a band of Sentinels blocked the exit ahead of him. Vince stopped too. Another band of greencoats, headed by Lieutenant Hancock, entered the arcade behind him.

"Leave him to me!" Vince said.

James stood with his troops at the exit. "I don't think so, Vince. Not this time." He held up a musket.

"Dammit, James. Supposed to wait until we had them all in one place!"

"Which was all well and good until they stole from us. We couldn't very well stand by and do nothing, now could we?"

The crack of the musket shot echoed through the arcade. The shot struck Lambshead's leg, and he crumpled to the ground crying out in agony.

Vince ran to him. "Enough!"

Another volley of musket fire came from outside and rang through the arcade, the sound bouncing from wall to ceiling.

"My officers are making short work of your little riflemen," James said to Lambshead.

"Don't kill him." Vince balled his fists, ready to emphasise his point.

James was smiling. James was always smiling. "I have no intention of it." He grabbed Lambshead by the collar and dragged him along the ground. Lambshead shouted and screamed out for help. Vince moved to aid him but two bayonets prompted him to keep his distance.

James dragged Lambshead to the bridge, ducking the missiles being thrown from the windows of the Reach by children. When he crossed the bridge, the mood changed significantly. The people there cheered when they saw him. Vince kept his distance the whole time. Sorcha and Exeter ran to him.

"What happened?" Sorcha asked.

"Sentinels swarmed over the bridge, shot the sentries down like they were nothing. Listen." The cheering grew louder when James heaved Lambshead into a cart and paraded him in front of the crowd. "We've lost them," Vince said.

THE CHARCOAL NIB crumbled onto the page as Vince worked. He brushed away the pieces, making pleasing streaks across his drawing of Crabmeat. He shaded in some more of the dog's ear, trying to capture where the firelight fell upon it. A knock at the door roused Crabmeat from his slumber by the fireplace, and he barked, half-heartedly.

"Told you to keep still." Vince slid the drawing under a stack of blank sheets and wiped his hands on an old rag. He opened the door to find James Godgrave standing there, holding a bottle of Scottish whisky.

"I hope you don't mind me calling unannounced," James said. That bleddy smile was still on his stupid, handsome face.

Vince invited him inside. Crabmeat wagged his tail a couple of times and then immediately fell back asleep.

James set the bottle onto a table, hung up his overcoat, and bent to gaze out of the grimy window to the bridge beyond. "This is where you're living now?"

"Came with the position." Vince was glad he'd taken some time to tidy up and polish every surface. The little dwelling probably hadn't been this clean in years. "Not out celebrating? Half the town wants to buy you a drink."

"And the other half wants to slit my throat. I wanted to come round and explain myself."

"No need."

"Nonetheless, here I am. I couldn't let you take Hugo Lambshead away. I needed the public to see my Sentinels taking him to the magistrates. It's quite a victory for us." He sat by the fireplace.

"Good bribe and he'll be out by morning."

"That doesn't matter tonight. Tonight, the Gunbrides are rudderless. Thanks to my Blackrabbit Sentinels."

"Thanks to you, you mean. All for you, isn't it?"

James toyed with the ring on his little finger. "I'd be lying if I said no. How about this—why don't we simply merge the Watch with my Sentinels?"

"Under your command."

"I believe I'm best suited. The Watch can then continue their duties."

"But we'll report to you."

"It won't be so bad. You've been under me before. I don't remember hearing you complain." His sage-green eyes twinkled in the firelight.

"Should have waited," Vince said. "Wasn't the plan."

"Oh, come off it, man. My hands were tied!" His voice turned sharper, his eyes colder. "They stole from us. We knew where they were. I couldn't very well just ignore it. And the longer I waited, the more chance they'd take the weapons and ammunition somewhere else, hidden it somewhere, or parcelled it out amongst themselves. I couldn't take the risk. Not even for you."

Vince opened the bottle and poured it into two of the cleanest glasses he had to hand. "Can't fault your honesty." He handed a tumbler to James. "Took a while for you to find it, mind."

"I wasn't certain I could trust you before. I have no reason to lie to you now."

"Sad state of affairs when I'm not even worth lying to." He clinked his glass against James's.

"Thought you should taste some proper whisky, for once," James said.

Vince took a mouthful and swallowed. It burned his throat in a good way. "Escaped Gunbrides will need to be rounded up."

"Oh, we'll find them soon enough, I'm certain of it. I'm sure from where you're sitting it looks as though I betrayed you. I wanted you to know that was never my intention. I'm as bound by my duty as I am by my word." James's striking features glowed in the firelight. The flames brought out the red in his smart beard.

Vince finished his drink and poured himself another glass. He couldn't remember tasting a finer quality. While they talked, Vince lifted a stick of charcoal from a little burnt tin and idly dragged it across a page.

"Why don't you just leave me to it, hmm?" James asked. "You don't appear to be a natural fit for this work."

"Took enough from this town over the years," Vince said. "Trying to give something back." He swirled the charcoal, lifting and striking as he went.

"Why? What does it matter?"

"Right thing to do."

"There's got to be more to it." He held his glass up while Vince refilled it.

"A guilty conscience is a powerful engine. It can drive a man to all manner of extremes. It can keep a man up at night only so long before he's compelled to assuage it." James didn't so much talk as purr his words out, like a contented tiger in a waistcoat. He smiled when he talked, when he wanted to get a person on his side, when he wanted to endear himself. As he spoke, his eyes disappeared, becoming little slits, like upturned crescent moons. But when serious, his eyes widened and his smile sank as if never to return, buried under a stony glare. "I think you're afraid."

Vince spluttered into his drink "Of?"

"I think you're afraid of me. Of my Sentinels. Of your Watch being absorbed into my organisation. And shall I tell you what else I think?"

"Could I stop you?"

"Certainly not—how rude. I'm a guest," James said with a laugh. "I think your years spent at the top of the chain of command gave you a taste for it. I think you'd be utterly incapable of taking orders from me or from anyone else. I've seen the way you bristle when Rabbit talks to you. You're used to being in charge, and you don't want to give it up."

"Wrong," Vince said.

"Well?"

"Mudge gave the orders. Not me. His plan, his vision. After a while, started to see him for what he was. But I was trapped. No way out without ending up in his sights. Had to stay to protect myself. Now he's gone, it's time for me to fix what I broke. No one else can do it. Time to clean up my own mess."

"And if you don't?"

"Might as well stay here. Drink myself to the grave."

James set his glass down. "I didn't bring quite enough whisky for that."

Vince admired James's face. The way his eyebrows lifted when he spoke. The way the neat curls of his moustache accented the curves of his slightly chubby cheeks. And then there was the confident boom and crystal clarity of his voice. The self-assured tone of it. He'd have made a fine actor, treading the boards of London. Vince turned his attention to the page, using his wide thumb to smooth and blend the charcoal. "Used to know who my enemies were," he said. "Used to be obvious."

James smiled more widely. "I told you already, I am not your enemy, Vince. I know you're used to seeing the world in those terms, but we want the same thing. To bring justice and peace to the town."

"Can't work together though. People think the Watch needs help from the Sentinels, it makes us look weak. Rabbit doesn't want it either."

"Very well. Maybe we can't work together out there," James said, rising from his chair. He placed his hand on Vince's shoulder. "But behind closed doors, there's no limit to what we can do." He leaned down and kissed him. He put his hand on Vince's face, stroking it. With his other, he lifted the portrait Vince had been drawing. "I don't think you've captured my nose quite right."

Vince stood and pulled him in close. He quickly flicked his blackened thumb onto James's nose, leaving a smoky smudge.

James chuckled and wiped it off before Vince kissed him again.

Vince led him to his bedroom and began to strip. They caressed each another, slowly, deliberately. James nibbled at Vince's bull neck, causing him to moan loudly.

James stroked Vince's broad, bare chest. "Let me get a proper look at you."

Their encounters in the cherry house had been in wan candlelight. There in Vince's bedroom, they had plenty of lantern light and plenty of time.

James slipped Vince's braces off his heavy shoulders and helped him to pull off his shirt. He rubbed his hands over Vince's tattoos. "A painted man is a work of art in itself." His fingers stopped on one of the many scars. Lightly, he tracked it, a raised welt on Vince's side. "A musket wound," James said. "Who did this to you?" He lightly touched the eyepatch and motioned to lift it.

Vince stopped him. "Not tonight."

They kicked off their boots and trousers and fell onto the bed. Vince groped at James's sturdy frame, his hairy chest, his powerful thighs. He ran his thumb across the mole at the base of James's throat. James grabbed between Vince's legs, squeezing and groping enough to make Vince moan. As Vince kissed James's ear, there came a loud, wet slobbering. Vince stopped and frowned.

James stared at the doorway. "Does he have to be in the room with us? It's somewhat...disconcerting."

Crabmeat sat with his head tilted and tail wagging before licking his soggy lips again and drooling all over himself.

"Crabmeat, out. Go." Vince clicked his fingers.

The dog turned and happily padded back downstairs.

"What sort of a name is that for a dog?" James asked.

"Had it when I got him," Vince said. "Too old to change now."

CHAPTER TWENTY-TWO

VINCE LAY NAKED on his bed as James dressed—first his shirt, then his breeches, then his boots. He closed the buttons of his silk waistcoat—charcoal grey, embroidered with flowers and little bees—and pulled on his overcoat. He stood before a looking glass and fixed his auburn hair.

"Don't need to be fussy," Vince said. "No one knows you round here."

"I'm not doing it for the benefit of other people. I'm doing it for myself. A tidy appearance for a tidy mind, as my father always says."

"Never met my dad," Vince said. "Turned out to be a

pirate. Dead now.”

"A pirate? I wonder if he and my father ever crossed paths? He was a noted pirate hunter, as it happens. At sea for most of my childhood. They may well have tussled on the open waves. My mother was left to raise me alone. Much like you from the sounds of it.”

Vince shook his head. “Mum got the local orphanage to do it. Wasn't any use to her until I was old enough to push a broom or carry a coal scuttle. Runs the asylum now. Worked for her before the Watch.”

James faced him, his eyes softening, his hands open by his side. Crabmeat plodded up the stairs and lay outside the open bedroom door.

Vince fiddled with the corner of his pillow. “Could have anyone you want,” he said. “Came here instead.”

James sat on the edge of the bed. “I have no plans to propose, if that's what you're thinking. I find you attractive. I think I'm right in saying the feeling is mutual. Whatever is happening in our professional lives, I see no reason why we can't enjoy each other's company from time to time.” He leaned in and kissed Vince on the forehead.

Vince fell quiet for a moment. “Usually the way. Only good for bedding and brawling.”

"And so very good at both," James said. "But speaking of professional life, what about these gang leaders? Lambshead and the rest? Did you know them from before?"

Vince lay with one arm behind his head. The other on James's thigh. He nodded.

"I suppose they must have been your lieutenants?"

"Just grunts. Talented ones, mind. Best people I had died when the hurricane struck. Last year. All of us were in a pub called the Dogtooth. Over in Gull's Reach. Hurricane took a whole tenement building down on our heads. Buried me alive. No light. Just darkness and dust. Like being in my grave."

James laid his hand on Vince's and gripped it tightly.

"Thought about just lying there," Vince said. "On my back. Letting the darkness swallow me. Forever. But started digging instead. Tried to get closer to the noise. Hurricane was still raging. Felt air on my skin. Followed it. Burst through to the surface. Shouted to others. No answer. All dead."

"That must have been horrendous." James's bluster had gone entirely. His voice mellow and soothing, his beetle-brow narrowed.

"Still dream about it sometimes," Vince said. "Wake up with a weight on my chest. Can't breathe properly. Anyway.

Two other gang members, Penhallow and Palk, filled the void. Useless pair. Schemers. Tried to kill me a few months ago. How I ended up wearing this." He gestured to his eyepatch. "In the gaolhouse now. Both of them. Crabmeat was theirs first. Liked me better though. Didn't you, boy?"

Crabmeat wagged his tail without lifting his head from the floor.

"So," James said, "the current gang leaders were below those two? I'm sorry, I can only think of it all in terms of rank."

"Not too dissimilar," Vince said. "Penhallow and Palk went into hiding when I left. Always crowing about taking over from me. Chance came but they bottled it." He hesitated then, uncertain how much more he should say. But then he remembered the cheering of the crowd at Bezzle Bridge. "Know how the gangs were at war for a while? Celeste, Lambshead, and Littletar came up with an idea–concocted the fanciful notion of a dangerous fourth gang to keep everyone in line. Truth is–the three of them formed what they're calling a Shadow Council. Controlling everything from behind the scenes. Like I used to."

"I see." James rubbed his thumb across the back of Vince's hand as he spoke. "They've done quite a job of it.

Since you're trusting me with this information, are you going to let me see under your eyepatch now?"

"Better leave some mystery," Vince said.

On his way out, James insisted that Vince sign the portrait he'd drawn. Vince did so with a just simple *V.*

James then rolled up the portrait and slipped it into his pocket. "A memento of a memorable evening," he said.

After escorting James out of the house and locking the door, Vince returned to his bed. He should have been at the Watch House, but what was the point? The council was clearly going to give the Night Watch duties over to the Sentinels, sooner or later. And James had been right. Vince couldn't take orders. He couldn't traipse around town with greencoat troops who were armed to the teeth and ready to shoot anyone who stepped out of line.

Crabmeat climbed up and made himself comfortable on the end of the bed. Vince rubbed him behind the ear. It would still be a couple of hours until sunset and the start of his shift on the Watch. He rolled over, pulled the blankets up to his chest, and fell into a deep sleep.

THE COUNCIL OF Blackrabbit had gathered around their polished oak table. Above them, the domed ceiling of the council chamber painted with stars. Everyone was in attendance, except for Fox who would be last to enter, as usual.

Rabbit sat bolt upright and fidgeted with her mask. She'd been in politics long enough to feel when there was something new in the air, some change in atmosphere. She cursed the feathered masks they all wore, covering the top half of every face and preventing her from reading the expressions of her fellow councillors. Although perhaps that was part of the point of them. Perhaps their forebears had devised the ideal system to put everyone on equal footing.

Mr Uglow opened the chamber doors to admit Fox. She strode in, unapologetic for her lateness, and took her seat, smiling broadly all the while. She wore white, as she usually did. A stole of rabbit fur. Fox wasn't given to subtlety.

Swan knocked the table to get everyone's attention. "I think we all know why we're here. The Watch's failure to subdue the uprising in Gull's Reach must surely be the final straw."

Rabbit used her most imperious voice. "Mr Knight assures me he was well on his way to solving the tensions without violence."

Badger laughed and held his hand up. "Surely you jest? Mr Knight doesn't know anything but violence."

"He's trying his best," Rabbit said.

"This town needs more than Mr Knight's best," Swan said. "It deserves more. Which is why I believe it's time we end Rabbit's little experiment and hand the duty of keeping this town safe over to Captain Godgrave and the Blackrabbit Sentinels. Day *and* night."

Badger and Magpie both nodded in agreement.

Rabbit turned to Fox and held her hands out. "Well? Aren't you going to speak up? Isn't the whole point of Fox to be the dissenting voice?"

"It is," Fox said, "but I think you're playing my part today, darling. Look, we all admire you for giving Mr Knight a chance—"

"Speak for yourself," Swan said.

"—but even you must see he's just not up to the task. He's had two substantial failures of late, not to mention the fact the public are deathly afraid of him. It was a good and noble effort on your part to try to help him redeem himself, but I think it's time we wake up to the truth and put the good of the town first."

VINCE AWOKE TO the furious barking of Crabmeat. And then he started coughing. He rolled out of bed, landing with a thump on the bare floorboards in his smoke-filled bedroom. Staying low, he grabbed his boots and trousers, and scrambled downstairs to his front door. Someone banged on it, over and over. He undid the latch and fell out on the road beneath the bridge, coughing and retching.

On his hands and knees, with Crabmeat licking at his face, it took him a moment to come to his senses. The Watch House burned. A crowd of neighbours had gathered, some carrying buckets of water. Vince rose to his feet. "Anyone come out of there?"

Exeter came running from around the corner and skidded to a stop. "Vince! What's happened?"

"Supposed to be watching the prisoners!"

"I had to go out. I was only gone five minut— Where are you going?"

Still nude, Vince slipped his wide feet with their stubby toes into his boots. He wrapped his trousers around his neck to cover his nose and mouth and ran headlong into the closed door of the Watch House. It burst under his force, belching out black, acrid smoke. He kept his head down and made his way to the cell doors, banging his legs against the desks as he went. The cells were still locked, the prisoners within panicking. They rattled the bars, shouting at him, swearing at him. Some fell to the floor, trying to escape the smoke choking their lungs, burning their throats. Walter stared at him, tears in his eyes, without saying a word.

Cursing himself for leaving the keys upstairs, Vince fought through the smoke to his desk. He took his cane from the wall and pulled on the octopus handle, revealing a short sword blade. Still coughing, he jabbed the blade into the cell door lock and heaved. The lock popped. The sword's tip snapped. The prisoners ran for the door, pushing past one another in a rush to escape the blaze. Last of all, Walter fell out and into Vince's arms.

Clutching the now-sheathed octopus sword in one hand and Walter's arm in the other, Vince pushed on through the flames. He lay Walter on the ground outside while Exeter brought him some water. The prisoners all scattered and ran. Vince had no intentions of chasing after them.

He stood before the burning Watch House, his naked flesh tigered with soot. The fire wrapped its fingers around his workplace, around his quarters, pulling them down, brick by brick. The warming light of it danced across his bare, inked skin. He roared at the top of his voice, causing the onlookers to flinch.

"Um, I think you should put some clothes on," Exeter said.

Vince pulled on his trousers, fixing the braces in place over his heavy shoulders.

One of his neighbours had deployed a set of horological bellows by attaching them to a set of pipes on a building across the road. The bellows pumped the water from the pipes through a long, leather hose and onto the Watch House. Other neighbours continued dumping bucket after bucket of water onto the blaze. The flames crackled as they licked from the windows of his lodgings, like angry tongues from angry mouths.

The rest of the Watch had arrived, expecting to report for duty, but instead pitched in to help douse the fire. After several hours, they succeeded. One neighbour had brought Vince a coral-coloured banyan just about big enough to put on but not up to the task of closing over his belly. Under a starry night sky, he stood before the smouldering ruins of his new home. Crabmeat sat against his leg.

"Good of the neighbours to help," Sorcha said.

"Just worried about their own houses."

"We spoke to some young lads who were nearby," Sorcha said. "They saw some people lurking behind the Watch House. They must have waited for Exeter to leave and then set the fire. The boys saw two men. One was bald, had a little purple gemstone earring."

"Philip Talan," Vince said. "Warning from the Gunbrides."

"More than that," Sorcha said. "You could have been killed. So could Walter and the other prisoners."

Walter had been propped up against a wall by a neighbour and kindly given a cup of brandy to calm his nerves. He hadn't budged an inch since. "They knew we were in there," he said softly. "They didn't care. They didn't care."

"There goes the cache of weapons from the docks," Exeter said. "I suppose if the Gunbrides couldn't have them then no one could."

"Where you will stay tonight?" Sorcha asked.

Vince snorted. "Go back to the asylum, I suppose. Still have a room there."

"You can't travel all that way tonight," Sorcha said. "You can stay with me."

Vince shook his head. "Can't put you in danger."

"This was my workplace too. I could have just as easily been in there. I'm already in danger," Sorcha said. "Come on."

THE WATCH GATHERED in the Quick tailor shop. Vince, still in his ill-fitting banyan, leaned on the counter while Frank and Clive squeezed onto a chaise lounge. Mr Norton stood with his back to the door, crossed his arms, stared at the floor, and occasionally shook his head.

"What will you do now?" Sorcha lit another striker lantern. "And don't just grunt at me."

"Don't know," Vince said. "Sleep here. See what the world looks like tomorrow."

Clive fiddled with the mechanism in his metal leg. "Well, we can't go on patrol without our equipment."

"And I've lost this month's records," Mr Norton said.

Sorcha hopped up onto the shop counter and swung her legs. "We'll all have to warn our families to take extra care. In case the Gunbrides attack our houses too. Having you here is—"

"Risky," Vince said.

"I was going to say extra protection."

"I've had word from a friend who works at the town hall," Mr Norton said. "The council have officially decided to allow the Sentinels to patrol the town. Day and night."

"That's it, then," said Sorcha. "We're done."

Vince cracked one of his knuckles. "James said there was a place for us in the Sentinels."

"I didn't realise you were on first name terms with Captain Godgrave," Mr Norton said.

Sorcha rolled her eyes. "I won't be signing up to the C.T.C. any time soon."

Clive raised his eyebrows. "I've done my time with them. And I can't really picture you as a greencoat, Vince."

"Well, if you're not going to wear a uniform, you'll need some other clothes," Sorcha said. "Stand up straight. Come on. Let me measure you."

"Have my measurements from the shirt you made?"

"Unless you have a stash of clothes in Captain's God-grave's bedroom, you're going to need some new trousers." She produced a tape measure from a drawer, ran it around his generous waist, then up his inside leg.

"Steady," Vince said.

"Calm down. You're not my type. I prefer men who aren't covered in soot and old enough to be my grandfather."

"Oi! Cheeky brat!"

"What? You are. And the white hair makes you look even older." She jotted some figures in a book and sighed. "I suppose I'll have to get used to this. Looks as though Orla got her way. I'll be working in the family business after all."

"I thought you hated your sister," Mr Norton said.

Sorcha shot a look to the back of the shop and gritted her teeth. "Keep your voice down! I don't hate her. We just...don't get on the way we used to. And I didn't want to spend my life running my hands up old men's legs. But it's not as if I have much choice now."

Vince squinted at her before turning to Exeter. "You. Explain."

Exeter had been ignoring most of the conversation from

the corner where he stood. "What's to explain?"

"Supposed to be guarding the prisoners," Vince said.

"I was," Exeter said. "I guarded them all day long, while you were off in Gull's Reach with your friends in the Gun-brides."

Vince thumped his fist on the counter.

Exeter raised his voice and avoided looking at him. "I can't have been gone more than ten minutes."

"Not what you said when you arrived at the fire. Said you'd been gone five minutes."

Exeter thrust his hands into the pockets of his overcoat. "Five, ten, what's the difference?"

"Could have been the difference between the Watch House going up in flames or not."

"I had to go and see a friend, if you must know."

"Friend," Vince said. "Explains why you came back in that state."

Exeter looked down and tucked in his errant shirt tail. "It was your idea to build cells in the Watch House. Pardon me if I'm not prepared to adjourn my entire life to accommodate your whims."

"Don't need to worry about my whims any longer," Vince said.

"The gangs won't like them," Walter said from the corner. "The Sentinel patrols, I mean. You think things are bad now, wait until the gangs start rubbing up against armed officers on their streets. Mark my words, it will be trouble."

"Well, it won't be our problem," Mr Norton said. "Why are you still here, by the way? Why haven't you run off yet?"

"I've got nowhere else to go. I've seen what everyone thinks of me. I'm expendable. I'm safer here with you lot."

Mr Norton lifted his coat and turned the doorknob. "Well, if there's no more Watch, there's no sense in my being here." On his way out he stopped and turned to Vince. "Who would have thought you'd be more of a threat to the Watch by working with us instead of against us?"

Once the rest of the Watch had left, Sorcha fetched a blanket and some pillows for Walter. He settled on the floor by the fireplace. Crabmeat sniffed him a few times before laying with his head on Walter's lap.

After washing the soot from himself, Vince followed Sorcha to a tiny room on the top floor of the shop decorated with floral wallpaper. She closed the door behind her, leaving Vince alone with his thoughts. He lay on the soft, skinny bed and stared at the ceiling.

He'd been handed everything he'd needed on a silver

plate. A position of worth, a roof over his head, a chance to make up for his past misdeeds. And now look. How quickly it had all slipped from his grasp. How poorly he'd handled the situation. How perfectly he'd failed.

CHAPTER TWENTY-THREE

JAMES FED A ragged chunk of fish to his peregrine falcon, Maclaren. "I suppose you've seen the newspaper today?"

Perty lifted the paper from his desk. "My, my. They certainly are on board with us, aren't they?"

"Article after article of praise for our actions in Gull's Reach yesterday. Well done, Perty."

"Thank you, sir."

James beamed from ear to ear. The articles were exactly the sort of thing he needed to see. His talk with Ms Hawkmoor had clearly done the trick. "The Courant makes particular mention of how the Sentinels stopped any violence from spilling over the bridge and into the rest of the town."

Perty turned the page, quickly perusing the contents. "I don't see any mention of the two Sentinels who lost their lives in the process."

James waved his hand. "The public doesn't need to know about that sort of thing. It would only frighten them. We'll have a plaque made for the front office. In honour of those who gave their lives during the inaugural operation of the Blackrabbit Sentinels."

"Have you seen this? About the fire at the Watch House?"

James didn't flinch. "Ah, yes, I did. I wonder if you might, discretely, ascertain the current whereabouts of Watch Commander Knight? I know he was living at the Watch House at the time."

Perty squinted at the page. "The story doesn't mention any casualties."

"I'm sure he escaped, but I think it's wise for the Sentinels to know where all the Watch members reside. In case they should attempt any reprisals for their usurpation. It is far easier to round up dissenters when one already knows where to find them." He wiped fish scales from his hands on a rag.

"Yes, sir." Perty could always be relied on for her

discretion.

"Besides, the burden of locating the murderer of dear Sergeant Spradbery now falls to us, and we may need to ask the Watch for any pertinent information. Oh, and can you ask someone to set up a standing order at the market for fresh fish every morning? Maclaren deserves the very best catch of the day. Don't you, my dear?" James rubbed the backs of his fingers along his falcon's chest.

"Of course, sir," Perty said.

By noon, James's Sentinels were combing the streets for gang members. Without any input from the Watch, they had no idea who was and who was not a member, but that proved no deterrent. Their patrols began rounding up anyone they felt to be a possible candidate. They trotted them off to the magistrates for trial, and from there they would be shipped off to Blackrabbit Gaol with hardly a word spoken against them.

By nightfall, word of the arrests had spread and a noticeable shift in the attitudes of the townsfolk became the talk of what James had named Sentinel Garrison. His people spoke of hostile encounters ranging from thrown insults to thrown fruit and vegetables. The presence of an armed force watching the townsfolk's every move was bad enough but the supposed reckless disregard for the innocence of the prisoners was positively galling. Several officers reported a growing sense of unease in their duties.

James soon put them right. He assured his people any change would naturally be met with resistance and scepticism. If the Sentinels carried on doing their duties and providing a firm hand to steer the town towards justice and order, the people would soon accept them as though they had always been there. "I would go so far as to say they will, in fact, find it difficult to imagine life without us."

He unpacked the last of his belongings—his brass compass—and set it on his desk, turning it this way and that until it sat in the perfect spot. A voice from the doorway startled him.

"You had this all ready to go, didn't you?" Rabbit asked.

James offered her a seat. "The Chase Trading Company is very organised."

"This building was completed weeks ago. You and Swan conspired from the beginning. You were always meant to take over from the Watch. It's the real reason you're here."

James sat back and smiled. "Swan knew the C.T.C. was best suited to keep order on Blackrabbit. We've always been the obvious choice."

"The people don't want greencoats controlling every aspect of their lives. They are already the biggest employer in

Port Knot, the person who runs the company is on the ruling council, they own everything from the docks to Pudding Quarter, and a good deal more besides."

"Success is nothing to be ashamed of."

Rabbit squinted, deepening the wrinkles about her eyes. Some people found the masks of the council unsettling but James found Rabbit to be a good deal more fearsome without hers. Her attention flicked briefly to the framed charcoal portrait of James hanging on the wall. "What do you intend to do about the Watch?"

"Oh, I didn't think we needed a Watch any longer," James said. "They were fine at the time, but the world is changing fast. A more aggressive approach is what's needed now."

"That's as may be. However, you'd be a fool to deny the wealth of knowledge the Watch represents. The experience. And you strike me as many things, Captain Godgrave, among which a fool does not number."

James smiled and toyed with the silver ring on his finger. "I already spoke to Commander Knight and told him serving Watch members would be most welcome to join my Sentinels."

"Something tells me Mr Knight would not be entirely

keen on taking orders. Could the Watch not continue to serve as an independent unit? Supplementing the force of the Sentinels?"

James leaned back in his chair. "The council put me in charge of law and order in Port Knot. I can't very well have a band of untrained ruffians running about, knocking heads, and claiming to be in positions of authority. It would be much too confusing for the common man. No, given how coolly my offer was received, I'm sorry to say the time of the Watch has passed. A bright new future beckons for Port Knot. And I stand at the forefront of it."

ORLA STOOD AT the head of the table and dished out a bowlful of lamb stew. "Have you given any more thought to Apricate Maunder?"

Sorcha blinked at her and shrugged her shoulders.

"Mrs Maunder's son. The one she's been trying to get you to court for weeks."

"Ach, I haven't time for any of that," Sorcha said. "Not

with everything going on with the Watch and Vince."

"Speaking of which, how long is he staying for?"

Sorcha shrugged again and dug her spoon in. Steam rose in ghostly curls. "I don't know, however long it takes for him to find somewhere else, I suppose."

Orla slumped onto her chair. "There's no room for him here, Sorcha. Look at the size of this place." She lowered her voice. "He can hardly fit through our doors. He certainly wouldn't fit round this table with us."

"For one thing, he can hardly fit through any doors," Sorcha said, "not just ours. And I don't think he's going to be joining us for meals. He's not an elderly aunt come to visit." She blew on a lump of stringy meat to cool it.

"No, he's a criminal mastermind being targeted by arsonists!" Orla kept checking over her shoulder as she spoke.

"*Mastermind* feels like a stretch, to be honest. It sounds like Councillor Mudge was the brains behind it all. Vince was just the muscle."

"Except he wasn't, was he?" Orla still hadn't eaten any of her stew. "He wasn't *just* the muscle. He controlled the gangs. He was the one the scary people were scared of! And now he's asleep upstairs! What happens when the Gunbrides come to finish him off? You think they'll politely ask for him to step outside before they do him in? No, they'll take us and the shop with him!"

"Oh, for... What would you have me do, Orla? He doesn't have anywhere else to go!"

"He must have friends or family he can stay with?"

Sorcha took a chunk of potato from her bowl and swallowed it. "He said he could go back to the asylum. He used to work there, but sure, it's a ways out in the countryside. Look, I'll talk to him."

"Tonight."

"Let the man sleep. Tomorrow is plenty of time."

"And what about him?" Orla pointed to the other end of the table where Walter sat quietly eating his stew.

"I keep forgetting he's here," Sorcha said.

Walter smiled and sat up straight. "One of my best qualities, that," he said. "Celeste told me one of the greatest tools a thief can have is the ability to go unnoticed."

"I suppose he could help you in the shop? What about it, Walter? Any good with a needle?"

"Oh, no," Walter said, licking his spoon. "Although I am a dab hand with a bodice."

Orla and Sorcha just stared at him.

"No, no, not like that! I can thread whale bone into a

corset like nobody's business. Little hands, you see." He held them up to give Orla and Sorcha a better look.

"Huh," Orla said. "I might be able to use you, after all."

ON THE SENTINEL'S first official day, Perty Hancock attended a meeting in Captain Godgrave's office to learn what her new role would entail. He quickly made it clear to her that while he would oversee the Sentinels as a whole, the performing of day-to-day duties would be left to her discretion.

"I trust you know what's best for your home town," he said.

Perty took to her new role with rampant enthusiasm. Her first order took the battle to the heart of the problems, as she saw it. She insisted on posting a Sentinel outside every tavern, inn, and alehouse in the town. From the Jack Thistle in the north to the Lion Lies Waiting in the south, from the Star We Sail By in the east to the Salt Pocket in the west, these and every other drinking establishment would be watched from opening to closing.

The innkeepers and tavern owners were opposed to this measure, to say nothing of the patrons, but what could they do about it? She knew where some of the less than legal drinking dens were to be found and even managed to ferret out the location of a few more. She closed several down before the moon had risen that evening.

On the second day of the Sentinels' reign, Perty had guards posted across the harbour market. She then had her people inspect every stall for illegal or untaxed goods. They moved methodically, starting at the outside and moving in. By the end of trading, more than fifteen stalls had been permanently closed. Forty stall owners were issued with heavy fines. Three stall owners had been arrested after they tried to flee from the inspections, and a handful of market customers had ended up with injuries after attempting to help the market traders escape. Multiple arrests were made for refusing to co-operate or for attempting to hide contraband.

Talk amongst the townsfolk had the Sentinels painted as nothing better than thugs muscling in on new territory. Perty paid no heed to it. For every voice raised in anger, two more praised the Sentinel's no-nonsense approach to crime. Perty explained to her troops how she had a plan to starve the gangs of the supplies they needed to function.

The next stage of said plan caused even more uproar. Stretching her resources to their limit, Perty insisted every crate and barrel that rolled off a ship docked in Port Knot harbour had to be inspected. "In the interests of public safety," she said. "After what happened with the Pennymen trying to smuggle weapons and ammunition into the town, I am not prepared to risk any illegal contraband sneaking ashore. It is in everyone's interests that checks are made."

When asked how long these checks would be in place, Perty had just stared blankly. "Until Port Knot is safe," she said.

This caused an even greater split among the townsfolk. People had shouting matches in the streets over the checks. Some said they were too much, a gross invasion of civil liberty, a show of mistrust, while others said they were only a temporary measure, necessary to starve the gangs out. The Blackrabbit Courant posted articles praising the activities of the Sentinels and their thorough, conscientious approach to law-keeping, lending even more fuel to the fires of debate.

Perty had gathered around herself a pack of her favourite officers to form her own personal guard. With them, she targeted a set of very specific businesses in town, mostly in the Tangles. They went from place to place, vigorously overturning stock, checking tax records, and searching for any minor infraction to use as a reason to issue a fine or make an arrest.

"Perty Hancock, as I live and breathe."

Perty tipped her cap to the shop owner, one Mr Spin Gastrell, not out of deference, but out of spite. "Spin. You've done well for yourself."

He wiped his hands on a rag. "Better than you. What brings the daughter of Hangman Hancock back here? Last I heard, you'd run off to sea. Pity it washed you back to our shores."

"I feel very much the same way," she said. "Tell me—these gin bottles—they're taxed, are they? You have records?"

"I... Of course I do." He rummaged in a desk under his counter and produced a tattered black book.

Perty opened it and flicked through the pages. "Oh, dear. I don't see any mention of customs duties being paid."

His face flushed red, and his eyes narrowed. The rag moved from his hands to the back of his pink neck. "It's never been an issue before, Perty."

"Well, it is now." She clapped the book closed in her hand. "And my name is Lieutenant Hancock."

CHAPTER TWENTY-FOUR

ON THE THIRD day, Sorcha finally snapped. She'd been as calm as possible, kept Orla at bay, but her patience had finally been worn out. She marched upstairs to her spare room. Or Vince's room, as it had become. Crabmeat lay at the closed door, as he had done since Vince sealed himself away from the world. Upon seeing her, Crabmeat wagged his tail once, a perfunctory response, like a head nod to a barely liked neighbour.

"Go on, you. Get out of the way. Shoo." She waggled her foot at the dog, and he plodded over to the top of the stairs. She banged her fist on the door. "You'd better be decent because I'm coming in, and I don't want to see an aul lad's tackle." She shoved the door open.

Vince lay on his bed shirtless, the braces of his trousers by his sides, his feet bare. On the floor laid several bottles of gin, all empty.

"For feck sake, will you ever open a window? It smells like a brewer's carthorse died in here." She flung open the curtains, threw up the sash window, and in rushed the clacking of hooves and the chattering town chorus. She started to clear up the empty bottles.

"Don't need you picking up after me," Vince said, his voice rusty, his lips dry.

"Someone has to do it."

"Not you."

"Oh, I'm sorry, I didn't realise all your other friends were here to rally around you. Where are they? Under the bed, are they? Or maybe they're hiding in the wardrobe? Or is it just me? Am I the only person on the entire island who cares about what's happening to you?"

Vince kicked the bedclothes away. He heaved himself up so as to sit against the wall with his feet touching the floor.

Crabmeat wandered in, found the borrowed coral banyan crumpled up into a ball, and lay on it.

Sorcha sighed and sat beside Vince on the little bed. She almost tipped into the well that had formed around him. Her feet dangled over the edge of the frame. She slipped off her shoes and wiggled her toes by his. "Look at my perfect little fillets next to your bloated gammon joints." He didn't respond, and so she sighed again. "Really, though, no one has come around to check on you. Do you...have anyone? Friends?"

Vince shook his head. "Not on Blackrabbit. Haven't had since I was a young lad. Not really. Told myself I don't get lonely. Tricked myself into believing it. Can believe anything if you have to."

"You have family, though, don't you? A mother?"

"Runs the asylum. Have a brother too. Innkeeper on Merryapple. Wants me to work there with him."

"That sounds nice, doesn't it? Would you not consider it now the Watch is done?"

Vince licked his cracked lips. "Wouldn't be safe for him. Too many people want me to suffer. Might take it out on him. His husband. His family. Took this role to clean up my mess. Make it so I can go back to Merryapple safely one day. Didn't work."

"What are you going to do now, then? Because I hate to

break it to you, but you're not staying in here until you drink yourself to death. I'll not be left to look after that mangy dog of yours."

"Won't have to drink myself to death. Only a matter of time before someone comes to finish me off."

"Oh, wonderful, so I'll have a gallon of blood to clear up as well."

He fell quiet again. Sorcha scratched at her arm, trying to think of what to say. "You never struck me as the type to mope about. I had you pegged as a man of action, you know? I thought you'd face any crisis head-on, take it by the throat and shake it until the answer fell out."

"Come after me last year, things would have been differ-ent. Philip Talan would be lying face down in the Lowena. Lambshead would be a sticky smear under my boot. Can't do that now. Got to be a better way."

"What's brought this on?"

Vince lay his thumb over his forefinger and loudly cracked the knuckle. "Something Celeste said. About how they all looked up to me. How I abandoned them. Asked me what I'd be without them or the Watch. Didn't have an an-swer. Still don't. Can't just be a brawler my whole life. Has to be more to me than that. Have to try to be more."

"You took a lot of young people off the streets, didn't you? That's what we always heard. You trained them from an early age. Or had them trained, at least."

"Easier that way. Made them more loyal, in the long run."

"It's no wonder they looked up to you, no wonder they felt betrayed when you walked out on them. They've known you most of their lives. You provided for them, in a way. Gave them the tools to survive. And now you've rejected them. Started a new life without them. On the other side of the law, as well. It's as if everything you told them was a lie."

"Celeste said the same thing." Vince leaned his head against the cold wall. "Sorcha, you don't know what it's like. To have lived a life of violence. To know your own life will end in violence. To have waited for it every day. To know you deserve it." His breathing turned shallow, his voice quivered. He covered his face with his hand. He might have sniffed away a tear; she couldn't be sure. "Still so young," he said. "Hours are fat when you're young. All the time in the world to sit and ponder. Hours are lean as whippets at my age. Don't know what it's like. Thought I knew who I was. How my life would be. All changed now."

Sorcha frowned and clasped her hands. "It must be quite frightening. I suppose it's like being unmoored. Cast adrift.

You worked hard to make things better. That's a start, isn't it? You're a good many things, but you're no fool. I know you didn't think you could wipe your slate clean with one good shift on the Night Watch. Could it be, though, that maybe you didn't realise just how steep a mountain you had to climb?"

Vince rubbed his face and still wouldn't look at her.

She nudged his brawny arm and smiled. "People don't climb mountains alone, you know. And you don't have to, either."

He nodded then, and his weighty shoulders dropped. He stared dead ahead.

"Mind you," Sorcha said, "I wouldn't count on Orla's help. She wants you out of here as soon as possible."

"Didn't fancy breaking it to me gently?"

"Ah, sure it's not as if you didn't know already. She thinks you're a bad influence on me."

"Might be right. Never been known to have a positive effect on people."

"Well if I start to feel the urge to pick a pocket or hold up a coach at musket point, I'll be sure to let you know." She slouched against the wall.

"Sit up straight. Bad for your posture." Vince picked at the dirt under his fingernail. "Never lost your accent."

"Ah, sure, Irish accents are carved in stone. A thousand years at sea couldn't weather them away. I like how you Pellans talk, mind. All bleddy this and backalong that."

"One of us too, now, aren't you? Been here long enough. Thought about going back? To Ireland?"

Sorcha fell quiet for a touch too long. "I don't think it would be a good idea. We've built a life for ourselves here. To be honest, we have more here than we ever would have had at home. Besides, I've enough trouble with an overbearing sister, I don't need to go back to an overbearing mother."

"Orla took care of you. Provided for you."

"And now she thinks she owns me." Sorcha tucked her legs under herself. "When we were sleeping rough, we had people offering to help. They wanted to train us to survive. To steal. And pick pockets. They were part of a gang, they said."

Vince clasped his hands together in his lap. "So, if Orla hadn't found work..."

"I'd have ended up working for you."

"Still did."

"Hah, true enough, I suppose." Still no smile on his stony face, but at least he looked at her now. It broke her heart a little to see him in such a state.

"Sounds to me like Orla worries about you, is all. Feels responsible for you. Heart's in the right place. Good thing to have people who worry about you. Only met my brother for the first time last year. Known him sooner, it might not have taken me so long to see what I was. Life is better with family."

"Not all family."

"Really think Orla is as bad as your mother?"

Sorcha scratched at her arm again. "Ah, no, I wouldn't go that far. I'm just being mean because it feels nice, sometimes. It does, doesn't it? Just to be a little bit of a mean aul cow? Warms the blood. I just wish she'd loosen the apron strings a little."

"Could have a word."

"That's sweet but I'm not sure scaring her would help in the long run."

Vince frowned, catching the band of his eyepatch in a forehead furrow. "Wasn't going to scare her. Just have a chat."

"You're scary when you chat. It's the voice. And the eyepatch. And the lingering air of menace."

Crabmeat rolled onto his back and whined until Vince rubbed his belly.

Sorcha picked her words carefully. "Can I ask, if you weren't here, if you were still above the Watch House, what would you be doing with your time? Eating some beef, downing a bottle of gin, falling asleep in your chair?"

"Not always beef. Sometimes ham."

"Being Watch Commander, that was it for you, wasn't it? Your last chance."

His frown deepened. "Bit personal."

"Push through it," she said, patting his knee. "Come on. Be a big, brave boy."

"Very well. Yes. Watch was my last chance. Happy?"

"Oh my, no, not at all."

Crabmeat clambered up on the bed and onto Vince's lap. Vince laid his giant hand on Crabmeat's head. He looked like he could have crushed the dog's skull if he wanted to.

"Going to talk to Orla?" he asked.

"I don't know. I don't think there's any point. I just...I just want her to understand not everyone wants to put on a pretty dress and find a nice man to settle down with."

"Don't like men?"

"I like them. I just don't want to marry one. Not yet."

"Not even Alfie Exeter?"

Sorcha snorted out something like a giggle. "Now who's being personal? But while we're talking, can you do one thing for me? Please?"

Vince raised his chin and nodded.

"Please have a wash," she said with a laugh. "Please. I'm begging you. Your fancy man won't want you if you don't."

"Who?"

"Your man, Captain whatshisname, with the perfect moustache and the neat-as-pins beard. I've seen the way he looks at you, all moon eyes and smiles. Sure he's mad about you, so he is. It's plain as day, the way he looks at you."

Vince stopped petting Crabmeat. "Not like that. Just screwing."

"Oh. Well. That's...well."

"Sorcha Fontaine blushing. Never thought I'd see the day."

She scrunched her nose and made a face. "It's just the thought of two aul fellas lapping at each other like thirsty dogs at a water bowl."

"Because the thought of your gangly limbs failing about like a newborn foal is so arousing?"

She straightened her spine. "Excuse me, I am not gangly—I am graceful."

Vince let one of his hands go limp and slapped it against his thigh. "Like a daddy-long-legs banging against a window-pane."

Sorcha snorted another laugh. "I think I liked it better when you hardly talked."

"Only talk to people I trust."

"Ah, you trust me! Sure that speaks very well of you, so it does." She sat up and wiggled her shoulders, pleased with herself.

"Mixing giblets with a man I knew wanted to put me out of work. That speak well of me?"

"It says you must really like him."

"Never met anyone quite like James. Hard to think straight when he's around. Want him to look at me like he wants me. Want him to like me."

Sorcha thought about the day Captain Godgrave had come striding into the Watch House in his immaculate uniform. "He is very handsome, in fairness. For an aul lad."

"Not old. James is younger than me."

"Sure, that's not saying much. The cliffs of Blackrabbit are younger than you."

"Rude brat."

"I'm only rude to people I trust," she said, flicking her long dark hair over her shoulder.

"Not true at all, is it?"

"It's not, no, not even a little bit," she said. "No, I'm rude to everyone. I just don't think it's fair to play favourites." She curled her lips and held her hands open. "Oh, come on, you're still not going to give me even one little smile?"

"And take away your only reason for getting up every morning?"

CHAPTER TWENTY-FIVE

VINCE HAULED HIMSELF off the bed and washed in the little room at the top of the stairs. He needed to buy a new straight razor to tidy up the edges of his beard but after running his fingers through it a few times, it settled down into a pleasant-enough state. He fixed his snowy white hair as best he could by parting it at the side. James had told him once he liked how it looked.

After breakfast, he sat awkwardly in the little periwinkle parlour of Sorcha's home. He'd been given a cup of tea so small he was almost certain it was from a doll's house. While he had been washing himself, Sorcha had taken it upon herself to wash the banyan he'd been loaned. He had wanted to leave but didn't want to walk around outside without a shirt.

He was not a man prone to embarrassment but something about sitting shirtless in those surroundings felt wildly inappropriate. His tattoos sat clumsily against the floral wallpaper and doilies, as if the inked creatures on his frame were fighting through a forest of heather and tulips and peonies.

He had asked to borrow a pen and some paper and was in the middle of sketching when Orla finally spoke to him.

"How long do you intend to remain ensconced with us, Mr Knight?" She feigned politeness just well enough, though her plastered-on smile threatened to crack at any second.

Vince struggled to see the family resemblance between this sandy-haired woman and Sorcha.

"Not long," he said. "Need to get some clothes first." His beefy chest flexed involuntarily as he spoke, making inky tentacles move, and the sails of a tall ship ripple.

Orla couldn't take her eyes off them. "Sorcha should be back any moment. She and Walter went to the market."

"Good girl, is Sorcha," Vince said. "Told me about how you came to Blackrabbit. Hard start in life. Could have turned out very differently. Speaks to her good nature. Raising her alone can't have been easy."

Orla sipped at her tea. "The hardest part was stopping your gangs from getting their hooks in her."

Vince didn't rise to the bait. "Grown now though. Able to make her own decisions."

Before Orla could respond, the bell above the shop door jingled.

"We're back," Sorcha shouted.

A door led from the parlour to behind the shop counter. Sorcha popped her head around and asked Vince to join her. He carefully folded his sketch and put it into his pocket.

On the shop floor, she hunted through a tea crate filled with material. "I was rummaging through the sewing room this morning and I found you a shirt to wear. It should fit you." She pulled out a cream top shirt with lace fastenings.

Vince pulled off his braces, careful not to let his trousers fall, and slipped the shirt on.

"Perfect," Sorcha said. "There are some breeches over there you can wear. I know you prefer a trouser but they are all I could find."

Vince grunted his gratitude. He found breeches much too tight and constricting, but he wasn't in a position to refuse.

"I found you an overcoat too." From a deep trunk covered in cracked green leather and held together with iron fittings, she pulled a high-collared, naval-style, claret-coloured coat with black trim. "I seem to remember hearing you favoured this colour. And it's too big for anyone else, so you might as well have it. We had an order for a dozen coats, all in different sizes. The customer decided they weren't red enough so wouldn't pay for them. Honestly, some people. Maybe I'll start a rumour they're helping the gangs, get the greencoats to haul them off to the gaolhouse."

"Don't joke about that," Orla said. "I've heard what they've been up to. Awful. Parading around like they own the place, watching everything we do. I can't relax."

Vince rubbed the fabric of the coat sleeve between his thumb and forefinger. "Had one this colour. Left it behind in a friend's house. On Merryapple."

"Oh, so you do have friends, then?" Orla asked.

Vince glared at her.

"Well, you can't blame me for being surprised."

"Suppose not," Vince said. "Will pay you for this, soon as I can."

"You'd better," Sorcha said. "I know where you live. Hah! I don't believe it; I swear I just saw a flicker of a grin on your face."

"Rubbish."

"No, there was definitely movement there."

"Suppressing a sneeze is all." Vince lifted the black breeches and went behind a screen to try them on.

"Now all you need is a new tricorne," Sorcha said.

"You won't be getting one of them for free," said Orla. "You've gotten enough as it is."

Vince pulled on the breeches and boots. "Told you I'd pay."

"See that you do." She turned for the work room just as the shop door burst open, and two men swaggered in.

The older of the two, a man with a high mop of chestnut hair and a wry smile, closed the door and leaned against it. The other—a young man with large ears, a heavy brow, and short, cropped hair —marched up to the counter and slapped a knife onto it. "Are you the proprietor of this fine establishment? You are? Excellent. I'm sure you've heard the stories about the greencoats going around, snatching up good and honourable business owners, claiming they've been harbouring gang members. My associate and I—say hello, Mr Culpepper—think it's a terrible state of affairs."

"Absolutely reprehensible, Mr Diamond," Mr Culpepper said.

"We think business people such as yourself should be

free to work without the threat of violent arrest. And we'd like to help you."

"Really?" Sorcha moved behind the counter to stand beside her sister. "And how do you plan to do that?"

"Well, now the Watch has been disbanded—and we are terribly sorry to hear it, Ms Fontaine—we are prepared to provide protection for your fine premises and all who dwell within. And at a very reasonable rate."

"Reasonable and mandatory?" Sorcha asked.

Mr Diamond smiled and laughed. "Mandatory is such an ugly word. I think you'll agree in this uncertain world, no price is too high for safety."

Sorcha and Orla looked at each other and both crossed their arms. "I think you'll find we're already in safe hands." Sorcha nodded over his shoulder.

Vince, having watched the whole scene from behind the screen, stepped out into the light. Mr Culpepper turned slack-jawed at the sight of him, the colour draining from his face. Mr Diamond lifted his knife, uncertain if he should attack. With one smooth motion, Vince grabbed Mr Culpepper by the collar, lifting him off the ground while also slapping the knife from Mr Diamond's hand and taking him by the neck. "Door, please."

The two men gurgled and struggled while Sorcha opened the shop door. Vince carried them both out in the road and threw them as hard as he could across it. They thumped into the wall on the far side, banging their heads on the copper piping with a terrific clang. They lay there, dazed and sweating. People emerged from doorways to see what the noise was. Passers-by stopped in their tracks.

Vince stood over the men and drew himself to his full height. "Tailor shop is protected." He spoke loud enough for the whole road to hear. "Any one of you step inside to make trouble, you'll be carried out in a box. Understand?"

Mr Culpepper and Mr Diamond nodded and bolted away from him as fast as they could. The people on the road carried on walking, avoiding eye contact with Vince.

"That should do it," Sorcha said. "Who were they? Pennymen?"

Walter had emerged from the shop doorway. "Not any I know."

"Opportunists," Vince said. "Recognised one of them. Related to the landlord of the Star We Sail By. Part of the Diamond family. Troublemakers, the lot of them."

A red-faced Mr Norton appeared from around a corner, running and waving to them. "Ataraxy Crimp's been spotted."

"Where?"

"The cherry house, on Capstone Over."

Sorcha pulled off her apron and handed it to Orla, who grabbed her by the arm. "Just a minute. Where do you think you're going?"

Vince hurried off after Mr Norton.

"With them," Sorcha said, pulling her arm free.

"To some cherry house? Absolutely not."

"I don't need your permission, Orla."

Sorcha broke free and ran along the road. She easily caught up with Vince and Mr Norton. "How did you find out where she was?"

"I still have a few informants dotted about the place," Mr Norton said. "I forgot to tell them I wouldn't be needing their services any longer."

"Forgot?" Vince asked.

"Fine, I didn't forget. But the Sentinels don't appear to be interested in finding out what happened. I might not be a Watchman now, but I still have a civic duty."

When they arrived at the cherry house, Vince hammered at the door with his fist. It opened, just a fraction.

Queenie held the blood-red door with her painted hands and peered around. "Oh, no, Mr Knight, we don't want the

Watch in here." She tried to close the door but Vince set his wide hand on it and held it fast.

"Not here for trouble, Queenie. Just need to talk to someone. Important."

"Of course he knows the owner," Mr Norton said, rolling his eyes.

Vince shoved the door, careful not to hurt Queenie. He apologised as the rest of his former Watch rushed in. The cherry house had plenty of life about it, even at that hour of the morning. Vince leaned over Queenie. "Ataraxy Crimp. She here?"

Queenie baulked at his presence. "I don't—"

"*No,*" Vince barked, causing her to jump. "No. Not doing that. Tell me. Not in trouble. Just need to talk."

Queenie drew close, keeping her voice low. "Mr Knight, she's in hiding. Scared for her life."

"Want to help her. Can protect her."

Queenie hesitated. "She's upstairs. Second door on the right."

Sorcha led the charge up to the room where she politely knocked. Tutting, Vince lifted both of his huge fists and slammed them on the door. It burst open and he charged in.

Ms Ataraxy Crimp sat on the floor, propped up against

the bed.

"Too late," Vince said. He leaned her body forward to find the same knife wound as in Sergeant Spradbery.

Sorcha dashed to the open window and pointed. "There!" She hopped out and landed on a slanted roof before dropping to the ground.

Vince followed her. The tiles of the mostly flat roof rattled and creaked under his heft and threatened to give way. He quickly lowered himself to the road, huffing the entire time. He ran off after Sorcha.

"I saw a man," she said. "He headed this way."

They ran at full pelt through the busy, narrow lanes of Port Knot. People jumped out of their way, although Vince still knocked shoulders with some of them.

"There he is!" Sorcha pointed to a flash of a grey coat as it disappeared around a corner.

Vince grabbed her arm and pulled her into an Entry. "This way." He led them both through a series of the town's arteries, cutting off the major roads and lanes. He burst out just ahead of their target and grabbed him, throwing him onto the ground.

The man's cap fell off.

Sorcha caught up with them. "Alfie?"

CHAPTER TWENTY-SIX

VINCE GRABBED ALFIE Exeter by the collar and pulled him close to his face. "Explain!"

"I was chasing after the murderer, you gorilla," Exeter said, struggling to get free. "He'll be long gone by now."

"Don't believe you." Vince didn't loosen his grip one iota. "Knew Crimp was here. How?"

"Mr Norton told me," Exeter said. "He saw me on the street when he was on his way to fetch you. I told him I'd come on ahead. I'm faster than the lot of you put together, and I was still too late!"

Sorcha put her hand on Vince's arm. "Let him go,

Commander."

Vince stared into Exeter's eyes for a moment, then dropped him. "Saw the killer?"

"I couldn't get a good look at him," Exeter said. "All I saw was a glint of something, might have been an earring. It all happened so fast."

Vince rubbed his mouth with the back of his hand. He shouted at the sky. Mr Norton arrived, huffing and puffing. He doubled over, trying to catch his breath.

Exeter stood and dusted himself off. "What now?"

"The killer has gotten rid of the only witness," Sorcha said. "There's nothing more we can do."

"What about the cherry house?" Exeter asked. "Did anyone see Crimp arrive?"

"Queenie did," Vince said.

"Let's go talk to her," Exeter said. "Crimp might have told her something useful."

"Go without me," Vince said. "Scared Queenie enough for one day. Meet back at the shop later."

"What are you going to do?" Sorcha asked.

"Ms Crimp had friends. Family. Deserve to know what happened before it's spread all over town."

"I'll come with you, then," Sorcha said. "Mr Norton can

go with Alfie."

"Don't need you to—"

Sorcha held up her hands. "I cannot begin to imagine what those poor people are about to go through, but I expect it would be ten times worse coming from you."

Mr Norton held his side and winced as he followed Exeter towards the entrance to the cherry house.

Vince stomped around the alley. An old crate took the brunt of his frustrations and several kicks quickly reduced it to splinters.

"I don't think that crate is the killer," Sorcha said.

Vince kept his back to her. He considered going straight to the Star We Sail By, Crimp's favourite haunt. A good many bedworkers plied their trade from the Star's sailboat balcony. Crimp's friends would be there. Vince knew her family—a brother and grandmother—but doubted they'd want to see him. He thrust his hands into the pockets of his claret overcoat and sulked all the way to Lodestone Lane.

Sorcha followed him, making idle chit-chat all the while. He knew she was trying to keep his spirits up but he found himself blocking out the sound of her voice. Not hearing what he didn't want to hear had always been one of his talents.

They found the Crimp house, a shambling wreck held

together by plaster and hope. Sorcha knocked on the door. After several minutes, the door creaked open, then slammed shut again.

Vince huffed and took a moment to calm himself. He balled his fist and knocked. "Please," he said. "Have news. About Ataraxy."

The door opened, and they found themselves invited into a murky parlour by a small woman in a shawl, using two walking sticks. Her head bobbed beyond her control.

"Won't stay long," Vince said.

Sorcha perched herself on the edge of a chair like a bird on a branch. "We have some bad news, I'm afraid."

Before she could say anything else, Ataraxy's brother rushed in through the front door, carrying a stick. Vince instinctively raised his fists.

"Stop!" Sorcha said. "Stop. Please. We're not here for a fight. Please, just put that down for a minute."

Ataraxy's brother looked Vince up and down before lowering the stick. "What have you done?"

Vince lowered his head. "Ataraxy died. Think she saw a murder happen. Murderer got to her before we could."

The old woman dropped onto a chair without a word. Ataraxy's brother's eyes filled with tears but he scowled, trying to hold them in. Vince sat and told them what happened. Her family hadn't heard from her in almost two weeks. He told them he would make the arrangements for the burial. They left the Crimp household after an hour or so and walked the length of Lodestone Lane.

"Why did you offer to pay for her funeral?" Sorcha asked. "You didn't know her that well, did you?"

"Failed her," he said. "Least I can do."

"He was afraid of you. Ms Crimp's brother."

"Not surprised," Vince said. "Beat him up once. Years ago. Group of his friends tried to take over a cherry house Ataraxy was working in. Over in Ironworks. One of my business interests. Had to step in to settle things down."

Sorcha had walked on a few paces before realising Vince had stopped outside the collapsed and charred ruins of a house. "Who lived here?"

"Used to be my house," Vince said. "When I worked for Mudge."

"I thought you'd have taken a house in Gravel Hill," Sorcha said. "You must have made quite a bit of coin in those days."

"More than a bit. Was the whole point. Was raised in an orphanage, then went to work in Chase Manor–one of the island's great houses. Went from abject poverty to a place of wealth beyond my imagination. Any wonder I preferred the latter? Wasn't lucky enough to be born to it so I decided somehow, some day, I'd take it. Made no sense to me that some people can have so much while the rest of us scrabble in the muck just to get by.

"Took a house here to keep me close to my people. Thought it better to stay humble. Must have been burned down after I left, last Midwinter. Suppose the locals didn't want me back." He set his hand on the scorched remains of a wall. "Can't say I blame them."

WHEN THEY RETURNED to the tailor shop, they found Lieutenant Hancock standing outside, looking up at the sign.

"Ah, Mr Knight, there you are. I was told I could find you here. I wondered if I might have a word?"

They led her inside. Orla had a number of fabric swatches on the counter.

Mrs Maunder stopped leafing through them and stared at Lieutenant Hancock. "Oh! I recognise you; you're one of the Sentinels! Let me say what wonderful work you are doing." She glanced briefly at Vince. "It's about time someone did something about the riffraff in this town."

Vince snorted through his nose at her, causing her to quail. He guided Lieutenant Hancock through to the floral parlour.

"Captain Godgrave wanted me to ask you about the Spradbery murder," she said.

Vince leaned against the mantelpiece and tipped tobacco into his pipe. "So ask."

Lieutenant Hancock stared at him. "Since the Watch is no longer a going concern and the Sentinels have taken over the peacekeeping duties in the town, Captain Godgrave feels we should pick up the search for Sergeant Spradbery's killer. Have you made any headway?"

Vince puffed on his pipe. "Found a witness," he said. "Bedworker named Crimp."

"Oh, that's a start. Where is—"

"Dead," Vince said. "Killer got to her first."

"Ah." Lieutenant Hancock crossed her legs and rested her hands on her knees. "Anything else?"

"There was a man." Sorcha took off her cap and threw it on the settee. "Mr Exeter saw a man at the cherry house. He ran after him but he, umm, didn't catch him."

"Just a vague sighting of a man?"

"A man with an earring, maybe," Sorcha said.

"It's not a lot to go on but I don't know what else I expected from civilians." Lieutenant Hancock stood and straightened her tunic. "If you hear anything else, let us know as soon as possible." She nodded and Sorcha saw her to the door.

Before long, Mr Norton and Alfie Exeter arrived. Alfie flumped onto the settee, narrowly avoiding Sorcha's cap. "This is a bit of a step up from the old Watch House," he said. "Much more comfortable."

"This is not your new Watch House!" Orla shouted from the hallway. "And get your feet off the furniture!"

"We're not the Watch, so we don't need a Watch House," Mr Norton said. "Frank and Clive have taken up work at the docks. And Ruth has gone back to working behind the bar at the Jack Thistle."

"The Sentinels are going to take up the hunt for Sergeant Spradbery's killer," Sorcha said.

"What's left for us to do?" Mr Norton asked.

"Want to find the killer," Vince said. "Important."

"Why?" Exeter asked. "Why not just leave it to the green-coats?"

Vince puffed his pipe. Clouds hung about his head, like at the shrouded peak of a mountain. "Need to have something to show for my time as Watch Commander. Can't have been a complete failure. Won't let it."

Mr Norton sat in the window seat. "Queenie confirmed Ms Crimp came to her and asked her for a place to hide. She'd only been there a short time before we arrived."

"Who told you she was at the cherry house?" Sorcha asked.

"One of the staff, Mrs Marjory Winkleigh. She works there as a cleaner."

Vince puffed out a cloud of smoke. "Another of your informants?"

"I asked her to keep an eye out for Ms Crimp. It's the only cherry house in town, if a bedworker wanted someplace familiar to lay low, I knew that's where they'd go. Mrs Winkeligh came and told me she'd spotted Ms Crimp, I came and told all of you."

"So we're no closer to finding the killer," Sorcha said. "That's it. They've gotten away with it."

"Not yet, they haven't." Vince puffed on his pipe again. "One chance left to find them."

CHAPTER TWENTY-SEVEN

VINCE STOOD RELIEVING himself in the shop's water closet when Sorcha called for him. He took his time, being careful not to splash the floor this time. He didn't want another earful from Orla.

"Did you not hear me?" Sorcha asked. "I've been looking for you. That boy is downstairs."

He hurried to the shop floor to find young Brendan standing patiently with his little hands behind his back.

"I've found it, sir."

"Show me."

He led Vince several streets away to a dingy little

pawnshop tucked away down an alley. Vince removed his tricorne and ducked into the doorway, keeping his head down as they passed rows of books, old rocking horses, trinkets of brass and copper, and box after box of tarnished silver cutlery.

At the rear of the shop, Brendan took from his pocket a piece of paper. He unfolded it and pointed to a tray of jewellery on the counter. "See? It's just like the one you drew for me."

Vince lifted a ring and examined it. He clenched his jaw, his face suddenly flushed red.

"You have a good eye, sir," said the shop owner. A small fellow in a chestnut waistcoat and strung with a gold chain.

Vince turned to face him and the man gulped. Vince reached into his own pocket and withdrew two crowns. He handed them to Brendan, whose eyes lit up on seeing the coins. "Good work," Vince said. "Go home."

He sprinted out of the shop, giggling to himself.

The shop owner held his hands up, eyes wide and lip quivering. "I don't want any trouble, Vince."

"Trouble follows you Pennymen. Thought you'd be used to it by now." He held the silver ring up to the shop owner's face. "Tell me about this."

"Why, it's been in my collection for some years now."

Vince's eye narrowed, and his voice boomed. "Don't you lie to me, you twopenny-halfpenny little scut!" He grabbed the man's thumb and pulled it back.

"Ow, ow!"

He held the ring up close to the man's face so he could get a good look at the wolf engraved into it. "Ring was taken from the finger of a murdered greencoat sergeant. Want to know who sold it to you." He squeezed the man's thumb again. "Want to know now."

"Be reasonable, Vince. You know I can't reveal that. Pennyman rules. If the others find out, they'll—"

"Feel like a night at a cherry house compared to what I'll do." He pulled the thumb again, harder.

"Ow, stop. Please, stop. You're going to break it!" the man said. "I don't know his name. Ow, I don't, honestly! I don't know it but...you might."

"I DIDN'T MEAN to break it," Sorcha said. "I'm sure I can fix it..." She scooped the pieces of the clockwork sewing device onto a tray and started poking through them.

"Just leave it. I barely use it," Orla said. "Come over here. Hold this."

Sorcha held the hem of Mrs Maunder's gown and sighed.

"Do you have to do that quite so loudly?" Orla asked.

"I can start tutting if you think it'll add some spice to the occasion?"

Orla glared at her. "I'm sorry about my sister's abhorrent behaviour, Mrs Maunder."

"Don't worry about it for another moment, Ms Fontaine," Mrs Maunder said. She was standing on a plinth in the middle of the shop floor, admiring her reflection. She turned slightly; to better appreciate the purple silk brocade and lace cuffs. Her fingers alighted on one of the bright embroidered sunflowers. The gown–which bore no resemblance to her initial brief–was almost complete, at last.

She jolted when the door of the shop burst open. Orla all but spat the pins from her mouth. "Oi, what do you think you're doing? This isn't your Watch House. You can't just—"

"Shut your face," Vince said with a growl.

"I beg your pardon!"

"Ah, here now, steady on, Commander," Sorcha said.

"Will apologise later." Vince barged past them into the

parlour where Alfie Exeter lounged on the settee. Vince picked him up, dragged him to the hallway, and shoved him into the sewing room at the back of the shop. Walter looked up from his box of whale bone.

"*Get out!*" Vince yelled at him.

Walter scurried out of the room as Vince pushed Alfie onto a chair. Sorcha entered, shutting the door behind her.

"Out," Vince said.

"No. I'm staying," Sorcha said. "I want to know what's going on."

"Sorcha, *get out,* damn you!" Vince threw his claret overcoat against the wall.

It thumped against a shelf near her head, knocking a box of thread to the floor. The spindles rolled across the room. Sorcha didn't budge an inch. She balled her fists and stared up at him, breathing heavily and forcing herself not to look away. He was so damn big it was like facing down an angry polar bear. He roared at her, his icy stare hardening. Still, she didn't move. She held her ground.

Vince snorted and turned his attention to Alfie. "Explain. *Now.*"

Alfie glared at him and breathed loudly through his nose. He said nothing. His beautiful eyes darted, taking in every inch of Vince's round face. He ground his jaw but kept his ruby lips tightly sealed.

Vince loomed over him in the windowless room, his lantern-fed shadow monstrous on the wall. He pulled out a ring from his pocket. "Start with this."

"I've never seen it before," Alfie said.

"What is it?" Sorcha asked.

Vince didn't answer her. He threw the ring in Alfie's face. "Found in a pawnshop. Sold by you after you took it from Spradbery's body."

"I—"

"All of James's senior officers from the *Lancelot Striking* have them. Specially made. Only a handful in the whole world."

Sorcha bent to retrieve the silver ring from the floor. She ran a thumb across the engraved wolf.

Alfie gripped the armrests of the chair. "I took it after Ruth left to fetch you, the day we found Spradbery's body. He was already dead, and I needed the money. I didn't see the harm in it."

Vince squinted at him. "Lying. Done it once too often. Can smell it now. Tell me about Crimp."

Alfie kept his mouth shut.

"Very well," Vince said. "Killed Crimp because she saw you kill Sergeant Spradbery, yes? First night we met. Late for your shift. Had just killed Spradbery, hadn't you? Why him?"

Alfie spoke through gritted teeth. "For the fun of it." He squeaked when Vince slapped his cheek, leaving a pink mark.

"No," Vince said. "Not that sort of killer. Met plenty of them. No more lies."

Alfie rubbed his cheek. Sorcha turned away and put her hand on the wall to steady herself.

Vince sat on the chair facing him. "Look. Seen how you are. Angry. Always spoiling for a fight. Been where you are, right now. All starts here. Road you choose now is the one you follow for the rest of your life. Don't want to end up like me. Trust me."

"What, feared? Respected?"

"Alone." Vince stood and paced the floor. "Killed someone in a room like this once. No windows, one candle, two chairs. Took a knife and ran it across their throat. Ever seen how far blood can shoot? Farther than you'd imagine. Painted the walls, the ceiling. Killing you've done was the coward's way. In the back. Didn't have to look them in the eye. Didn't have to see their lights go out."

Sorcha stared at Vince as though she'd never seen him

before. He loomed large in the room, shrouded in shadow.

He laid his hands—his rough, powerful hands—on the armrest of Alfie's chair and leaned into him. "Won't always be that way. Won't always get away without a scratch. Want to end up like me? Because that's where you're headed. All leads to me. Leads to this!" In a flash, Vince straightened up and pulled his shirt off, holding his long arms out wide. He turned on the spot, letting Exeter get a good look at him.

Aside from a gallery of tattoos, his bulky frame was peppered with long pink lines, raised white lumps, and fleshy ridges. His voice had grown louder and louder until it filled the room and shook Sorcha's bones.

His face turned red. "Want to end up like this, do you? Scarred and marked by every terrible thing you've ever done? Want to get stabbed? Want to get shot? Want to end up a walking scab?" Globs of saliva flew out of his mouth as he shouted. "Want to be beaten so badly you lose your damn eye? So badly that your brains stop...that...that...that your words don't... They don't..." He turned his back on Exeter then and covered his mouth with his hand. The sudden silence was thick enough to bury them all.

Alfie folded his hands in his lap. "I paid Ms Crimp to be at the alehouse that night. I told her to get Spradbery's attention and to bring him to Quither Pier, where I would be waiting."

"To kill him?" Vince asked, still not facing them. "Why?"

Alfie hesitated for a moment. Vince grabbed him out of the seat with one hand and raised his fist.

"I had no choice!" Alfie said.

"Name."

"I can't tell you."

"*Name!*"

"I can't tell you! You know I can't!" he said. "You know how these people operate. You taught them how to do it! If I tell you, I'm as good as dead. I owe a lot of money to some very bad people. They said if I do this one job for them, my slate will be wiped clean."

Vince's nostrils flared. He stared at Alfie. "Don't need you to tell me his name. Know exactly who paid you. And where to find him."

CHAPTER TWENTY-EIGHT

VINCE HUNTED ABOUT for the key to the sewing room and finally found it at the back of a drawer filled with spindles. He locked the door and handed the key to Orla, with strict instructions not to open it until he returned. He insisted on going alone.

Sorcha told him she didn't care what he wanted and bundled herself into the carriage with him. "If I'm ever going to be of any use in this town I need to know what you know about its underbelly."

"Watch is gone," he said. "Planning to join the Sentinels?"

Sorcha raised an eyebrow. "No chance. But even they can't be everywhere. I want to help, and if I have to do it outside the law, so be it."

Vince said he thought it was hardly just an underbelly any longer. When he had been in charge, there was an order to the disorder, so to speak. Criminals had grown bolder of late, pushing their luck. He disapproved of the heavy-handed approach of the Sentinels but understood why it appealed to some citizens. When a wound starts to bleed you don't just patiently mop up the blood, you sew up the hole so it can never leak again.

The carriage rocked from side to side on the uneven roads and more than once the horse whinnied at someone who ran out in front of it.

"Say something," Vince said.

"I'm sorry. Are you really telling me to talk? Being a bit too stoic for your tastes, am I?"

Vince grumbled and shifted about. "Doesn't do any good to bottle things up. Man you love just confessed to murder."

"First of all, I don't love Alfie Exeter, I just want to kiss his stupid face, and run my hands through his stupid hair, and squeeze his stupid peachy bum. Second of all, how I feel about him is none of your business, Commander."

"Third of all?"

She threw her hands in the air. "How could he lie to me so brazenly? He wasn't chasing Ms Crimp's killer; he was running away from us! He looked me right in the face and lied."

"Perfectly reasonable to be upset."

"I'm not upset. I'm angry. I'm feckin' furious, actually. I could throttle him, so I could."

"Perfectly reasonable too."

Sorcha tugged aside the carriage curtain as they drew up at the Frost & Thaw Tearoom. "What are we doing here?"

Vince leapt out of the carriage and made straight for the main entrance.

Sorcha hurried along beside him, keeping her voice low. "If we're looking for whoever coerced Alfie, wouldn't we be better off going softly?"

"Surprise is good," Vince said. "Shock is better."

He slammed open the doors without breaking his stride and marched inside. A man at the door tried to stop him. Vince slapped a clockwork flamingo to the floor. It clattered to pieces. The man howled as he tried to find all the parts before they rolled away.

The great tearoom, with its glass walls held in place by black, coiling metal bars, wouldn't get going until later in the evening. Still, its owner, Ms Clementine Frost, was in attendance, making sure everything would be ready for the evening's entertainment.

Vince's voice filled the space. "Bring him out here! *Now!*"

Most of Ms Frost's attendants scurried about, some ducked, and some froze on the spot like frightened deer.

Ms Frost held up her hands. "Mr Knight, I'll have to ask you to leave."

Vince slipped his fingers under a table laden with glassware and flipped it over. The shattering echoed through the tearoom. "Not until I've spoken with him."

Ms Frost, to her credit, didn't budge an inch. "I'm sure I don't know who you mean, and I can't imagine there is a single person on my premises who could possibly be of interest to you."

She held her ground in front of him, tilting her head as she stared him down. Her golden hair fell in curls over one shoulder.

In other circumstances, Vince would look at her in an entirely different light. "Quaintance," he said, in his most sonorous tone.

Ms Frost's eyebrow twitched. "*Mister* Quaintance isn't

here."

Vince leaned in close to her face. "Can tear this place apart looking for him. Or you can go get him."

"No need, my dear," came a voice from the balcony above. Mr Noss Quaintance, wearing a coral satin waistcoat and matching breeches, leaned on the railing.

Sorcha spoke out of the side of her mouth. "Are you sure you've got the right fella? He doesn't look the type."

"What type?" Ms Frost asked.

Vince pointed up at him, jabbing his finger as he spoke. "Pennyman filth. Arranges murder. Never gets his hands dirty. Coward."

"Steady on, Mr Knight," Ms Frost said. "My companion is not one of your rabble to be accused and accosted willy-nilly. And he most certainly is not involved with the Penny-men."

"It's well past time Mr Knight and I spoke," Quaintance said. "May we use your office?"

"Stay," Vince said to Sorcha. He paused and whispered, "Mean it this time. Keep an eye on her."

Ms Frost stepped to one side, and Vince stomped up the black spiral staircase to a little office at the top of the tearoom. More wood than glass, it offered a degree of privacy. The patterned carpet sank under Vince's boots, and the scent of honeysuckle filled the air.

Quaintance poured himself a gin and sat in a wingback chair. "You should try to control your temper when you're out in daylight, Mr Knight. The people here are not the petty crooks and cutthroats you are used to mingling with in the moonlight. We are not in the gutters now, you know."

"Any place with you in it is a gutter."

"You never used to speak to me like this," Quaintance said. "You used to know better."

"Town is out of balance. Old ways have been cast aside. No place for scum like you now."

"At least I can pass myself off in decent society," Quaintance said swirling his drink. "Look at you. You don't belong here, in a civilised place, among civilised people. You barely fit up that stairwell, you duck through every door, you darken every room you enter. You are an obscenity, Mr Knight. A rabid dog pretending to be a man."

Vince's blood started to boil, his ears started to burn. "Should drag you to the magistrates right now."

"And how do you imagine it will go? My dearest friend in all the world is on the ruling council. I have connections all across this town. I have money to pay off anyone I choose.

You, on the other hand, have burst in here and caused quite a bit of damage. And, as I understand it, your Watch no longer exists. What's to stop *me* from dragging *you* before the magistrates, Mr Knight?"

Vince stood tall and balled his fists. "Like to see you try."

Quaintance laughed into his drink. "I'm sure you would. Perhaps I'll send for a troop of Sentinels to take you away. Maybe I'll even have them rough you a bit first, what do you say to that, hmm? Hah. What are you doing here, you shambling wretch?"

"Alfie Exeter confessed to killing Spradbery. Did it to clear his debts. Led me right to you."

Quaintance sucked his teeth. "Now, Mr Exeter should have known better. He'll have to be punished. He really shouldn't have mentioned my name."

"Didn't. Didn't have to. Know how you operate. Recognised your handiwork. Find someone in dire straits. Offer to get them out of it. Little stabbing here. Little killing there. Debt goes away. All their problems solved. Seen you do it more than once. Waste of a life. Another vulnerable youngster manipulated. Exploited."

"Hah, are we talking about me or you?"

"Wasn't your idea to kill Spradbery. Want to know who

paid you."

"That would be frightfully bad for business. My clients do expect anonymity."

Vince set his hands on his hips and narrowed his gaze. "Port Knot changed when you weren't looking," he said. "Thought you could go about your business the way you always have. Problem you have now is I know all the dirty secrets of this town. Rabbit put me in charge for that very reason. Time was, what you got up to didn't matter to me. Weren't a threat to me or my operation. Had a use for you before. No longer. Should just do away with you. Snap your neck, and be done with it. But trying to be better. Give everyone a chance. Even scum like you."

"A chance to do what?"

"Change. Be better."

"Oh, but Vince," Quaintance said, almost laughing, "what if I just don't want to?"

Vince reached over and carefully plucked the glass from Quaintance's grip, setting it delicately onto the sideboard. Then he placed his hand around Quaintance's long, elegant neck and squeezed. He dragged the man to his knees and placed the nails of his thumb and forefinger around Quaintance's left eyeball.

"Find myself in need of a new eye," Vince said, his rumbling voice almost a whisper. "Wonder if yours will fit?" He flexed his fingers.

"Stop! Stop!" Quaintance said, his voice almost a shriek. "Lieutenant Hancock of the *Lancelot Striking* hired my services. She wanted Spradbery dead."

"Why?"

"She didn't say; they never do. And I don't ask. She just said it had to be done as soon as possible."

He could kill Quaintance. He could. Right now. No one could stop him. He would be swept away in the familiar and comforting red mist that consumed him at times like these, that moved his limbs, that kept him safe from his enemies. Instincts born in blood and finessed in a thousand fights. He would tell Rabbit that Quaintance pulled a knife. That he had no choice.

Vince's breathing grew faster and faster. He gritted his teeth. His vision started to blur. He tightened his grip. Quaintance started to gurgle. *He deserves it. He's arranged so many murders. He has so much blood on his hands.* But then, so had Vince. And if Vince was serious about this new life of his, if he was really serious, he was going to have to try hard to curb these tendencies. To silence these voices. He didn't fear reprisal; he feared what it would to do him...inside. How could he look Sorcha in the eye and tell her he was doing his best to change? Or his brother? His mother? He'd worked so hard this past year, he couldn't throw it all away, not for the likes of Quaintance. And he would be throwing it away, he knew that for certain. It would be the thin end of the wedge. The start of a very slippery slope. His chest tightened, his neck grew sore and stiff.

Quaintance could not simply be left unpunished. He had to know his place. What had Vince said to Sorcha? Surprise is good. Shock is better. He leaned in close and whispered into Quaintance's ear. "Always have to be the dandy, don't you? Always the gillyflower—never a hair out of place."

He suddenly let go and Quaintance dropped to the floor, panting on his hands and knees. Sneering, Vince stood over him and undid the buttons of his own fall front breeches. He withdrew his member and relieved himself on the back of Quaintance's head. Quaintance spluttered and fell back against his chair, Vince's stream following him. Quaintance wheezed and wiped his own face. The urine left dark islands in the ocean of plush, blue carpet.

Quaintance gasped as he tried to shield himself. "What are you doing, you animal!"

"Even a rabid dog marks his territory." Vince shook his manhood and tucked it away. "Seems you forgot Port Knot is mine. All of it. Always has been. Always will be. No matter what side of the law I'm on. Your assassins try it with me, I'm feeding them to my dog. Then I'm coming back for that eye. Behave yourself in my town."

CHAPTER TWENTY-NINE

SORCHA PICKED UP the enamel eyes of a tin flamingo from the floor and apologised to Ms Frost for Vince's actions. "I didn't know what he was planning to do."

"He doesn't seem the planning sort," Ms Frost said. "More a wild animal acting on instinct."

Vince's boots clanged on the metal steps of the spiral staircase, and Sorcha braced herself for another altercation. Instead, he simply walked straight past her and Ms Frost without a word. She forced a smile, handed the eyes to Ms Frost, and then ran after Vince.

He stared at the floor of the carriage on the journey back

to the shop. Sorcha fiddled with her braces as she tried to work up the courage to ask him if he'd left Quaintance alive.

"Wasn't easy," Vince said. "Not one of mine. Never has been. But everything's different now. All have to try to adapt."

"Did you find out about the killings?"

"Lieutenant Hancock paid for Spradbery's murder."

Sorcha crossed her arms. "And we know where she gets her orders from."

"James isn't responsible," Vince said a little too quickly.

"Are you sure? Think about it for a second. The murder of gang members is unfortunate but understandable. But to murder an officer of the Chase Trading Company? On Blackrabbit? It's horrific. Unconscionable. Outrageous. Sergeant Spradbery's murder was one more nail in the Watch's coffin. One more reason to get rid of us. One more piece of evidence we weren't up to the task of protecting the town. It must have helped the council to decide to give the greencoats control. Who benefits most? Captain Godgrave."

Vince shook his head. "James isn't that ruthless."

"Are you sure?" Sorcha asked. "You know him that well, do you? Because I was under the impression you'd only just met him recently."

Vince glared at her and said nothing for the rest of the

way. When they reached the shop, Sorcha disembarked but Vince didn't. He slammed the door and banged the side of the carriage. It carried on its way.

Inside the shop, Sorcha pulled up a chair to the locked door of the sewing room. "Now, what are we going to do with you?"

The voice from the other side was muffled but tinged with anger. "You're not the Watch anymore. None of us are."

"We're still citizens of Port Knot. We still have a civic duty to protect the people from murderers."

Alfie's piercing laugh cut right through her. "What about the one you're working for?"

Sorcha didn't have an answer. Vince was a murderer; there could be no getting around the fact. She'd heard the stories, of course, but could have easily dismissed them as tall tales. If she hadn't heard it from his own lips.

Orla shook her head. "Can I have my sewing room back now?"

"I'm not opening this door until Vince comes back," Sorcha said.

"Good girl, do what you're told," Alfie said.

"What's that supposed to mean?"

"Good little Sorcha, always willing to please," Alfie said.

"I think Mr Norton would disagree with you there," Sorcha said. "And Orla."

"Hah! You fall over yourself to make your sister happy."

"If only that were true," Orla said.

"She stays in this shop for you, you know, Orla. She tells people you're suffocating her. She wants to get away and see the world, not live and die in this squalid little hole. But deep down she knows she can't because she couldn't live with the guilt of leaving you alone."

"That's not true," Sorcha said. "It isn't." Tears welled in her eyes.

"I know you better than most," Alfie said. "You told me so much about yourself, hoping to worm your way into my favour."

Sorcha covered her face, her shoulders rattling as the tears flowed down her face.

"Stop it," Orla said, slapping the door with her palm.

"As if I'd ever be interested in the likes of you."

Orla rapped the door over and over with her fist. "Stop it. That's enough. Horrible little man. Leave the door locked. Let him starve in there."

VINCE BANGED ON the door of the townhouse until Mr Norton opened it wearing only a tawny cotton banyan. Vince barged past him.

"What are you doing here?"

"Need to check your books. From the Watch." He barrelled upstairs and into the room he and James had used to spy on the Gunbrides robbery. He pulled some books from a crate, checking the years.

"Don't just throw them on the floor! You're making a mess. Do you need a hand?"

"Know what I'm looking for."

Mr Norton stood with his hands on his hips, tutting.

Two women hurried out from another room, barely dressed. The older of the two, wide-mouthed with sharp cheekbones and a pile of golden ringlets atop her head, led the way. "What's all the ruckus?"

"Oh, nothing," Mr Norton said. "Just my former Watch Commander come to rifle through our things."

"Not things," Vince said without looking up. "Records.

Detailed records. Names. Dates. Crimes committed." He cast book after book aside until he found a likely candidate. He opened it and ran his finger down the column of names.

"This is Mr Vince Knight," Mr Norton said. "And these are my wives, Temerity and Holly."

Vince flicked the page over and paused. "Wives? Managed to convince two women to marry you?"

The younger woman, Holly, had nut-brown hair and wore a low-cut bodice. She frowned at Mr Norton, her hands rapidly forming shapes in the air.

"She says you really are as rude as I described," Mr Norton said.

Vince growled at him and set the book down. He held his hands up and made the sign for *sorry*, and then the one for *necessary*. Holly's eyes widened, and Mr Norton's arms dropped by his sides, his mouth slightly agape.

"Learned a few things over the years." Vince flicked the page again and stopped. He leapt to his feet and held the book in his hand. "Need to borrow this."

THE FARTHER VINCE got through the docklands, the angrier he became. Though the marketplace was in full swing, he heard almost none of the din from the crowds, so loud was the pulsing of his heart and the throbbing in his ears. He should have asked for help, for support, but he knew he wouldn't be able to get the words out. He knew his moods, and he knew when best to work alone.

He pushed his way through the rabble, keeping his target in sight.

"Mr Knight, stop!"

Ignoring the guards, he barged through the doors of the new Sentinel building and onto the mezzanine. Below him, the rank and file worked at their desks. The two guards from the front door had chased after him. He grabbed the nearest one by the collar. "Where's Hancock?"

The guard, barely more than a boy, whimpered a response and pointed.

Lieutenant Hancock stood outside her office, her hands on the railing. "Would you mind terribly unhanding my soldier, Mr Knight?"

Vince dropped the man while Lieutenant Hancock approached him.

"Now, what's all this shouting about?"

Vince pointed at her. "Coming with me." He moved to grab her arm but found himself surrounded by armed Sentinels, one rifle levelled at his head, another at his heart.

"I'm not going anywhere with you, Mr Knight. Even if you were still with the Watch, this is Sentinel Garrison, and I will not be dragged from it like a tavern brawler."

A voice boomed from behind her. "What is the meaning of this?" James Godgrave strode out of his office in his full uniform. "Mr Knight, explain your presence in my headquarters."

"Need to have words with your lieutenant."

"Then you may do so in my office. Lieutenant Hancock, do you have any objection?"

"None, sir."

James stood aside to let her pass. He waved the armed guards away and followed Vince.

"Sit," James said. "Both of you. Now, what exactly is all this about?"

Vince struggled to fit into the little chair. "Hancock here paid for the murder of your Sergeant Spradbery."

Lieutenant Hancock laughed. "Preposterous."

"What on earth makes you think that, Mr Knight?" James asked. For once, his smile was nowhere to be seen.

"Killer was one of my Watchmen. Exeter. Hired by a Pennyman named Quaintance."

"Surely you can't mean Mr Noss Quaintance?" James asked. "Companion to Fox?"

Vince nodded. "Known to me. Want someone done away with, get him. Knows people who can get it done. Whole point of the Pennymen is they can get you anything you need. Even an assassin. Hancock paid Quaintance to do away with Spradbery."

"But why, man? Whatever for?"

"Came to ask Hancock that very question."

"It's no secret Sergeant Spradbery and I never saw eye to eye," Hancock said, "but I didn't have him killed. How could I?"

"Been thinking about that," Vince said. "Blackrabbiter, aren't you? Guessing you know Mr Dowland Hancock?"

"Your father's name, wasn't it?" James asked.

"Hangman Hancock, they called him," Vince said. "Did some digging." He threw the Watch record book onto James's desk and opened it. "Hancock family comes from the Tangles. Roughest part of a rough town. Beadle Norton keeps records. Found a name in there. Mr Dowland Hancock. Arrested for murder. Paid to do it by an unnamed person. Said he did it to clear a gambling debt. Only one person in Port Knot takes murder as payment. Quaintance buys debts. Coerces people into killing."

"This doesn't prove anything," James said.

"Means she had a connection to Quaintance through her father. Knew about him. Knew how he operates. Said you and Spradbery never got along. Why?"

Perty swallowed hard and looked to James.

"I don't believe a word of this," James said, "but I would like to know the particulars as well, Perty. What harm can it do now?"

Perty looked to her hands in her lap. "Sergeant Spradbery is a Blackrabbiter too. He is—or rather he was— from Little Acorn. He knew about my father, and he never let me forget. Spradbery and I served together on several ships before being assigned to the *Lancelot Striking*. He liked to needle me about my father every chance he got. When we took up on a new ship, and he thought I was getting along too well with my crewmates, he'd tell them what my father did to try to turn them against me. When I was promoted to Lieutenant ahead of him, well, it was more than he could take." She sniffed away a tear.

"The day he was murdered, he and I went for a drink in

a tavern in town. The Star We Sail By. We tried to make amends. I did my best to assure him my success did not scupper his chances of advancement. I tried to make him see how serving in Port Knot could be good for him. We didn't exactly part ways as friends, but we made a start." She looked Vince square in the eye. "I didn't kill him, Mr Knight, nor did I have him killed."

"Heard confession from Exeter and Quaintance himself."

James squinted at him. "The killers, you mean?"

"Exeter is a Watchman of five years standing."

"I'm afraid I'm going to need a bit more than that," James said. "And as for this Quaintance person, I met him at Silver Hope and found him to be a wonderfully erudite gentleman. You can't seriously expect me to believe he's some...I don't even know what you would call him. A broker for assassins? This is all quite ridiculous. You can go, Lieutenant."

Vince stood to object. "Wait just a damn—"

"We are in *my* headquarters, and *I* give the orders!" James's eyes turned quite nasty when he bellowed.

Vince considered the dozens of armed officers outside and bit his tongue.

When they were alone, James closed his office door. His

demeanour changed and his smile returned. "Now, Vince, really, what did you expect to happen? I'd just let you come in here and take my most trusted officer away?"

"Trusted? Paid to have another officer killed!"

"So says a confessed killer."

Vince frowned at him. "Talking about Exeter or me?"

"I consider Perty Hancock a friend," James said. "When you smear her name, you call into question my judgement both as a captain and as a man. You should have come to me directly with this. I can't let my Sentinels see me siding with you, not after the way you behaved. Until you can produce some kind of evidence—proper evidence—I cannot let you do anything. Law and order on Blackrabbit are under the purview of my Sentinels. If there is guilt to be apportioned, we will see to it. You can trust us." He laid his hand on Vince's shoulder, squeezing it. "Or at the very least, you can trust me."

Vince studied James's face. "Starting to wonder."

"Now what could that mean?"

"No secret Spradbery's death did you a favour. Helped you get what you want."

James dropped his hand from Vince's shoulder and took a step back. "What a terrible thing to say, Vince. It's beneath you."

"Wrong, is it?"

James returned to his seat. With his elbows on the arm-rests and his hands over his chest, he turned the ring on his little finger. "You do not believe I had any hand in the death of my own sergeant. You are losing the run of yourself. Seeing enemies everywhere you turn. Forgive me, but you don't strike me as a man with a lot of friends. It's perhaps ill-judged of you to alienate the ones you have."

Vince's glower faltered, just for an instant. "Just answer this. Was there time?"

"Time for what?"

"Between your first meeting with Swan and Spradbery's body being found. Was there time for Hancock to speak to Quaintance?"

"I think perhaps you'd better leave."

Vince slammed the door on his way out.

CHAPTER THIRTY

WITH A FLICK of the lever on her armrest, Emmeline Hawksmoor guided her wheeled chair out of the doorway and down the busy road. A flick left and she dodged slow walkers. A flick right took her around piles of rotting vegetables. She'd had word of the greencoats harassing a chandler over an undocumented delivery of soap and wanted to catch them in the act.

As she passed by an Entry, she became aware of a man approaching from behind. She spun her chair round and tilted her neck back to stare up into the eyepatch of Mr Vince Knight.

"Think it's time we had a little chat," he said.

Emmeline had once heard the distant grumble of rocks sliding from the white cliffs of Blackrabbit. His voice reminded her of that moment. "Stay back, you." Her eyes darted around, seeking help.

"Not going to hurt you. Already be hurt, otherwise. Just need to talk."

Across the road, a coffee house promised sanctuary. "How about over there?" she asked. "Where there are plenty of witnesses?"

In the airy coffee house, with its high ceiling and wood-panelled walls, they sat by the window in full view of the road and the other customers. One corner held a table of notable young local playwrights arguing over some tedious point of grammar or other. Another held a couple clearly in the early stages of an affair but desperate to appear as though they were merely friends catching up. If they wished to maintain the ruse, Emmeline thought, they may want to ask for a longer tablecloth. If she had noticed the woman's hand kneading beneath the flap of the man's breeches, so might others.

Mr Knight barely fit behind the table where he sat hunched over. One of his brawny legs stuck out, on the knee of which he rested his huge, rough, scarred hand. How many throats had it been round, Emmeline wondered? How many noses had it broken? How many necks?

His claret overcoat showed no signs of wear whatever, nor his tight, black breeches. New purchases, Emmeline supposed. Perhaps an attempt to tidy up his image? He had a reputation for many things among which sartorial elegance did not number. Ah, the fire. Emmeline had heard the new Commander had taken up residence above the Watch House. He must have lost his possessions in the blaze.

They ordered two coffees, for which Mr Knight insisted on paying. The cup was laughably tiny in his hand. One wrong move from him and it would shatter. He leaned over it a little and appeared to take in the aroma. His nose, small for his face, but somewhat bulbous, had been broken in the past and ran just a smidge kinked.

"What's this about, Mr Knight?"

"Don't like that. Name's Vince."

"Very well, Vince," she said as she pulled a notebook from her satchel. "You may address me as Ms Hawksmoor." She flipped open a new page and readied her pencil.

"Story you ran about me when I took over as Watch Commander. Very harsh, I thought."

"But accurate, to the best of my knowledge?"

He grumbled, or snorted, or made some other explosion of air from his nostrils, like a disgruntled bull. He rubbed a hand over his short, snowy white beard. "Think it made my work harder."

"In what way?"

"Need the people of the town on my side. Can't fight them and the gangs."

"It's my understanding you won't need to do either. Hasn't your Watch been disbanded?"

His icy blue eye stared at her as if trying to see right through.

Her blood ran a touch cooler and it made her glad for his other eye to be covered by a leather patch. Being under the full glare of both eyes would be frightful. "How did you know where to find me?"

"Make it my business to know."

"That's not really an answer."

He sighed. This was not a man used to explaining himself to anyone. "Know you work at the Courant office. Road outside here is shortest way from there to your house. Thought if I had any chance of running into you, would be here."

"And how do you know where I live?"

"Told you."

"It's your business to know, yes, you said." She scribbled some notes down onto the page. Mostly so she would not forget but partially so he wouldn't notice her hand shaking.

"Only a handful of people in this town have any power over it," he said. "Helps to know where they are."

"You think I have power?"

"Telling people what to think is power, no?"

Emmeline tutted and lifted her coffee cup. "I do nothing of the kind. I report events and let people make up their own minds." How she wished that were so.

There was the snort again. "Paper told everyone I was a monster."

"The paper laid out the facts as presented to us."

"Presented by the greencoats," he said. "Told you to bad-mouth me, didn't they?"

Emmeline composed herself. "The Chase Trading Company prefers to let the Courant run independently, whenever possible. At times, they come to us with information they deem necessary for the public good." She didn't really believe it. And she could tell Vince didn't either.

"Seem like a monster now?" he asked.

"A little bit, yes," Emmeline said, taking a sip of her coffee. But that wasn't really true, was it? He frightened her, certainly. He had an aura about him, his voice so gravelly and low as to be felt as much as heard, but he was far from the murderous beast she'd been told about. Something about the way he talked, his odd use of language that she found disarming. She'd met his type before, or so she'd thought. She had spoken to killers and cutthroats but they'd lacked the light behind their eyes she'd noticed in Vince. Or eye, in his case.

He sat back and folded his beefy arms, the claret wool of his overcoat stretching to its limit. If she didn't know better, she'd call it pouting. "Heard anything about the murder of Sergeant Spradbery?" he asked.

"No, the Sentinels have been very tight-lipped. Why? What do you know?" She set her pencil to the page once again.

He rubbed his nose with his hand. "Don't want this coming from me."

"I have to—"

"Forget it, then." He went to rise from his chair, but Emmeline reached out and touched his sleeve.

"Wait. Wait. If you were to *accidentally* let some information slip in the course of a casual conversation..."

He settled himself again and checked around for prying ears. He leaned in so close Emmeline could smell the coffee on his breath. "Heard the Sentinels ignored an allegation. Heard Lieutenant Hancock of the *Lancelot Striking* was involved. Paid a Pennyman to hire a local Watchman named Exeter to do away with Sergeant Spradbery."

"You've heard quite a bit."

He held his hands up and leaned back. "Friendly chat, is all."

"And we are such good friends," Emmeline said.

Vince held his cup to her as if making a toast, then noisily drained it.

"My editor won't like this. He's wary of criticising the Sentinels for fear of incurring the wrath of the C.T.C. admiralty. Or even of Swan herself. But I think I can talk him around. His brother's shop was harassed by the Sentinels over a minor customs issue. I had a meeting with Captain Godgrave about a week ago. He tried to get ahead of any bad publicity surrounding the Sentinel patrols. Tried to charm me into taking his side. Honey-tongued snake. I suspect he often uses that smile of his to get his own way."

Vince's silvery eyebrows flickered, just a touch, and Emmeline wondered if Captain Godgrave had tried his charms on Vince too. "If this were to get out, though, it wouldn't do you much good," she said. "A Watchman accused of murder?

Hardly the thing to get the public on your side."

"Said it yourself—Watch is disbanded."

Emmeline set the pencil against her lip. "I assumed this was part of some effort to discredit the Sentinels and restore your Watch? Or is this just petty revenge?"

He fixed her with that glare again. "Careful," he said, "else we might not stay friends for long."

CHAPTER THIRTY-ONE

SPOILING FOR A fight, James gathered two of his Sentinels and took a carriage through the mist to the town hall. In his hand, he gripped the day's edition of the Blackrabbit Courant so tightly his knuckles had turned white.

He once again ignored the obsequious fellow outside the council chamber and burst through the doors to find the council meeting already in session. The five members had gathered around the polished oval table in their animal masks.

"You're late," Rabbit said.

James threw off his hat and waved his copy of the Blackrabbit Courant above his head. "Absolutely outrageous!

Slanderous!" He slapped the paper on the table.

"Captain, yes, welcome. This is what we wanted to discuss with you."

He sat in the only vacant seat, red-faced and ranting. His attendants, Mr Spry and Mr Bodmyn, hovered by the doors until he yelled at them to get out. They backed away, pulling the doors closed behind them.

"It's all anyone has been talking about this morning," Fox said. "I was stopped and asked about it several times on my way here."

"The people are demanding answers," Badger said.

James could not stop himself from bellowing. "Here's the ruddy answer—it's twaddle! Malicious, fallacious twaddle!"

"So the rumours are untrue?" Badger asked. "The Sentinels have had no such allegations made?"

"The allegations were made, yes, but they're unfounded," James said. "No proof has been brought forward. Just the word of a confessed killer, who by the by, still hasn't been handed over either to my Sentinels or to the magistrates."

Rabbit exchanged a glance with Fox, who smiled.

"Nevertheless," Fox said, "it would do little for the public profile of your new-found venture if the Sentinels were thought to ignore allegations of corruption?"

"It's preposterous," Swan said. "My officers are the finest, most upstanding members of society."

Fox tilted her head to one side as she spoke. "Might I remind Swan she serves at the pleasure of all the people of the island, not just the upstanding ones. And certainly not just the ones on the Chase Trading Company payroll?"

"And given Lieutenant Hancock's innocence," Rabbit said, "surely she would have no qualms about stating her case before the magistrates?"

James's voice turned volcanic. "What!"

"Rabbit, please, you must see how unnecessary this is!" Swan said.

"It will be a simple matter to settle in the public eye before it gets out of hand," Rabbit said. "This Watchman—Mr Exeter—will state his case, the lieutenant will refute it, and the magistrates will note the lack of evidence and make a judgement. Captain, you will kindly make your lieutenant available for the hearing."

"I'll do no such bloody thing."

Rabbit leaned to one side, propping her elbow on an armrest. "I would hate to have to call on the services of the Sentinels to bring in a suspected criminal."

James slammed his hand on the table in frustration. His attempt at getting on Ms Hawkmoor's good side had clearly been in vain.

"Do we know who told the newspaper about the allegation?" Rabbit asked.

James stood and tucked his hat under his arm. "I know exactly who told them."

JAMES BARKED ORDERS at his attendants on the road outside the Quick tailor shop, instructing them to wait and to not allow anyone else to enter. He pushed his hat into the hands of Mr Spry, who clutched it tightly. They nervously stood by the carriage as he threw open the door to the shop and marched in, head held high.

A young woman approached with her measuring ribbon drawn. "Can I help you, sir?"

James all but spat his words out. "Do I look as though I'm in dire need of a tailor?"

"Well, you have just burst into a tailor shop..."

"Blast it, woman, I'm here to see Mr Knight. I was told he could be found within though I cannot begin to fathom why. Are sausage fingers suddenly advantageous in a seamstress?"

"Oh," she said, rolling her eyes. "Yes, he's here. I'll fetch him. After all, what am I here for if not to attend the needs of the mighty Mr Knight?"

"Don't bother," Vince said from the door. "Heard him. Whole road heard him. Come through."

"Yes, yes," said the woman, "go on through. Apparently this is Mr Knight's headquarters now."

"Don't be so impertinent," James said as he passed. "It's a woefully unattractive trait in a person your age."

James followed Vince through the back of the shop and into a small parlour with entirely too many floral patterns—the wall, the curtains, the carpets, the cushions. He felt as though he'd stepped into a Dutch market. "Now look here," he said, jabbing a finger against Vince's chest. "Just what do you think you're playing at, running off to the press like that? Don't you know the trouble you've caused? For me and for you?"

Vince settled himself on a gaudy couch. His top shirt hung open to the navel, as usual, and James forced himself not to get distracted by the octopus tentacles and ship's rigging inked onto the warm, bare flesh of his massive frame.

"Used to trouble," Vince said.

James threw his hands in the air. "You could at least deny it! Do me that courtesy."

"No point. Both know I did it."

"But what on earth did you do it for? How does this help you?"

"Not about me."

James pulled off his emerald-green-and-white overcoat and sank onto an armchair by the cold fireplace. "You're punishing me. Don't deny it. You're punishing me for taking the Watch away from you. I can restore it if it will make you happy."

"Already talked about that."

"Then I can hire you and the rest of the Watch. You don't have to join the C.T.C. I can make you all civilian advisors or something. We can work out the details later. I have the power to do it."

"And Hancock?"

"Dammit, man, she didn't do anything! Hounding her isn't helping you! What are you going to do, stand up before the magistrates and tell them what happened? One killer confessed to you—another killer—that an officer of the Chase

Trading Company orchestrated it all? You have no reputation to tarnish but Perty Hancock does."

"Going to be a trial, then?"

"The Council is pushing for one. As you bloody well knew they would. And what about this Exeter chap, come to think of it? Shouldn't he be behind bars as we speak?"

"Keeping him safe."

"Safe from whom?"

Vince glared at him with his single icy blue eye. How intense he must have looked when he still had two.

"You can't honestly think Perty Hancock..." James closed his eyes so as not to lose his temper any further.

"Exeter is the only one who can explain what happened," Vince said. "Much as I hate to admit it, Quaintance is untouchable. Legally, anyway. Need to keep Exeter out of harm's way until the trial."

"He's here, isn't he? You've hidden him under a pile of lace or something."

Vince didn't respond.

"Oh, so now you don't trust me either," James said.

"Do any different in my shoes?"

James sat up straighter. "I'd understand my word as a criminal and a murderer carried no weight whatsoever. I'd understand that even if Perty Hancock did have a hand in the death of Sergeant Spradbery and that bedworker, there are more important things at stake."

"More important than two dead people?"

"Frankly, yes. My Sentinels are the only ones who can stop the gangs from damaging this town any more than they already have. If some sacrifices have to be made along the way, so be it. It's a dirty business."

Vince's gaze never wavered from James. "Keep calling me a killer, like you've never taken a life."

James's spine straightened enough to snap. "I, sir, am a captain in the Chase Trading Company. I have fought pirates, and Spanish, and French. The lives I have taken have been for a cause greater than myself. The lives you have taken were..."

"Go on."

James sat back in the armchair and played with one end of his gently curving moustache.

"Don't know, do you?" Vince asked. "Heard the broad strokes, not the specifics."

"The details of crime don't interest me."

"Funny position for the head of the new town Watch to take."

"We're not a Watch," James said. "We're something else. Something new."

Vince's face remained unreadable. A statue would have had more life about it. "Lives I took were other criminals. Other killers."

"How terribly noble of you."

"Nothing noble about it. Did it to protect my territory. Or for revenge. For the death of my people. Murder of my husband."

James squinted at him, trying to decide if he was lying or not. "I didn't know you were a widow."

"No reason you should."

"What was his name?"

"Martin. Showed me I could be more. Before him, was only ever useful to people on my back or in a brawl. People didn't care what I had to say. Last time you and I spoke made me remember what it felt like. Don't like that. Don't like being ignored."

James's thumb turned the silver ring around his finger. He never imagined a man as big as Vince could be insecure about not being seen or heard. "I never intended to make you feel that way."

"Did anyway. Not your fault. Old pain is like a building

you pass every day. Always there but you stop noticing it. Until the day you do. Then you see something new. Some aspect of it you hadn't seen before."

"I don't know which is the more painful—the loss of a spouse or the loss of a child."

"Hope you never find out," Vince said, his voice gentler than before.

"A person must be more than a catalogue of their tragedies," James said. "Though had I suffered as you have, I do not believe my heart could take it. I don't think I could let myself get close to anyone else ever again."

In the misty morning light, Vince's snowy white hair almost glowed like a mountain peak. "Hurts but it's worth it. Don't want to be alone forever. Both of us have blood on our hands. Both have our reasons. Port Knot is a bad town filled with bad people. Compromises have to be made or nothing will ever get done. Rabbit understood that when she hired me. Past is done. Future beckons. Have to make the best we can of it."

James sighed and slid down into his seat. "Perty Hancock and Spradbery hated one another," he said. "Still, I can't accept she had any hand in his death."

"Trial will show that," Vince said.

"And then what?" James asked. "If it comes out Hancock is innocent, what becomes of your Mr Exeter?"

"Confessed to killing Ataraxy Crimp. Has to be punished for it, no matter what happens. Magistrates will send him to Blackrabbit gaolhouse. C.T.C. run it. Some greencoat guard will find out what he did and take revenge."

"You have a very low opinion of my organisation."

"Born of experience. Even greencoats are human. Human needs. Human frailties."

"I can try to make sure he's safe," James said.

"Some things are beyond even your power," Vince said.

CHAPTER THIRTY-TWO

STANDING BEFORE THE looking glass in her cabin, Perty Hancock straightened the lieutenant insignia on her epaulette and imagined how she might look as a captain. With both hands, she smoothed her hair. She tied her scabbard onto her belt and checked her collar.

She had almost finished packing the last of her belongings, ready for the move to the small cottage next to Sentinel Garrison. It had been earmarked for Captain Godgrave, but he'd turned his nose up at it–claiming it to be entirely too cramped for his liking–and so it had passed to her. A knock on the cabin door stirred her.

She opened it to Sergeant Tresome who handed her a newspaper. "I think you should see this, Lieutenant."

"Why, what...?" She stopped when she spotted her own name in the first story and quickly scanned the rest of it.

"It's not true, is it, ma'am? You weren't involved in Carter Spradbery's death, were you?"

Perty's feet turned cold, her hands too. "Of course not! Get back to your duties before I have you flogged."

Tresome hurried off without another word. Perty slammed the door to her tiny cabin. She crumpled the newspaper and threw it against the bulkhead. Fixing the last button of her emerald-green-and-white overcoat, she slid her sword into the scabbard on her belt and marched to the weather deck of the ship. "Sergeant Tresome. See to it all copies of that libellous rag are removed from this ship. And I don't wish to see another edition of it cross our gangplank. Is that understood?" She lifted her chin and addressed the crew within earshot. "There's a nasty, bitter streak running through the people of this town. I've seen it first-hand many times. They will even stoop so low as to besmirch the name of a Chase Trading Company officer. I intend to pay the offices of the Blackrabbit Courant a visit and ensure it doesn't happen again."

She marched down the gangplank to the dock and

walked to the far end of the harbour, well out of sight of her ship. She passed through the bustling market, stopping to purchase a length of rope which she secreted under her long coat. She searched about the harbour until she found a lone sailor tending to his little boat. "You there," she called.

"Winkleigh," the man said.

"Yes, very good, Mr Winkleigh. I should like you to take me across to the gaolhouse."

"What, now?"

"Yes, now!"

"But I've got to be home in an hour or Marjory will shout at me. She's made a special luncheon for us, y'see, and—"

"You shall be home in plenty of time, Mr Winkleigh, and with a crown to show for it."

Mr Winkleigh cleared space in his boat and offered his hand to help Perty aboard. She slapped it away. "I'm not some damsel in need of assistance. Cast off and let's be away."

The crossing went smoothly, despite the pervasive mist clinging fast to the sea. The gaol and lighthouse sat on the same clump of rock to the northeast of Blackrabbit. When the bells of the gaol rang, they could be heard clear across Port Knot.

The slight and weather-beaten Mr Winkleigh moored the boat to the little dock.

"Wait here until I return," Perty said.

"But...but...but...my Marjory. Luncheon."

Perty stared at him. "Would two crowns lessen your wife's anger?"

Mr Winkleigh beamed, showing his remaining teeth. "I'm certain it would, ma'am."

The gaolhouse was a suitably gloomy affair—all smooth, grey blocks and black iron bars. The C.T.C. had always run the prison; indeed, it had been built and paid for by the then-head of the company, the late Lord Marley Chase. As such, the guards fell under Perty's command. She nodded to the C.T.C. soldiers on the entrance and headed inside where she was greeted by a man in want of a good wash. The white of his uniform was more of a creamy yellow, and the green closer to brown.

As he spoke, he picked his teeth, such as they were. "Can I help you, miss?"

"Lieutenant," she said. "Stand up straight and get your fingers out of your mouth when you're talking to me. Which way is Hugo Lambshead's cell?"

"Well, it's just down that corridor and to the right, miss,

um, ma'am, um, Lieutenant."

"Good, I need to speak with him."

He stepped in front of her. "We're not supposed to let anyone in to see him. Orders and that."

"Would you like to explain to Captain Godgrave why you prevented me from carrying out my duties?"

The man gulped and lifted a ring of keys. Clearly, the captain's reputation had penetrated even these dense walls.

"Give them here," Perty said, snatching the keys from his grimy hands. "Which ones do I need?"

She left the foul-smelling man behind and hurried down the damp corridor lined with empty cells. Patches of mould gathered in every corner of the place and the air was thick enough to lick. She found Lambshead lying deathly still in his cage. Her heart jumped. If he were dead, her plans lay in ruins. She rattled the bars of his cell door.

"Keep it down, some of us are trying to sleep."

She sighed and drew out the keys. "Get up, Lambshead, you've got work to do."

"Do I know you?"

She slid the key into the flaking lock. "Not yet," she said.

"But by nightfall, you're going to think of me as your very closest friend." She unlocked the door and swung it open.

"Why are you letting me out?"

"Because I need you to keep the Sentinels busy for a while. There's somewhere I need to be, and I don't want any interference from them."

Lambshead sprung to his feet in the blink of an eye. He stifled a wince and grabbed his wounded leg, but still managed to cross the filthy cell floor like a peacock strutting before a mate. He leaned against the bars. "My friends like to do me favours," he said. "They find it keeps me happy."

"Letting you out of this cell is a favour, is it not?"

"Mmm, no, it's not," he said. "Because you're just doing it for your own sake." He took a few steps backwards. "In fact, I don't see why I shouldn't just remain here and call for the guards."

"What is it you want?"

He splayed his arms wide and almost sang. "I want Port Knot on fire and on its knees, begging me for forgiveness."

Perty had met plenty of men like him before. All bravado and arrogance. Angry at everything. Exactly how she wanted him to be. "Isn't there something in the C.T.C. headquarters that can help you? Something new and powerful?" She handed him the rope from beneath her coat. Perty had always found the best way to get a man to do what she wanted was to let him think it was his idea in the first place.

PERTY RETURNED TO the unkempt jailer. "I thought you said Lambshead was at the end of this corridor?"

The jailer jumped to his feet. "You mean he isn't?" He grabbed the keys from her hand and hobbled on broken boots to the unlocked and empty cell. He searched it anyway, throwing blankets in the air and checking under the cot before returning to his desk. He turned a lever on the wall, setting alarm bells ringing.

A group of guards arrived, rifles drawn, and Perty despatched them to the top of the gaolhouse to commence their search. She would search the gates and dock. She ordered the jailer to remain at his post.

As the guards rushed past her, Perty made for the gates where she ordered the two guardsmen to join the search inside.

"We're not supposed to leave our posts," one said.

Perty splayed her hands and gestured to the small dock. "He's obviously not here! If he escapes, it will be on your head."

The guards sprinted inside to join their comrades. Perty hurried to where Mr Winkleigh had moored. As expected, Hugo Lambshead clambered to meet her. He'd used the rope to scale down the walls of the gaolhouse and secrete himself among the jagged rocks.

"Cast off," Perti said.

Mr Winkleigh glanced at Lambshead. "But the alarm…"

"I am an officer of the C.T.C., and I am commandeering this vessel. You will cast off immediately, Mr Winkleigh."

While Mr Winkleigh set them on their course back to the harbour, Perty removed her uniform overcoat and swapped it for Lambshead's soot-black coat. Next came their breeches and boots.

"Here, what are you two up to?" Mr Winkleigh asked. "I shall have to report this, Lieutenant."

Lambshead, now bedecked in Perty's uniform, nodded towards him. Perty hesitated before drawing her sword and lunging forward, covering Mr Winkleigh's mouth with one hand and driving the blade into his gut with the other. Together, she and Lambshead slid the body overboard and let it slip under the water.

"Why are you helping me?" Lambshead asked.

"This town needs to pay," Perty said. "And you and I are the only ones who can ensure that it does."

CHAPTER THIRTY-THREE

SINCE THE GUNBRIDES disaster at Gull's Reach, the road in and out of town had become significantly safer. Vince sat alone in his carriage as it rattled past hedgerow after hedgerow on its way into the countryside. Set a ways back from the road, the great circular gates of Silver Hope swept past on his left-hand side. A short while later, the carriage wheels crunched on the loose gravel outside Wolfe-Chase Asylum.

The broad steps to the front door had been washed that morning, as usual, and patches of slippery wet stone remained. Vince let himself into the spacious front hallway. The floor mosaic of the Chase Trading Company logo—a letter *C* entwined in a ship's wheel—had been covered in several large rugs.

A nurse looked to him and nodded. While he had never been antagonistic towards the medical staff, neither had he ever been especially friendly with them. He had been employed to lift heavy things and scare unruly patients into submission. And little else.

"Come back to us already?" his mother asked. "And I told you before—your animal is not allowed inside the house!"

Crabmeat whimpered and plodded back outside to wait on the steps.

A short, round woman in her seventies, Mrs Honor Knight kept the Asylum running as well as she'd kept the house running when it had been Chase Manor. She waited for him, unsmiling, on the branching staircase. They passed the great stuffed wolf on the landing, posed as if set to pounce on intruders at the front doors.

"Need to collect some things," Vince said.

His mother accompanied him to his room on the top floor. Everything had been left untouched. She stood at the doorway with her hands clasped. "I knew you'd be back before long."

"Always had such faith in me," Vince said.

The room, dustless, held a simple bed and table. He took a bag and filled it with clothes from the chest of drawers under the window overlooking the sweep of gardens at the rear of the manor. From under the bed he pulled a battered tricorne. He shook a spider loose from it.

"Your money is still under the floorboards," his mother said. "Where you left it."

Vince sighed. "Knew there was no point hiding it from you." With one hand, he shoved the chest of drawers over to one side. He knelt, removed a loose floorboard, and pulled out a small wooden box.

"You don't need to count it, it's all still there. I heard about the dissolution of the town Watch. You may resume your position here at your earliest convenience."

"Not sure I want that."

"I'm not sure you have much of a choice. What else will you do? Sign on with the Sentinels?"

The springs squeaked as he sat on the bed. "Going to be a trial tomorrow. One of my Watch killed two people."

"You do seem to attract that sort. Will you be attending? I know of your distaste for courthouses."

He rubbed his mouth with his hand. "Suppose I'll have to. Sentinels are involved too. Don't know if they'll come out unscathed."

"It sounds as though you don't want them to."

He sighed heavily. "Sentinels are going to hunt down and kill remaining gang members."

"I can understand how the idea of criminals being punished would be unpleasant for you."

Vince shot her a look. "Have plenty of convicts here. Know full well some people aren't responsible for their actions. Met a girl in Gull's Reach. Gunbride. Young. Things she said turned my stomach. Completely unhinged. Lambshead has her mind twisted. Not the only one, neither. My fault. Let him run wild. Gave him a chance to spread his ideas."

His mother moved into the room and stood closer to him. "You couldn't have known it would come to this."

"Not the point," he said. "All happening because of me. Sentinels won't give Gunbrides like her a chance. No one will." He turned the box of money over and over in his hands. "Asylum procedures. They work? They...help people?"

"You worked here for months; didn't you see any successes?"

Vince's gaze dropped to the floor. "Never paid much attention."

"That sounds right," she said. "It can be slow, but it works, yes. I was sceptical at first, but I've seen people heal. I've seen the doctors here calm the storms in their patients' heads, in their hearts." She stood by the window, watching the patients in the gardens. "I've seen people brought here—violent people, lost people, desperate people—and seen them walk out and rejoin society. Lady Eva Wolfe-Chase opened this place to give prisoners a chance to change. To give the magistrates an option besides locking people up forever. Not everyone needs that kind of punishment. Some just need a little compassion."

Doctor Cranch ran past the door, then doubled back. "There you are. Have you seen outside? There's smoke coming from the town."

A SCREAM FROM outside drew James to a window. Crowds of people flocked away from the docklands. He dashed outside, followed by several of his Sentinels.

The courthouse went first. Engulfed in flames, its ancient

wooden structure lit up like a bonfire, probably seen for miles. Several nearby businesses caught in the blaze were next to go.

James took a rifle from the nearest Sentinel. "Where's Lieutenant Hancock?" He took a pouch of powder and tied it to his belt.

"She went to the newspaper offices to speak to them," Sergeant Tresome said. "I haven't seen her since."

The boom that followed shook Sentinel Garrison. The force reverberated through the building, up through James's feet and legs. Had he not been on dry land, he would be absolutely certain a man-o-war had just unleashed its arsenal.

James hurried towards town, buttoning his jacket as he went. In the confusion, his Sentinels rushed around like headless chickens, trying to calm a hostile and frightened crowd. James grabbed one of his people by the arm. "Stop and think, you mutton-headed lobcock! Get some Sentinels on the street and direct the people inland. You, Spry, get help putting out the fire before it spreads. Bodmyn, Hamlyn, come with me."

Sergeant Werry approached him, clasping a wounded ear. "Clipped by a gunman," he said.

"What's happening?"

"Lambshead. He's back and he's riled up his gang. They're running wild, shooting at anything that moves."

"He's in the gaolhouse!" James said.

His lieutenant shook his head. "He escaped. Bribed his way out, most likely."

Just like Vince said he would. "Most of his surviving gang were imprisoned. Did he break them out?"

"No, sir. As far as I know, they're still in the gaolhouse. Some Gunbrides escaped Gull's Reach. Lambshead must have rounded them up before the attack."

Another explosion sounded. "There can only be a handful of Gunbrides left, then," James said. "Can't we subdue them?"

"They're using the road and bridges as cover," Lieutenant Werry said. "We chase them, but they lose us. We don't know the roads like they do. But, sir, that's not all."

Another boom shook the very cobbles under their feet.

"They raided the C.T.C. headquarters in the docklands. They've got the siege weapon."

James gritted his teeth. "How did they...? The raid. There were rumours of a new weapon circulating around town for weeks. When the Gunbrides stole from our ammunition and weapons store, they were really there to find out if the rumours were true."

"We can't stop them now, sir."

"Poppycock," James said. He readied his rifle. "On me!"

Lieutenant Werry joined Bodmyn, Hamlyn, and two other Sentinels. Together, they all sprinted up Quarrier's Run towards Pudding Quarter—the main commercial district of Port Knot. In the shadow of Hooves Heaving, one of the largest and steepest bridges in town, they found a band of Gunbrides firing wildly into business premises. One of the gang took aim at the bridge's ornate columns. His musket barked, creating a plume of smoke and snatching the nose from a great stone seahorse.

James aimed his rifle at them. "I order you to stop!"

The Gunbrides bolted, splitting into several directions at once. James held his troop together. "That one, follow that one!" He knew the plan was to split them up, making them easier targets. He wasn't about to be fooled so easily.

He and his Sentinels followed the gunman through the roads and into one Entry after another. After a minute or two, they all emerged into a square surrounded by high, butter-coloured walls.

James gave the order to take cover. From windows high above, shots rang out. Bodmyn and Hamlyn fell dead on the spot. Before they could fire a single round, Miller and Treffry followed. James and Lieutenant Werry ran towards another

Entry, out of the line of fire. James made it. Lieutenant Werry did not. James held tight to his rifle and ran.

He followed the sound of musket fire towards Trivia Place, at the heart of the town. There he hid in a doorway and peeked out at the assembled Gunbrides. Outside the gates of the town hall, they danced around like maniacs, hooting and singing as they fired, intoxicated by the power of their prize—the siege engine.

A great armoured contraption of cannons and wheels making a noise like nothing he'd ever heard before. Eight rapid bursts, a clicking pause, then another eight. Sixteen cannons working in succession to subdue a whole street.

The cannons, monstrous versions of the pepper-box muskets the Gunbrides used, whirred and clicked as they fired. When one battery emptied, it rose up and fell backwards. From the automated cabin behind, each of the battery's eight barrels filled with shot and powder, ready to be redeployed when the other battery finished firing.

In action, the process took seconds. Under a metal roof, three Gunbrides constantly worked to feed gunpowder into the recharging cabin. Four blinkered horses, armoured like the steeds of medieval knights, slowly pulled the whole lumbering affair forward. The horses were guarded by a number of Gunbrides walking alongside. The force of the cannon fire cracked bricks and broke pipes. Water sprayed out onto the streets like fountains.

Embers floated past on acrid air as James leaned back into the doorway and rubbed his face. "Damn it, Perty, where are you?"

"I DON'T KNOW where he is." Sorcha closed the curtains in the tall bay windows of the shop. "He said something about needing money."

"The town is on fire, and it's your fault." Orla heaved a heavy box against the window. "You and your lout friend. I don't even want to think about how he's getting money."

"How is this our fault?"

"You were supposed to suppress the gangs!"

Sorcha took another box and set it on top of the first, adding to the makeshift barricade. "We tried! We weren't given a chance before the council turned the town over to the Sentinels. Why aren't you yelling at them?"

"If they were here, I feckin' well would!"

In a flash, the door to the shop flew open, and Lieutenant Hancock ran in, grabbing Orla by the arm and twisting it as she spun round behind her. She held her sword to Orla's bare throat.

Sorcha's heart nearly stopped beating. "Don't hurt her!"

The lieutenant's dark eyes held her gaze steadily, calmly. "Where is he?"

"Who?" Sorcha asked.

"Exeter! Where is he?"

"I...I don't know."

Lieutenant Hancock gritted her teeth and turned the blade of her sword.

Sorcha held her hands out. "I don't know where he is! He was here, we had him locked up in our sewing room, but Vince took him somewhere to keep him safe! He didn't tell us where. After what Exeter did, I don't think he trusts any of us."

"Don't lie to me, girl." She twisted Orla's arm enough to make her scream.

"He's at the asylum!" Sorcha said.

She twisted Orla's arm again, harder this time.

"It's true," Sorcha said. "Vince used to work there. His

mother runs the place. It's the best place to hide someone."

"The asylum is too far away," Lieutenant Hancock said. "Vince would want to be able to get to him quickly." She tensed her hand, preparing to slice. "I warned you not to lie to me."

"The Courant!" Orla said quickly. "I heard Vince say he was taking him to the Courant."

"Orla, no!"

Lieutenant Hancock shoved Orla towards Sorcha. As she stumbled, Lieutenant Hancock ran out of the shop. Orla slammed the door closed behind her.

Sorcha stared at her. "What are you after doing?"

Moments later, the door burst open again. Orla screamed.

Vince held the door and looked around the shop. "Sorcha! Anyone hurt?"

"No, we're all fine. But Vince, wait. Hancock was here, looking for Exeter. Orla told her where to find him."

Vince's face turned red, and he roared so loud, Sorcha jumped. "Bleddy tuss! Put Exeter in danger."

"You put us in danger by being here!" Orla said. "I wasn't about to have my throat cut to protect some murderer!"

"Exeter isn't alone. Told Ms Hawksmoor to keep an eye

on him." Vince slammed the door and ran.

"I didn't know that," Orla called after him. "I didn't know."

"I...I know you didn't," Sorcha said.

Orla dropped onto a chair. "Are you going after him?"

Sorcha stood with her hand on the doorknob. She bolted the shop door. "Someone has to stay here and look after you."

"I'm supposed to be the one taking care of you."

"No, you're not," Sorcha said, still facing the door. "I don't need taking care of. I'm on the Watch. My role is to protect you and the rest of the town, and so help me, if you say there is no Watch anymore, I will scream the feckin' shop down, so I will." She lowered herself into a chair and crossed her arms.

Orla licked her own lips in the way she always did when there was something she was trying not to say. Somewhere in the distance, a deep boom rumbled, followed by a shattering of glass. "I can't believe I brought us all the way here just to have it end like this."

"It's not the end," Sorcha said. "Vince will stop it. He will. He'll stop it."

CHAPTER THIRTY-FOUR

IN THE STREETS of Port Knot, townsfolk ran from their homes and businesses. They didn't stop to check on their neighbours. They didn't stop to help put out fires. And they didn't stop to assist the wounded. Instead, they ran aimlessly from one place to the next, seeking shelter. Loud bangs caused them to stagger as though they were swimmers pummelled by waves. Pillars of black smoke rose where buildings had been set alight.

Perty Hancock stuck close to the honey-hued walls. The home of the Blackrabbit Courant stood at the end of Five Brothers Road, behind Quarrier's Run. Crossing it would be dangerous. While no road in Port Knot could be described as wide, Quarrier's Run differed by being the most open.

Perty sidled along the Entry and waited. A thunderous boom from around the bend caused her to duck and cover her head. A trail of broken glass and splintered wood ran along the main road, and there, in the middle of it all, she spotted a flat cap. She sprinted to it, scooped it up, and carried on to the other side. She fixed the cap on her head and pulled it low over her eyes. She ran east, away from the centre of town. A few people with bloodied clothes huddling in shop doorways screamed when they saw her but she carried on past them.

She reached a long Entry that ran from the road and led directly to the back of the Blackrabbit Courant offices. A risky option, as once inside an Entry there was no way out but to continue through to the other end. Still, she preferred it to remaining out in the open.

She rang along the narrow lane. Cold, sand-coloured bricks on either side towered high above her. Washing lines stretched from one side to the other, hung with shirts and bed-clothes which floated above her head like the ghosts of distant ancestors, watching her, egging her on, or perhaps trying to warn her away.

At the rear of the newspaper offices, she rattled a door-knob in vain. She held her newfound cap over her hand and waited for the rhythmic sound of cannon fire. Eight. A pause. Eight. A pause. She smashed a window as the eight blasts fired, reached in, and quietly unlocked the door.

VINCE RAN THROUGH the town, keeping away from the Entries and avoiding musket fire. He knew he'd be lucky to make it to the Blackrabbit Courant office without encountering trouble. On Pit Lung Lane, his luck ran out.

He hurtled around a corner and collided with an unsuspecting Gunbride, knocking them backwards into a shop window. Vince doubled back, balled his fist, and with one blow punched the Gunbride straight through it. The Gunbride landed inside the shop, with shattered glass jabbing into his back and arms. The shards stuck from his body like glass feathers.

Another Gunbride turned, ready to fire, but Vince knocked the pistol from his hand, grabbed his collar, and pulled him close, head-butting him. Vince's tricorne cap fell from his head as the Gunbride's nose broke and a tooth flew from his mouth. Vince kicked his legs from under him and punched his head against the cobblestones.

The man he knocked through the window recovered his pepper-box pistol but before he could shoot, Crabmeat sank his jaws into the man's leg. The man shrieked and smacked the dog with his pistol.

Vince dived at him, pulling him through the broken window out onto the street, where he began to pummel the man's head and chest. "Never—" *Thump.* "—touch—" *Thump.* "—my—" *Thump.* "—dog." *Thump.* When the man stopped moving, Vince dropped him.

A musket shot rang out. Vince spun on his heels. A woman fell, clutching her chest.

"She was on your blind side," James said, reloading his flintlock musket. He stooped to retrieve Vince's tricorne and handed it to hm.

Vince grabbed James's shoulder and squeezed it. "Come with me."

"Where?"

"Courant. Exeter's there."

"We have more to worry about right now than him."

Vince carried on walking. "Not alone. Reporter with him. Gunbrides can wait."

"Why did you leave him with a reporter?" James asked.

"Exeter knows his life is in danger," Vince said. "Hiding. Ms Hawksmoor offered to stay with him. Thought it would be safest place for both of them. And make a good story."

James took Vince by the arm, pulling him to a stop. "Wait, I know you think Mr Exeter is in danger from the C.T.C., but everyone is focused on the Gunbrides attack."

Vince fixed him with a steely gaze. "Not the C.T.C. Just Hancock."

PERTY CREPT THROUGH the small and poorly lit ground floor of the Blackrabbit Courant building, careful not to make a sound. She hung her cap on a newel and clasped a handrail, ready to descend into the basement when a floorboard above her creaked. She slowly drew her sword and made her way to the other staircase where she hesitated. Across from it, she found a horological lift. She'd seen similar devices used for moving grain. She pulled the lever, sending the lift steadily up to the next floor. She hurried back to the staircase and crept up as silently as she could.

The distraction worked as she had hoped. Two figures had crouched behind a desk, with their backs to her. One was Alfie Exeter, the other was a young woman in a wheeled chair. Could it be Emmeline Hawksmoor, the reporter? Could Perty be that lucky? She paced along the floor, quiet as a cat. She struck out with her sword. Exeter ducked away at the last moment. He jumped to his feet and kicked Perty's arm. She held fast to her blade.

Exeter hunched his back and held his hands wide open, ready to move again. "How did you find me?"

"Your commander gave you up before I sliced him from ear to ear." Perty swished her blade through the air, narrowly missing Exeter each time.

"Vince is dead?" Exeter asked.

"Very much so," Perty said, enjoying the lie. "I presume this is the nosy Ms Hawksmoor?"

With the flick of a lever, Emmeline Hawksmoor reversed her chair across the floor, away from the fight. "Who are you?"

"This is Lieutenant Pertinacity Hancock," Exeter said.

"The reason Mr Quaintance paid me to kill Sergeant Spradbery."

Perty sliced the air, missing Exeter's chest by a hair's breadth but removing a button from his coat. It sailed through the air and tapped down the staircase. He stumbled backwards but quickly found his footing. He lifted a box of blackened printing blocks and threw it at her. The box smashed against a pillar, casting lettered blocks onto the floor.

"You couldn't even kill one drunken dolt without being seen," Perty said. "Why are you cowering in the dark here? Why didn't you leave town the moment Vince's back was turned?"

"Vince told me Quaintance had sent someone after me. It's why I agreed to hide here."

She struck out again but Exeter deflected her blow. "Hah, the big oaf lied to you. Quaintance doesn't care about you."

"He didn't send you?"

She sliced her blade through the air again. "Of course not! I hired him. I'm not his assassin! It's just as well you're pretty because you are not very bright."

Something thwacked into her back. She turned to find Ms Hawksmoor holding an ink roller with a scared look on her face. Perty slashed at her with her sword.

Ms Hawksmoor screamed and dropped the roller. She clasped the open wound on her arm and pulled the lever on her armrest, sending her chair whirring backwards. "Why did you want Spradbery dead?"

"He was a bottle-headed hog," Perty said. "He thought he could soften me up, full of false apologies and flattery."

"So you had him killed?"

"I needed to show the Council how the Watch wasn't up to the task of protecting this town. Swan and Godgrave were scheming behind the Council's back, getting him ready to take over. I couldn't take the chance that it wouldn't go ahead."

Ms Hawksmoor backed farther away. "Why did it matter so much to you? So much you were prepared to kill to make it happen?"

"Because this is little Perty Hancock, the daughter of Hangman Hancock," Exeter said. "Her dad killed a man, hung him from the rafters until his neck broke. Everyone knew about it. Used to make fun of her for it."

"*Fun?*" Perty hacked again and again at Exeter, missing each time as he hopped away. "They didn't *make fun*, they spat at me. They threw rotten meat at me. They hid dead mice in my clothes, in my food. I had my hair set on fire twice by

Spin Gastrell and his snotty brother! But now I'm in charge. And I'm going to make this grotty little town pay."

Ms Hawksmoor distracted Perty for just a moment and from behind, Exeter grabbed Perty's arms, pinning them down. Perty reared up and kicked Hawksmoor in the stomach, sending her hurtling backwards and smacking against a heavy desk. Her chair tipped over, spilling her out. She cracked her head loudly on the edge of the desk and crumpled to the floor.

"That's one," Perty said. She stamped on Exeter's foot and broke free from his grip.

Another boom shook the glass in the window frames. "Lambshead and his friends found the engine. As distractions go, I think you'll agree it's a good one."

"They'll destroy the whole town."

"Good," Perty said. "It's no more than it deserves. I'll sing in its ashes."

"I can't believe you did all this because some children were mean to you when you were young."

"It's not just the children. The adults were just as bad. Talking about me. Pointing. Whispering. They made my mother's life a living nightmare. Is it any wonder she left? There's a sickness in this town. A vein of malice running deeper than the mines. And I'm going to cut it out."

Exeter dived at her again but in one fluid movement, she spun on her heels and jabbed the sword under his ribs. The blade emerged from his back, red and slick. He sank to his knees and toppled face first onto the floor. Blood pooled around him where he lay.

Perty laughed and wiped her face on the back of her hand. She could scarcely believe it. The luck of finding Ms Hawksmoor here. She'd planned to pay her a visit later. Good-for-nothing busybody printing her business for all and sundry to read. She deserved to be done away with.

Perty wiped the blood from her blade and sheathed it in her belt. By the shiny base of a copper lantern, she fixed her hair into place, straightened her collar and sleeves, and dusted down her coat. Well, Lambshead's coat, really. She'd need to get rid of it shortly. She'd needed his clothes to blend in with the townsfolk, and he'd needed her uniform to help get him inside the C.T.C. headquarters and steal the siege weapon.

By now, the Sentinels should be engaging the enemy in the south side of town. They would likely have called in eveyone from the Garrison. She could slip back inside and change into her spare uniform. Then she would head off to find that blowhard, Godgrave, and help him kill Lambshead and anyone else causing a nuisance.

Calmly as could be, she marched downstairs, retrieved the cap from the newel, and walked out the front door into the street. She hummed a little as she walked. She hoped the Gunbrides wouldn't flatten all the theatres. When the dust settled, she quite fancied taking in an opera.

With all of the chaos around her, she hardly registered the boom of the musket shot that struck her. She had thought it just a bang like any other that had been popping off all morning. The cobblestones jumped up to greet her as her legs gave way. She wanted to stand, to run, but try as she might, her legs simply refused to move. Next, her fingertips tingled as her arms gradually turned completely numb.

She lay there on her side as boots ran by, narrowly missing her face. Skirts ruffled over her head, people screamed, and somewhere, somehow, music played. She was certain of it. Two Gunbrides walked past her, pointing their pepper-box muskets at her. One barrel still had wisps of smoke, probably from the shot which felled her.

In the middle of Quarrier's Run, in the town she hated more than anything in the world, and humming along to Handel's *Agrippina*, Lieutenant Pertinacity Hancock of the Blackrabbit Sentinels closed her eyes for the last time.

CHAPTER THIRTY-FIVE

JAMES'S EYES STUNG from the smoke and ash whipping through the air. He hurried after Vince, with Crabmeat in tow. Debris from the town's battered and burning buildings clogged the streets. The early morning mist had refused to shift and mixed now with musket smoke. Bodies lay in the roads. Over carts. In shop windows. James had been in battles before but nothing like this. He'd never before witnessed a town at war with itself.

Vince led them through several of the town's myriad narrow, piss-reeking Entries. There would be no question of him and Vince moving side-by-side through them. In fact, Vince had to turn sideways at several points just to fit through. James struggled in places as well. Only a place thoroughly opposed to planning and without a shred of consideration for its citizens could produce something like these. They begged for criminals to stalk them. They served no other purpose. When the gangs were finally subdued, James decided his first act would be to have the Entries walled up. There would be no hiding places in his Port Knot.

"Stop." Vince held out his huge hand to James's chest and pushed him flat against a wall. Vince peered around the corner. "Courant is at the other end of this road. Too many people. Need to cross." Checking the going was clear, Vince kept his head down and ran across the road. James did likewise.

A shot rang out and whizzed past James's ear. He shouted. Vince shouted. Some Gunbrides shouted, appearing from a doorway with their muskets levelled. Vince pounced on them in an instant, a tiger in a tricorne. With a smooth uppercut, he cracked the jaw of one and kicked out the knee of another. James lay into the nearest of the gang, pulling the musket from his hand while punching him in the side of the head. He and Vince stood back-to-back, arms raised, fists clenched, ready for the next attack. None came.

"Boxer's stance," Vince said.

"I know how to handle my fists," James said. "I used to do a bit in my school days. It never leaves you."

Vince led them along an Entry strewn with washing lines to the rear of the Courant offices.

"The window's been smashed," James said. "The door's open." He held the musket like a club. Without any powder, he had no other use for it. He regretted leaving his sword in his office.

He'd followed Vince the whole way there, not a position he felt comfortable in. If Perty Hancock was indeed after Mr Exeter, it would be James who dealt with her, not Vince. He remained convinced there was some explanation, some reason for her actions. He led the way through the dark and silent newspaper office.

On the first floor, they found Mr Exeter.

"Dead," Vince said.

Across the room, the body of a young woman lay slumped against a desk.

Vince lifted her head, gently, one thick finger under her chin. "Hawksmoor? *Hawksmoor?*"

The woman stirred, her lip quivering. "V-Vince?"

James drew a handkerchief from his pocket and held it

to the wound on the back of her head. Crabmeat licked her hand, wagging his tail the whole time.

"Hancock," she said, her words slow and unsteady. "Confessed to paying Quaintance. She killed Exeter."

James's heart sank. Vince laid his hand on his shoulder and squeezed it. Without a word, Vince lifted Ms Hawksmoor as if she weighed nothing and carried her downstairs. "Will come back for your chair," he said. "Promise."

"I'll take the lead this time, old chap," James said.

"Main door." Vince nodded his head toward the front of the building. "Can't carry her through the Entries."

James checked outside before waving Vince through. The main road of the town was peppered with people, some injured, some dead. Including a woman lying in the middle of the road. "That's a C.T.C. sword."

"Come back!" Vince kept close to the walls and hissed, "James!"

James crossed into the road and knelt by the woman's body. He glanced at the silver ring on her left hand as he removed the flat cap obscuring her face. He stood slowly and returned to Vince and Ms Hawksmoor. "We won't be needing a trial after all," he said.

VINCE CARRIED MS Hawksmoor through the tailor shop to the floral parlour where the former members of the Watch had gathered. Vince ignored them all. James took some cushions for her head and laid them on the settee. She winced but didn't complain.

"We need fresh dressing for her head," James said.

"What is this all over the shop floor? Is this blood?" Orla had followed the trail and stood open-mouthed and gesturing wildly.

"Wouldn't be any if you'd kept your trap shut," Vince said.

"I didn't know this would happen. Who is she, and why is she bleeding on my cushions?"

James turned to bark at Orla. "You, girl! Get some bandages!"

Orla pursed her lips. "I don't work for you! This is my home."

James barked almost loud enough to make Vince flinch. "Now, damn you!"

Orla all but leapt out of her skin and set off to find some gauze. All his time spent bellowing orders loudly enough to be heard in the middle of a cannon battle at sea had given James a voice that could rattle the dead.

Mr Norton stood behind the settee. "She needs a physician."

"It's too dangerous out there," James said. "I've seen plenty of head injuries in my time. We can keep her safe for now."

Orla returned with a bunch of fabric offcuts. "These were all I could find."

James stood and wiped his hands on a piece of cloth. "Don't let her fall asleep, you understand? She must be kept awake."

Vince finally acknowledged the presence of the Watch. His Watch. His failure. "Good of you all to come."

Clive nodded to him. "Someone needs to act. We thought you were... Well, we all thought you were the person best suited to organise a resistance against the Gunbrides."

Ruth stood and rested the head of her mace in her hand. "So what's the plan, Commander?"

From the far corner of the room, Walter stopped fidgeting and lifted his head. "I'm sure you've got some ideas."

Vince frowned and left the parlour, followed by James. They stood on the shop floor. Crates had been piled high against the windows. Though the curtains were drawn, light peeked in from the sides. Outside, people still screamed and shouted, musket fire still sounded. Vince stood with his hands on his hips.

"People are dying," James said.

"Sentinels?"

"They're all fighting or dead," James said. "I should be out there with them, not hiding in here with you."

"No sense rushing out without a plan. Without support."

"And where are we supposed to find it? Your Watch isn't enough. There aren't any C.T.C. soldiers permanently stationed here, just whoever is in port or at the headquarters. We need more people."

Vince slammed his palms onto the shop counter and kicked a trunk covered in cracked green leather. Then his eyebrows shot up. "Oh, no," he said. "Think I've just had a very bad idea."

WHILE THE WATCH muttered amongst themselves in the bay window, Sorcha knelt beside Orla. "He saved her," she said. "He didn't leave her there. He carried her all the way back so she'd be safe. He's not the person you think he is."

Orla sniffed, and Sorcha realised she was crying. "Working with the Watch, it's only a matter of time before some lout gets the better of you."

"Vince wouldn't let that happen. Neither would anyone else. That's what you've never understood about the Watch."

Orla sat quietly for a moment. "Was what he said true? Exeter, I mean. Do you want to leave?"

Sorcha breathed deeply. "Yes. I mean, I won't go, but yes, I do want to see more of the world. Eventually. Doesn't everyone?"

"I've seen enough of it." Orla soaked the cloth in a bowl of water. "This could have been you."

"But it wasn't."

"But it could have been!" Orla said. "It could so easily have been you, Sorcha. Why can't you see that? Why do you have to put yourself in the line of fire? I just want you to be happy!"

Ms Hawksmoor groaned a little, and Orla dabbed her head.

Sorcha sank deeper into herself. "Then let me do what makes me happy! Let me work with the Watch. Let me help the people of the town."

Orla brushed her hand over her own damp eyes. "You can still do all that, just with a man at your side. Or a woman. Just...someone."

"But what for? Why does it matter so much?"

Orla threw her hands in the air. "Because I need to know you'll be looked after when I'm gone!"

The Watch turned their heads and Sorcha waved them away. "What are you on about? I thought you didn't want to go anywhere. Where are you going?"

"Nowhere," Orla said. "Nothing. I just... If anything happens to me, I want to know you'll be taken care of. I want to know someone will make sure you're eating right and will keep a roof over your head."

"Why would you think something will happen to you? Orla? Are you ill?"

"No, it's nothing like that." She took a deep breath. "The night we left home, we crawled into the cart, remember? I put you in and had to run back for my bag."

"I remember," Sorcha said. "You were only gone for a minute."

"Mammy was there."

Sorcha's mouth dropped open. "What?"

Orla dropped a wad of bloody fabric into a bucket and replaced it with a fresh ball. "She was there with my bag. I froze on the spot. I thought she was going to... She just threw my bag at me. She told me it didn't matter where we went, she'd still find us. Find me. And make me sorry."

Sorcha hugged her arms around herself. She didn't know why; she just had to. "She didn't try to stop you? Why did you never tell me about this?"

"I didn't want you to worry. I think Mammy let us go, maybe even wanted us to. It meant fewer mouths for her to feed, I suppose. But I jump whenever I hear a door slam or feel someone walking behind me. I really think she meant it. I think one day she's going to find us. I don't know how or when, but she will."

"It's why we changed our last name," Sorcha said, taking her hand. "And it's all the more reason to keep Vince around."

"You're not marrying that man," Orla sniffed through tears.

"Don't be vile," Sorcha said, laughing. "And I'm not courting Apricate Maunder either, while we're at it. You know

I don't need someone to take care of me though. I can look after myself. You raised me well."

CHAPTER THIRTY-SIX

WHEN WALKING THROUGH the woods that summer, Vince had happened upon a tree which had grown around the skull of a deer. The white skull, its long antlers still attached, had been lifted from the ground and become an inextricable part of the trunk. Just as the old Wheal Boon engine house had become part of the buildings on Bow Leg Lane. They grew up around it, taking root in its walls, in its roof. If one didn't know where to look, it would be easy to miss. But Vince knew.

The front door had long since been boarded up, yet Vince's boot reduced it to kindling in one swift kick. He marched in, striking his octopus-handled cane on the dirty floor. Dust-flecked sunbeams fought through cracked walls. Hammocks slung from joists. Soiled sheets hung where walls once stood. The centre of the room held a table. One end covered with jars of food, the other with tools and spare parts.

Celeste sat at the table, her legs resting on it. She set down her newspaper. "You could have just knocked."

From behind the sheets, Flowers and Merlin appeared, blades in hand. Overhead, other Clockbreakers leaned over broken railings, whispering and muttering.

James and Clive Hext set a trunk covered in cracked green leather onto the table in front of Celeste. The iron fittings of the trunk formed three large X's across the lid. Vince opened the trunk and pulled out an overcoat.

Celeste rubbed her hands along a collar. "What's this?"

Sorcha and Walter entered through the ruined door, carrying crates and both wearing claret coats with black trim. Crabmeat padded in behind them, wearing a collar of the same colours.

"Oh, you've all got matching outfits!" Celeste said. "Even the dog!"

Walter raised his hand. "I made it for him. I didn't see why he should be left out."

"How adorable," Celeste said. "And how brave of you to return."

Walter took a couple of steps back, putting Vince between him and Celeste.

She pointed to James Godgrave. "I don't think much of his uniform though."

"Forget about him," Vince said. "Offering you a chance, Celeste. Last one you'll ever get. This or the gaolhouse. Me or the magistrates."

Celeste folded her newspaper, set it on the table, and rested her clasped hands upon it. "You took me off the street when I was just a girl," she said. "Gave me to my new family. It was raining the day you brought me to their door. Do you remember? *I* remember. I remember the water dripping from your cap. I remember thinking that finally, finally, I was safe. I thought you were my big, burly protector. It didn't take long to see what you were really doing. My new family worked for you."

James sighed and set his hands on his hips. "There isn't time for this."

Celeste's gaze never wavered from Vince. "You can't imagine the disappointment I felt when they put the first lock in front of me," she said. "Coaxed me into showing them how

I'd pick it. I thought all that was behind me. They trained me. Taught me how to be a better pickpocket. A better lock picker. A better housebreaker. They taught me how to make myself into the most valuable thing I could possibly hope to be in this world—useful to the great Vince Knight."

Vince pulled out a chair and sat. "Wanted to keep you safe."

"No, Vince. You don't get to rewrite my history. You—"

Vince held his hand up. "Not done." He swallowed hard. "Was going to say I put you where I needed you to be. Saw your potential early. Saw how you'd be useful to me. Didn't give you a chance at a real life. Only ever as a cog in my machine. Another weapon in my armoury. Didn't give a damn about who you were. Only what you could do for me." He cleared his throat and tried to look her in the eye. "Words don't come easy to me. Never have. Hard for me to get them out. To get them right. But the right words can save us. Words like sorry. Because I am sorry, Celeste. Sorry for what I did to you. Truly."

Celeste leaned back in her chair and laughed. She stared at him. "I never thought I'd hear you say that."

"Trying to make up for past mistakes. Watch was my second chance. Can be yours too." He stood and drew himself to his full height, his voice echoing around the empty walls. "Goes for all of you. Offering you all an apology. Everyone here is a victim of my ambition. Hurt you all. Broke you all—one way or another. Because of me, you were taken out of the world. Told you could never go back. Told there was no other place for you. Then I left you to rot. Wrong of me. Shirked my responsibility to you. Didn't see it before. Do now."

"You went back to the world and started hunting us down," Merlin said. "You started working for the very people you told us were responsible for our misfortunes."

Vince's bravado faltered, his eye twitched. "Met me before or not, all of you were told you'd be safe under my care. Still true, that. Making a promise to you. No Clockbreaker will see the inside of a gaolhouse cell. Not if you stand with me now."

"Ah, this is a press ganging!" Celeste said. "You're building yourself a new army, and you thought the best place to start was with these children. But then, that was always one of your skills, wasn't it, Vince? Getting the impressionable youth to heel."

"Different this time," Vince said.

Celeste squared up to him, baring her teeth. "All I see is another group of people trying to control the town. All I see is another gang."

"Rest of you?" Vince asked. "Want to hide in squalor for the rest of your miserable lives? Or do you want to earn an honest living for a change?"

"Have you lost your mind?" James asked. "You're going to send a pack of wolves after a pack of wolves! You're adding fuel to the fire, man!"

"Still young," Vince said. "Lied to. By me. Made mistakes. Weren't given a choice. All they need is a chance. All anyone needs is a chance."

Flowers stepped forward. "Walter, is he serious?"

Walter nodded. "I think so. Worth a go, at least? Or else we hide here until the Gunbrides decide what they want to do with us. And I think we can guess what that is. We don't mean anything to them. We've never meant anything to anyone, except to one another. Vince is offering a way out. I think it's worth trying. Besides, if the Gunbrides don't get us, the greencoats will."

"What's to stop Lambshead making them the same offer?" James asked.

"Swear an oath," Vince said. "Swear you'll serve your town. Serve me. Again. Help us put down the Gunbrides for good."

"After everything you've admitted, you're asking a lot," Flowers said. "However, there is safety in numbers. I don't know what this town will look like after today, but I do know I don't want to face it alone. I so swear. But I'm warning you—don't you dare let us down again."

"I so swear," said another boy.

Merlin took an overcoat but hesitated, looking to Celeste. "I'll go along with whatever you decide. But I don't trust him."

On and on it went, until the dozen remaining Clockbreakers had all agreed. Vince handed out coats to each of them. Some fit well. Some were much too large.

Vince held out a coat to Celeste. "Well?"

"It means taking orders again."

"Better than being in the gaolhouse."

Celeste clucked her tongue at her gang, all these young Clockbreakers signing up for a new cause. She stood with a hand on her hip. "Lambshead burned the Watch House knowing Flowers, Walter, and the others were inside. He didn't give a damn about them. He's not getting away with that."

"Not a revenge mission," Vince said. "With us now, with us for good."

She took the coat from Vince and slipped it on, rolling

the sleeves up to her elbows and admiring her reflection in a broken looking glass. "Lucky for you red is my colour. So, what, we're all Blackrabbit Sentinels now?"

Vince ripped open the crate of muskets and handed them out to his new recruits. Next came the gunpowder. "No. Not the Sentinels. Just the Watch." Around him, his new recruits loaded their muskets with shot and powder. "Not as fancy as Gunbrides muskets. Will have to do."

James touched the crate. "I thought these were destroyed in the Watch House fire?"

"Had Sorcha hide them at her shop. Told her I could smell trouble brewing."

"Aren't you taking one?" James asked, tucking a pouch of powder into his belt.

Vince shook his head and spoke to the Clockbreakers. "Don't get used to them, mind. For protection only. Not infantry. Won't be thrown in battle. Gunbrides are better shots than all of you. Use what you know. Still have your frogblades? Good. Need a map."

Walter produced one from his nook and spread it on the table for everyone to see. It had been marked with the houses the Clockbreakers had targeted, and ones they hadn't gotten around to yet.

Vince made a space for James. "Show me where."

James hesitated and ran his long finger over the map. "Here. I think."

"You think?" Sorcha asked.

"This town is a damn rabbit warren! How can I be expected to know one alleyway from the next? Look at all these Entries, they're like a spider's web. The last I saw the siege engine was outside the town hall. It's slow. It won't have gotten much farther."

"Were they attacking the town hall?" Sorcha asked.

"Not especially," James said. "They hadn't stopped outside it. Why?"

"I would have thought if there was some grand plan to take over the town, that would be the place to do it," Sorcha said.

Celeste frowned and shook her head. "I don't think that's what they're up to."

"I've seen the siege engine," Flowers said. "It's big, it will have to stay on the main roads. If it's already at Trivia Place then it'll move along Miner's Rest next. But how are we supposed to fight it?"

"The horses are the clear weakness," James said. "Take them out and the weapon is stuck. The cabin is armoured but the cannons only point out the rear of the contraption. We come up on it from the sides and overpower the people inside."

"Easier said than done," Flowers said. "It's guarded."

"Which is where you all come in," James said. "I need you to distract the guards. We'll be on the other side of the road, waiting."

"Can't we just go up high and pick them off?" Celeste asked.

"They designed it to be protected from those sorts of attacks," James said.

Vince examined the map. "Siege weapon is following the main road. Can use the Entries to draw out the guards. Rather, Celeste and the former Clockbreakers can. Guards are busy chasing you, we sweep over the weapon, remove the operators. Lambshead must be on board. Get him, we can stop all of this."

"Where do you want to start?" Celeste asked.

Vince ran his finger along the map until he reached a crossroads. "Here."

"That's a solid wall, you one-eyed fool," James said. "Unless you've also recruited a bunch of ghosts, how are we supposed to get to them?"

"Said it yourself. Port Knot is a warren. New places demolished and built all the time. Lots of places aren't on any map yet."

"Anyone who wants to patrol this town should know that," Walter said with a grin.

"You're welcome to the blasted place," James said.

CHAPTER THIRTY-SEVEN

VINCE NEEDN'T HAVE worried about finding the siege engine. He simply had to follow the thunderous booms and screaming. A good many buildings had been set alight. Burning embers wafted past and Vince tasted the familiar tang of smoke on his tongue.

When they drew close to Trivia Place, Vince ordered Merlin to scout ahead.

Celeste nodded her agreement, sending Merlin on her way. "I'm not thrilled about you using my people as bait."

"Not my intention," Vince said.

"Is this how it's going to be in your new Watch? Using

young people as grist for your mill?"

Vince stared at her. "Hadn't planned on it."

"I suspect you haven't planned much at all."

"Wrong, there. Was thinking this time you might prefer to have a say in how things are done."

Celeste raised an eyebrow.

"Going to need lieutenants of my own," Vince said.

"I thought the Watch had been officially disbanded?"

"Rabbit once told me anyone with the means can set up a Watch."

Celeste smiled at him with a wicked glint in her eye. "Fine. I'll be your lieutenant. For now. But I'll be commander one day. Just you watch me."

Merlin returned quickly, her eyes wide and face pale. "The engine will be round the corner in a minute or two. It's so... Celeste, I've never seen..."

"I know, I know," Celeste said, squeezing her elbow.

"We don't have to do this," Merlin said. "This isn't our fight. There are greencoats lying dead in the road. Let the C.T.C. take care of it."

"Lambshead tried to kill you," Celeste said. "I'm not letting him away with that. Get to the back. Everyone, get in position."

Vince divvied the Watch into teams and ordered them to hide at the crossroads and Entries.

The siege engine rumbled into view.

James peered around the corner. "Damn." On top of the recharging cabin were two rifle-toting Gunbrides. "They weren't there before."

The six-wheeled siege engine blasted volley after volley into the town. Brick dust gathered like clouds and wooden beams became no more than matchsticks. Whole buildings shook from the force of the assault. Vince's jaw dropped. This was the project Dick had told him about in the Star We Sail By. This was what the greencoats had been working on in secret. A way to bring about wanton, rampant destruction. His stomach turned at the thought of dozens of these machines trundling through towns and cities, at the horror they'd bring.

"It's the only one of its kind," James said.

"Better be," Vince said quietly. He ordered everyone to take their positions.

As the engine blasted its way along the road, it reached the Entries where new Watch members were hidden. A volley of musket fire rang out, toppling several of the guards walking alongside the engine. The rest returned fire, holding their position as the engine rumbled on.

Walter bounced about on his feet. "I don't know about this…"

Sorcha put her hand on his shoulder and smiled. "You can do it. Go on."

He ran along an Entry and, keeping his head low, darted into the road. He crept under the front of the carriage and in seconds he'd pulled the bolt. He rolled back into the road, slapping the nearest horse as he went.

The horse reared and kicked, throwing the guards from the carriage roof. Vince pounced on the nearest one in a flash, smashing the man's head against the ground. Ruth and her mace made short work of the other. Still tethered together, all four horses galloped forward, leaving the siege engine behind.

However, before the Watch could swarm onto the engine, one of the remaining Gunbrides pulled a lever and great metal plates embossed with the seal of the C.T.C. slid from the canopy and down over the sides, protecting its crew. It could no longer move but nor could the Watch get at the people inside.

"Back," James said. "Back, go, go!"

The Watch returned to their hiding places as the crew of the siege engine fired from slits in the armour. One round struck Merlin in the back, shredding her claret-and-black coat.

She cried out and fell hard on the cobbled road. Frank hesitated before running for cover. He caught Vince's eye and shook his head.

Celeste screamed at the Gunbrides every obscenity under the sun. She thumped Vince's arm, his head, his back. "She didn't trust you. She didn't trust you!" She sat with her back to the wall and wept.

Vince breathed heavily, wiping his mouth with the back of his hand.

"It's sitting there like a damn metal turtle," James said. "I've heard about a pirate stronghold that had something similar."

The great cannon batteries fell silent, one pointing forward, one still docked in the recharging cabin.

"They're stuck in place," James said.

Clive and Flowers arrived from a nearby Entry. "We got the ones who were chasing us. Now what do we do? We don't have anything strong enough to get through their amour. What's the plan now? Vince?"

Vince pounded the brick wall with the side of his fist. "Need a damn minute to think!"

"I might have an idea," Sorcha said.

JAMES HURRIED AFTER them, struggling to keep pace with the youngsters.

Sorcha kept looking to Flowers. "I'm sorry about Merlin."

Flowers frowned and turned away. He led her through the deserted roads.

James started to struggle for breath. "Vince said she'd be safe under his care."

Sorcha glanced at him over her shoulder. "Be fair. He can't stop musket balls."

James side-stepped around some broken glass. "It's a good reason for Celeste to hate Vince."

"She doesn't need another reason," Flowers said.

"He's taking quite a gamble putting a musket in her hand."

Flowers slowed to a stop. "Celeste isn't stupid. She can see that whatever else he may be, Vince is our best hope of surviving the coming days. And of staying out of the gaolhouse."

"And after that?" James asked.

Flowers pushed open the ruined door of the Wheal Boon engine house. "Who can say? I never thought I'd see the day those two worked side by side. I never thought I'd be helping a greencoat. I never thought I'd be on the Watch. None of us can see the future." He stood aside to let Sorcha in.

James insisted Flowers go first. "Mmm, well, if I were him, I wouldn't turn my back on any one of you."

"How many of them do you have?" Sorcha asked.

Flowers tore down the sheets separating one sleeping area from another. "Four that are definitely working. I was repairing two more but they're not ready." He lay the sheets on the ground. "We can put them in here. He can carry them." He pointed to James.

"I'm not a damn mule!"

"You're bigger than we are," Flowers said. "You want us to drag these through the streets? These are delicate machines. One wrong bump and they're ruined."

James grumbled under his breath. When they were ready, they tied a knot in the sheets.

James heaved the sack over his shoulder. One lock of his auburn hair tumbled over his eye, the most dishevelled

Sorcha had even seen him. "If my back gives way, I shall be very annoyed."

"How will we know the difference?" Sorcha asked. "Right, you head back to Vince and wait for us."

"What? Where are you two going?"

"Me and Flowers have some work to do."

THE STALEMATE IN town continued. Every now and then, one of the Gunbrides would fire out from their armoured engine at nothing in particular. Water gushed from broken pipes. Shattered glass lay in the road like glittering frost.

Against Vince's better judgement, Frank Rundle and Clive Hext had risked themselves retrieving the body of Merlin. Together with Celeste, they laid her inside a ruined shop. Celeste gently kissed Merlin's forehead before returning to Vince's side in time for James's arrival at the crossroads, red-faced and sweating.

He set the sack gently on the ground and sat on a

windowsill, trying to catch his breath. "Blasted roads twist like snakes."

Celeste untied the sheet. "Where is Flowers? What have you done with him?"

"He's here, he's here," Sorcha said, running up the road towards her with Flowers in tow. "I didn't think you'd miss him that much."

"How are we supposed to stop them from shooting us?" Celeste asked.

"Those slits in the armour were designed for rifles, not the Gunbrides pepper-box muskets," Sorcha said. "They don't have a good range of angles. Once we're up close, they can't hit us. We just need you to distract them. Me and Flowers will do the rest."

Celeste looked to Flowers for confirmation. He nodded his approval. Vince led the Watch through an Entry and in through the back door of a butcher's shop facing the engine. With its windows already shot out, it made the perfect spot to draw the Gunbride's fire.

The Watch fired their muskets, knowing full well they wouldn't cause any damage to the engine's armour, but it upset the Gunbrides within enough to get them to shoot back.

Exactly what Sorcha had hoped for. "Go, go!"

She and Flowers each took one side of the sheet and scrambled down the path to the other side of the engine. They deployed a number of Ticking Ginnys where the engine armour met the uneven cobbled road. They flicked the lever on each device. Long, thin prongs poked out, working their way easily underneath the armour. Then they started to lift. Another set of prongs pushed against the ground, balancing the devices.

Inside, one of the Gunbrides realised what was happening. He began shooting wildly from the slit above their heads. Sorcha and Flowers ducked, even knowing they couldn't be shot from that angle. The devices whirred and clicked as they worked. The Gunbrides tried to shoot the Ticking Ginnys from under the armour but couldn't get their barrels to aim that way.

The heavy armour caused the prongs to buckle but not before they'd done their job. Sorcha signalled to Flowers. They each pulled a tube from their claret coat pockets and lit the ends with a striker.

Sorcha shouted as she worked. "Please work, please work, please work..."

They each rolled their tubes under the armour—then another and then another. Thick pillows of smoke billowed out, filling the engine. Sorcha and Flowers ran for cover, keeping their heads low.

The Gunbrides kicked one of the smoke tubes from under the armour but within seconds, the plates had been retracted. Three Gunbrides fell out of the machine in a haze of smoke, coughing and hacking.

The Watch were on them in an instant. The smallest of the three quivered as James grabbed him by the arm.

"Where's Lambshead? *Where is he?*"

"He's not here!" the man said between coughs. "He went to Littletar's Emporium."

"Why would he go there?" James asked. "For reinforcements?"

"No," Vince said. "All this? Just a distraction. Come on. Might already be too late."

CHAPTER THIRTY-EIGHT

JAMES FOLLOWED VINCE and the newly expanded Watch through the streets of Port Knot. Vince had left Crabmeat with Frank, Clive, and a handful of former Clockbreakers to guard the siege engine and the captive Gunbrides.

Vince led them through buildings, under bridges, up steps, and along winding side streets. When they reached Littletar's Emporium, he split them into two groups. One led by him, one led by Celeste, much to James's annoyance. "I'm perfectly capable of commanding a bunch of young ruffians."

"Want you where I can keep my eye on you," Vince said.

Celeste took her troops into a nearby tavern and led them

up to the rooftops. When she was in position, she leaned over the roof and waved.

"Move," Vince said. Keeping his head low, he drew his octopus-handled sword and led the way inside.

The bazaar stood dark and silent. James and Vince crept through the shop floor and across to the staircase. James grabbed Vince's arm. Without a word, he pointed up. Muffled voices. Two, at least.

Slowly, they crept upstairs, never sharing the same step, careful not to make any noise. By the third floor, the voices had become louder and clearer.

Vince leaned in and whispered into James's ear, "Lambshead and Littletar." The warmth of his breath made James's skin tingle. He tried to ignore it.

At the top of the stairs, they found the first body. A woman, shot through the chest. Two men lay behind her and three more women behind them. All Pennymen, Vince whispered to him. All shot through the heart. That floor of the emporium had been given over to colourful horological animals. Birds and bats perched in cages. Monkeys and frogs hung from beams. Dogs and cats slept on heavy cabinets replete with drawers. Each automaton moved slightly, powered by its internal clockworks and springs. Heads clicked and turned, and jaws ticked as they opened. Chests whirred as they heaved and claws scraped as they flexed. Copper skins and enamel eyes glinted in the lantern light.

James's face flushed red when he realised Lambshead was wearing an ill-fitting C.T.C. uniform. He wanted to rush over and strip it from him, the way he had no doubt stripped it from the corpse of one of James's Sentinels.

In the centre of the room, a handful of Gunbrides encircled Lambshead and, James assumed, Fortitude Littletar.

On his knees, Littletar held his blood-soaked sleeve. "Thought you'd lost your weapon in Gull's Reach."

Lambshead laughed and threw his arm around the shoulders of a red-haired girl with freckles. "So did I! But gentle Kat Hookway here rescued her and kept her safe until we could be reunited. And I will be eternally grateful."

Kat Hookway smiled and tilted her head back.

Littletar winced and shivered. "Can't believe you did all this just to get at me."

Lambshead paced the floor, limping from his injury at Gull's Reach and rubbing his chin on the back of his hand. The hatchet head at the end of his musket dripped with blood. "I didn't do it. No, this was all the work of that green-coat, Hancock."

Vince turned to James, who scowled. His shoulders dropped, and he breathed heavily through his nose. It was true. All of it. His most trusted advisor, his best officer, his...friend...had lied to him.

"Hancock wanted a distraction so I gave her the biggest one I could find." Lambshead held open his uniform coat.

It must have been Perty's, James realised. She had swapped her uniform for his clothes. She'd helped him break into C.T.C. headquarters and steal the siege engine.

"And since I was causing a commotion anyway," Lambshead said, "I thought I might as well set my own plans in motion. This little system of yours, this Shadow Council, was never going to work in the long run. We all knew that going in."

Littletar shrugged and actually laughed. "I was going to get Celeste first. Then you. I suppose you've already gotten to her?"

Lambshead winced as he dropped to his haunches, his pepper-box musket swinging between his legs. "I'm saving her for last." He raised his pistol, but in a flash, Littletar grabbed it and pulled. Lambshead snarled, blobs of spit flying from his mouth. "I told you never to touch Summersong!" He pulled the trigger. The shot echoed through the building. Littletar fell to the floor, dead.

Still reeling from the revelation about Perty, James flinched, knocking his flintlock against a bannister. Lambshead's Gunbrides spotted them and opened fire. James and Vince both dove for cover behind thick cabinets.

Lambshead howled at him. "You're a dead man, Vince!"

About them, musket shot punched holes in the metal animals. Creatures fell from the ceiling, from the shelves and clattered onto the floor, the din of their parts scattering mixing with the roar of the flintlocks.

"Listen to him, Mr Lambshead." Walter held a pistol to Lambshead's back. James hadn't seen or heard Walter entering the room. He must have been a very skilled thief indeed.

"Don't move." Celeste held her weapon to the head of the farthest Gunbride.

Ruth, Sorcha, and Flowers filed out behind her, each pointing their muskets at a Gunbride. Walter stepped back as Lambshead turned round and round, unsure who to face.

He screamed in frustration, baring his teeth. "Celeste! You're with him? After everything he did?"

"He didn't try to burn my people alive! Your lot killed Merlin, shot her dead in the road like she was nothing! They knew her!"

The Gunbrides stood hunched, fingers flexing on the grips of their weapons. One wrong move now would get them all killed—gang and Watch alike.

James kept his musket pointed squarely at Lambshead.

Vince lowered his untipped sword and stepped forward, raising his voice. "Want to make you an offer. All of you. Surrender now. Won't be sent to gaolhouse. Asylum instead. For a time."

A short, prematurely balding man with hairy knuckles and a purple gemstone earring spoke first. "Asylum? What for?"

"Need help, Talan. All of you. Had your brains turned to mush by Lambshead. Not seeing things clearly. Asylum doctors can help you."

"Then what?" Talan asked.

"Then you join my Watch. Stand with me again."

Lambshead laughed, sending a spray of spittle into the air.

Vince ignored him. "Made Lambshead an offer. Back in Gull's Reach. Gave him a way out. Didn't take it. Now it's too late. No walking away from what you did today. Need to pay your debts to society. All of you. Either with me or in the gaolhouse."

Kat Hookway wobbled. Her eyes darted back and forth, from Lambshead to Vince and back again. She held her pepper-box musket with both hands, though it appeared much too large and heavy for her. James's aim hadn't wavered from Lambshead the entire time, but if Ms Hookway's finger slipped, someone would be killed.

"Why should we trust you?" Talan asked. "You turned your back on us once before."

"Recruited you," Vince said. "Some of the rest of you too. Offered you all a way to earn money. Doing it again now. But honestly this time. Better on this side, trust me. Won't let you down again. Won't abandon you again. Have my word."

James squinted at him. "I thought you wanted to get away from all of this?"

"Did," Vince said. "Can't though. Fooling myself to think otherwise. Have a responsibility to them. To all of them. Made my bed, have to lie in it."

The man Vince called Talan set his weapon on the floor and nodded to the other Gunbrides to do the same.

Lambshead moved to strike him, but Ruth's musket made him reconsider. "You're not seriously going to accept this?" Lambshead asked. "You can't trust him!"

Talan, hands raised, knitted his brow. "But it's Vince."

The vein on Lambshead's brow bulged as if to pop. His hand became a claw, trying to throttle Vince across the room. "You think I've turned their brains to mush? Look at the hold you have over them! You click your fingers, and they come running! I should shoot you in the face, show them you're just as human as the rest of us."

"Enough now, Lambshead," Vince said. "No more of this. Drop your musket."

"I don't take orders from you any longer!" Despite the injury James had given him, Lambshead moved quick as a cat and jumped clear through the glass of a nearby window.

James fired, missing Lambshead but taking the head from a tin parrot. Kat Hookway raised her pistol and fired, obliterating a clockwork elephant. Vince dashed out of the window after Lambshead, landing on a flat lower roof. James landed heavily behind him. They gave chase across the rooftop while a chorus of muskets rang out in the emporium.

THE TOWN CLOCK tower chimed as James huffed and

puffed his way across the flat roof. Lambshead forced open a glass-panelled door leading to a wide attic filled with plants. He levelled his musket and fired. The shot missed Vince by inches and took a chunk out of the chimney pot behind him. James hid and refilled his flintlock.

Lambshead's eyes were wide and unblinking. Every vein in his neck stood out. "I looked up to you more than anyone else did, but nothing I did was ever good enough." He fired again and again. The revolving barrels of Summersong whirred between each shot. "You overlooked me at every turn."

"Not true," Vince said. "Were one of the best. Most promising."

"But it's Celeste you went running to first to fill out your little Watch."

He ran to the other side of the attic, ducking behind some broad-leafed plants.

"Not making sense," Vince said. "Hardly likely to recruit you. Needed recruits to fight you."

"And had it been the other way around, had Celeste and her people been out there in the siege engine, would you have come to me for help?"

Vince hesitated.

"Exactly," Lambshead said.

While they argued, James crept around the attic and saw his chance. From behind a bushy plant, he stood, raised his weapon, and fired. It clicked. Nothing happened. Lambshead darted toward him, swatting the flintlock from his hand with one swipe of Summersong's hatchet. James braced himself, but before Lambshead could strike, Vince landed on him.

Vince chopped the air with his octopus sword but Lambshead moved too quickly. He raised Summersong in time to catch the hatchet on Vince's blade. Again and again, Vince lashed out, but each time Lambshead's hatchet bayonet deflected the blow. James lunged at him but the younger and faster Lambshead skirted away, kicking James in the belly and laying him out on the floor.

"James!" Vince roared at the top of his lungs.

Lambshead laughed. "That's what comes from having such a big target."

James lay on his back, holding his stomach and seeing stars. Again and again, Vince slashed his sword, harder and harder each time. He caught Lambshead on the hand, and Summersong clattered to the floor. Lambshead backed away, covering his face as Vince slashed his clothes, his arms. With a howl, Vince suddenly threw his blade away and began battering Lambshead with his enormous, heavy fists. They became a blur as they popped cartilage and snapped bone.

Lambshead's face turned red and then purple. Vince stopped and backed away, shaking the blood from his hands. Lambshead quivered and dragged himself through the glass attic door and outside to the flat roof. He hugged a chimney stack, frightening away a perched gull. With broken fingers, he clawed at the bricks, trying to stand.

"Done now," Vince said. "No more, Lambshead." He followed Lambshead outside. Pillars of black smoke rose higher and higher across the town.

"Done when I sa-say we're done," Lambshead said. "Wh-why do you always get to set the rules?"

"Because Port Knot is mine. Always has been. Only one who can control it. Only one who can steer it. Took my hands off the reins and look what happened. Never again." Vince's breathing had become heavier as he spoke. "Give it up. Not too late to make amends."

Lambshead laughed through broken teeth. "I'll never work for you again, you monster. You brute. You animal. Throw me in the gaolhouse. I don't care. How long do you think it can hold me? I'll be out in no time. And then I'm coming after you, old man. And Celeste. And the rest of your little Watch. One by one, I'll get all of you. S-sooner or later, I'll get you all."

A shot rang out, echoing across the rooftops. Lambshead doubled over and fell into a heap of ruined flesh.

Leaning against the attic doorway, James lowered Summersong. "I rather think you won't."

"No!" Vince knelt next to Lambshead. "Shouldn't have done this to you. Should have let you live your own life. Hugo, I'm sorry."

Lambshead's eyelids had swollen so much he couldn't open them. His words hissed out through puffed and split lips. "I don't...don't care. If there was any justice you'd be lying here instead of me. You're poison, old man. A vish...a vicious wolf...playing house. I hope you never know a moment's...a moment's peace." His breath rattled and wheezed, and then it stopped altogether.

Vince stood, shaking, his face red. He rushed towards James in a perfect rage. Before James could raise Summersong, Vince grabbed him by the shirt and screamed into his face. "Didn't have to kill him!" James had never before seen that look in Vince's eye. "Didn't deserve to die like this! Wanted him to have a chance too! Damned muskets—all they do is take and take!"

James's eyes narrowed. He grabbed Vince's wrist. "Hugo Lambshead was a killer! A dyed-in-the-wool killer! It was always going to end this way for him."

"Wasn't a threat!"

Sorcha and Celeste approached across the rooftop, slowly.

"Lambshead was always a threat," Celeste said. "Captain Godgrave did the town a favour." She crouched by Lambshead's body, checking for signs of life. "And frankly, if he didn't kill him, I would have. For Merlin."

Vince's whole body trembled with fury. "People keep dying! People I took in. People I hurt. People I damaged. All end up dead. Poisoned their lives, their minds, their hearts!" He dropped James and turned away. He wiped his hands on his claret overcoat, cleaning the blood from them. Lambshead's blood. He stalked back and forth across the flat roof, his cheeks wet, his arms shaking, his hands stretched and flexing uncontrollably. "Everything he did, my fault—"

James reached out to him. "It wasn't your fault, Vince!"

"Responsibility, then!"

James backed away from him, wide-eyed and scared. He tightened his grip on Summersong.

"Responsibility! Mine! Failed him then. Failed him now."

He rubbed his face, marking his snowy white beard with red streaks. He rubbed the tears from his eyes, knocking off his patch and revealing a scarred eye, intact but grey and clouded as an angry winter's sky.

"You told me the town had changed," James said. "That compromises had to be made."

"Not this."

"Yes, this! You think you're responsible? Well, I had a chance to kill him in Gull's Reach, and I didn't. So everyone out there, all those bodies on the streets, they are my responsibility. My Sentinels and the townsfolk alike. You are not in charge of the whole world. I made the decision to shoot him, and I stand by it."

Vince sank to his knees. "Needed to help him. Thought if someone gave him a chance..."

"You beat the man half to death with your bare hands, Vince. You knew—you *knew*—he couldn't be saved. Not everyone can."

Vince shook his head. "Don't believe that. Can't."

"Why not? Why is it so hard to accept?"

James lay his hand on Vince's shoulder as Vince's breathing grew heavier and heavier by the second.

Sorcha put herself in front of Vince. "Look at me. Look,

will you? You're neither poison nor a wild animal. If you were, sure, you wouldn't care so much." She lifted his eyepatch, wiping some dirt from it, and placed it back on his head.

Vince's voice had become a whisper, clanking and dry. "Hurts. Knowing the pain I caused."

"I know it does," James said, helping Vince to his feet.

They stood facing each other. James clamped his hand on the side of Vince's face. He rubbed his thumb along Vince's cheek.

"You can't change what's done," James said. "You're facing it, head-on. That's more than most people would do. More than most people *could* do."

"Lambshead was no worse than me," Vince said, the words catching in his throat. "Didn't deserve a chance, but somehow I do? Things I've done, people I've hurt...it's... Why did I deserve a chance to pick myself out of the muck, James? Why me but not him?"

"Why did you deserve a chance? The answer is simple." James pulled him in close, held him tightly, and looked him square in the eye. "It's because you wanted one."

CHAPTER THIRTY-NINE

RABBIT LOOKED UP from her papers when Swan entered the council chamber wearing her feathered mask.

"Am I early?"

"Not at all," Rabbit said. "I wanted a chance to speak to you before everyone else arrived. Whatever am I supposed to do with you?"

Swan dropped into her seat and pulled her teal coat closed. "I can't think what you mean."

Rabbit removed her mask and set it on the table. She fixed Swan with a stare. "You conspired with the Sentinels to take over the duties of the Watch with an eye towards ousting me. Don't try to deny it. I've seen such a change in you, this past year. Before, you were a timid, dull little creature on the outskirts of every social gathering. Banking on the Chase family name to get you through life. Since you became Swan, you've become more assured of yourself but more ruthless in your dealings with others. It's no way to live."

"Since when has ambition been a failing?" Swan toyed with the sleeves of her coat, avoiding Rabbit's gaze. "You're taking this much too personally, my darling. It's just politics."

Rabbit slammed her fist on the table. "It's just the bodies lying in our streets. It's just the homes and businesses left in smouldering ruins. It's just the livelihoods of the people who trusted us to take care of them."

"You cannot blame me for—"

"Had you been Rabbit instead of me, this town would still be on fire. You are not capable of performing my role, Dorothea, because when you look out of the window you don't see a town; you see a resource. You don't see people; you see workers.

"I have my shortcomings. I have had my lapses in judgement, but I have always tried to put the people of this town, of this island, first. You have been on the council for less than a year, and you thought you could just sweep me aside and take over. That is not ambition; that is hubris. I would be well within my rights to call for a vote on your dismissal from your post. However, despite your lack of compassion, you have performed well in your role. It would be a shame to waste your talents. But please, my dear Swan, don't try to run before you can walk."

RABBIT ADDRESSED THE assembled members in the domed council chamber. "I'd like to keep this short, everyone. We all have business to take care of, I'm sure. Mr Knight asked to come and speak to us today."

Vince nodded before speaking. "Came to ask you to formally reinstate the Watch."

"I think we've all taken that as read," Rabbit said. "Who do you recommend to succeed you as Watch Commander?"

Vince cleared his throat. "Thought I might stay. For a while. New, all this. Needs to be watched. So to speak. Guided. Was planning to form my own Watch if you lot didn't revive the old one, anyway."

Rabbit turned to each of the council in turn. "After your help in quelling the Gunbrides uprising, allowing you to remain in your role is the least we can do."

Badger raised his eyebrows. "Especially considering Captain Godgrave's failure."

"James didn't fail," Vince said. "Faced something outside his experience. Outside anyone's experience."

"You're being generous," Swan said. "You adapted to the situation. Captain Godgrave did not. More than half of his Sentinels were killed. Two are still being treated for their injuries. Dozens of townspeople are dead. It will take months to repair the damage caused by the siege engine. If you had not been here, I shudder to think what might have happened."

"Had I not been here to begin with none of it would have happened."

"A fact we all have to accept," Fox said. "You've made a good start on making up for past mistakes. You've shown your commitment to this town. It would be churlish to stand in your way any further."

"What of the Pennymen?" Rabbit asked. "With Fortitude Littletar dead, what becomes of them?"

Vince sighed and shrugged his shoulders. "Rudderless

now. Will make them the same offer I made the Clockbreakers: gaolhouse or Watch. Watch needs to operate in daytime. Assume it won't be an issue?"

Rabbit flicked over a page of the report. "The council charged you with breaking the gangs in any manner you saw fit."

"One dangling thread," Vince said. "Quaintance."

"Mr Quaintance has left the island," Fox said, folding her fingers. "I'm asking you to leave him in peace. He has been effectively exiled from his home, from his friends. I hope you will agree that's punishment enough?"

Vince sat forward, resting one forearm on the table. "People will say he should be tried for crimes. Chasing after him risks more lives. Not easy to say, but he's best forgotten." He raised a meaty finger and pointed at her. "Long as he never returns. Under any circumstances."

Fox splayed her hands wide and smiled. "You have my word. We had been friends for years, yet he lied to me. I had no idea what kind of man he really was. I hope to never lay eyes on him again."

Vince grunted and nodded. Her word was plenty for him. Blackrabbit had a difficult road ahead. The people were going to have to accept a pack of former criminals were now responsible for upholding its laws. Compromises were going to have to be made on all sides.

"Magpie and I have spoken with Mrs Damerell and other representatives from Gull's Reach," Rabbit said. "We have agreed to invest a significant amount of money in the area over the next five years. We've seen where neglect leads."

"I understand you've recommended the surviving Gunbrides be sent to the asylum?" Badger asked. "Whatever for? They ought to be locked up!"

Vince licked his lips and took a moment to compose himself. "Lot of those Gunbrides were young. Impressionable. Took everything Lambshead said to heart. Turned their minds around. Stopped them from seeing clearly. Youngest was a girl named Hookway. Injured in Littletar's Emporium but survived. Doesn't deserve to have her whole life ruined because of him. Because of me. None of them do.

"Asylum doctors can't help them, then send them to the gaolhouse. But give them a chance to get better first. Need to pay for their crimes, true. Can do that best by serving on the Watch."

"It certainly seems to have worked for you," Fox said.

A murmur of approval rumbled around the table.

"Kind," Vince said. "But let's not fool ourselves. Nothing

I do will ever wipe my slate clean. Not really. Some people will always hate me. Distrust me. Nothing I can do about it. Don't care, anyway. Doing this so I can sleep better at night."

"I, for one, hope it's working," Fox said. "You have a lot of work ahead of you. You'll need to be well-rested to keep your Watch under control."

"Watch can't function only at night any longer," Vince said. "Sentinels started something by working during the day. Showed the need for it."

"So long as you operate with a lighter touch than Captain Godgrave, I don't imagine it will be an issue."

"Don't intend to intrude on people's day-to-day lives," Vince said. "No more guarding alehouses. Won't be tax-checkers neither. But the Watch'll be there if people need help. Have another proposal." He cleared his throat, aware that what he was about to ask for would seem beyond the pale. "Want to make it illegal for anyone to carry a firearm on the island of Blackrabbit. Punishable by a fine and imprison-ment."

The council fell silent. Rabbit lay her chin on templed fingers.

"All saw the damage caused in recent days," Vince said. "No need for it. Let the greencoats keep their weapons on their ships. But nowhere else on the island. All saw what the siege engine could do. Next weapon that gets built might be worse. Smaller. Easier to move around. Seen those pepper-box muskets the Gunbrides used? Eight barrels. Eight lives on the line each time they're used. Could add another barrel to them. Another ten barrels. Faster reloading. More powerful powder. After that, who knows? People are only good at one thing—finding new ways to hurt one another. Have a chance to hinder that. Here. Today."

"And what happens the next time the island is besieged?" Badger asked. "Will you wave pointy sticks at the aggressors?"

"Won't be any weapons on the island for them to use," Vince said. "Foreign invaders have to get past the greencoats first. Might not be any use on land but unrivalled at sea."

"It might be a difficult thing to sell to the public," Fox said.

Swan had been unusually quiet throughout the meeting. "After everything that's happened, the people will be glad to see guns kept off our streets," she said. "I can promise you as much."

Rabbit laughed and sat back in her chair. "You walked into the Watch House a little over two weeks ago, Mr Knight. Two weeks is all it took for you to overhaul the Watch, begin a new approach to law and order on the island, and clear out the gangs from Port Knot. Imagine what you can do in two months. In two years."

"Better get started," Vince said.

CHAPTER FORTY

DRESSED IN HIS claret overcoat and black breeches, Vince pushed open the doors of the new Watch House. Behind him, Clive Hext and Philip Talan took a Pennyman by the arm and led him downstairs to the cells.

James leaned on the mezzanine railing overlooking the ground floor. Before him, the great glass turret offered a view of the busy harbour. Below, the new recruits were settling in.

In a dark corner, Sorcha and Flowers had their heads down over a box of spare parts, tinkering with some new contraption one of them had dreamed up. Ruth and Frank Rundle argued over who got the desk by the window until the beadle Norton bellowed at them from his records room. Walter scribbled a note and gave it to Brendan, who had become the official courier for the Watch. In Vince's office, Crabmeat lay snoring in his own little bed beneath the charcoal portrait of James.

James handed Vince a copy of the Blackrabbit Courant. "Have you seen today's edition?"

The lead story from Ms Emmeline Hawksmoor detailed her run-in with the bloodthirsty Lieutenant Pertinacity Hancock. It spoke of Lieutenant Hancock's confession, her murder of Alfie Exeter, and her subsequent death in the midst of the chaos she instigated. It also mentioned the failure of the Sentinels and the formation of the island's newest protectors— the Knights of Blackrabbit.

Vince snorted when he reached the line. "Not calling ourselves that."

"If it catches on with the public, you won't have much say in the matter." James pulled the silver ring from his finger and set it on the handrail. He slid it towards Vince.

"What this?" Vince asked.

"I told you before. It's a reminder."

Vince lifted the ring and slid it onto his little finger. It got stuck before it reached the first knuckle. He wiggled it at

James, who laughed.

"Damn, I thought it would be a nice gesture. Give it back then, you can have your own made. Or perhaps I'll have one forged and send it to you."

"Thought they were only for your crew?"

"Well, you've been under me, in a manner of speaking. I think that counts. And you've even taken the odd order or two." James wiggled his eyebrows. "Harder, faster, and so forth."

Vince couldn't help but laugh. "Incorrigible."

"What can I say? You've rubbed off on me," James said. "You know, I believe this is the first time I've seen you smile. You should try it more often."

"Ah-hah!" Sorcha called up to him and pointed. "A smile! At last!"

"Wasn't for you!" Vince said.

"It still counts!"

Vince laughed again and shook his head. "Put a light on. Ruin your eyesight, otherwise. Thought you wanted to go explore the world?"

Sorcha shrugged and held her hands out. "And leave you to run all this by yourself? You wouldn't last a day!"

"She's got a point," James said. "You have more work to

do now than ever."

Vince smiled at him. "Suppose I should thank you for giving us this building."

"It's of no use to us anymore," James said. "And besides, I think Swan felt guilty for her plans to remove Rabbit from office. This place had been created to serve the needs of the town protectors. That's you now. That's the Watch. Or should I say the Knights?"

"Careful," Vince said. "Almost sound bitter." He shuffled about where he stood. "Not sure I've forgiven you, you know. For Lambshead."

James squared his shoulders. "I was still Sentinel Commander at the time. Lambshead was a dangerous man. The responsibility was mine, and the decision was mine to make."

"Should have stopped you, should have—"

"You couldn't have stopped me if you'd tried." James's eyes hardened. He still smiled but in that way that let others know he was right and they were wrong. He gripped the lapels of his own waistcoat. "Let me be clear. I had always intended to do away with him. From the moment I learned of his existence, I knew there was only one way his reign of terror was going to end, and it wasn't going to be in the gaolhouse."

Vince gripped the railing and leaned forward a little.

"Had you been here, before, when I was—"

"I would have given you the same treatment. In a heart-beat." James's voice fired the words without hesitation. Shot from the siege engine of his mouth.

"Makes me feel better," Vince said. "In a way. Bit of a worry, actually. Can't be normal."

"Pfft, normal. Normal doesn't exist. Tell me one normal person you know. Just one. You can't." James leaned his ample rear end on the railing and crossed his arms. "You know, you think you've solved a problem, but you've created a whole new one. You've put a generation of rule-breakers in a position of authority. The power will go to their heads—mark my words. You've given them a chance, but they won't be satisfied for long. These hungry hearts. These crashing waves. These young wolves. You've ended up the head of another gang, and they'll come for you one day. They'll turn on you."

Vince lifted his chin and frowned. "Let them try. Now what?"

"Back to sea, old boy. Best place for me, I think. The land is complicated. The sea is simple. All you have to re-member is to stay on the top."

"Wanted a big house in the country, I thought?"

"And I'll have one," James said, "just as soon as I become

an admiral. Maclaren deserves some fields to fly over. Some trees to rest in." He put a hand on Vince's hip, leaned in, and kissed him on the lips. "Try not to get into any more trouble, will you?"

"No promises," Vince said, smiling. "Now get off my island."

James laughed and straightened his waistcoat as Celeste swung open the doors to the Watch house. "Right, you lot. Mrs Maunder's house has been burgled. Seems her fancy new dress drew a bit of attention. Someone's nicked it and all her jewellery. She's asked us to get it all back. Witness said the thieves headed inland. Commander Knight, you coming?"

"This is what you do now?" James asked. "Rush from one crime to the next? You're the Commander, man! Sit in your office and enjoy the privileges of rank. You have underlings for this sort of thing. You've earned some peace and quiet."

Vince grabbed his tricorne and made for the stairs. "Said it yourself, James. Calm seas carry no ships." He smiled and followed Celeste outside into the crisp November air.

ACKNOWLEDGEMENTS

I would like to thank my wonderful fiancé, Mark Wilson, for his support, his love, and his patience. My thanks as well to Tony Teehan, Christian Smith, and Alan McAteer for their feedback during the writing process. Thanks to @JailDice on Twitter for their ornithological advice, and most of all thanks to my late friend Damian Whyte, to whom this book is dedicated, for his advice and his friendship.

I'd also like to thank my publisher, Raevyn McCann, my brilliant editor, BJ Toth, Jaycee DeLorenzo for the gorgeous cover, and all the NineStar Press team.

About Glenn Quigley

Glenn Quigley is an author and artist originally from Tallaght in Dublin, Ireland, and now living in Lisburn, Northern Ireland with his partner of many years. His first novel, *The Moth and Moon*, was published in 2018. When not writing, he paints portraits in watercolours and tweets too many photos of lighthouses. He maintains a website of his latest work at www.glennquigley.com.

Email
glennquigley@gmail.com

Facebook
www.facebook.com/glennquigleyauthor

Twitter
@glennquigley

Website
www.glennquigley.com

Other NineStar books by this author

Moth and Moon Series
The Moth and Moon
The Lion Lies Waiting
We Cry the Sea

Use as Wallpaper

CONNECT WITH NINESTAR PRESS

WWW.NINESTARPRESS.COM

WWW.FACEBOOK.COM/NINESTARPRESS

WWW.FACEBOOK.COM/GROUPS/NINESTARNICHE

WWW.TWITTER.COM/NINESTARPRESS

WWW.INSTAGRAM.COM/NINESTARPRESS